MIRROR ISLAND

Mirror Island

SHEL GRAVES

Much love to fellow writers and teachers at Goddard College, Port Townsend, 2006-2008. Much love to Pam's Kids at the University of Washington, Popular Fiction program.

This book is dedicated to the Underdark Calligraphy Club — and to my beloved Sam.

CONTENTS

Dedication - iv
Prologue - viii

~~

Jump
1

~~

Doreena
8

~~

Moving
19

~~

Mango
34

~~

Retina
44

VI ~

~~

Marilyn
55

~~

Alonso
70

~~

Sales Meeting
84

~~

Surfers
98

~~

Baby Shower
112

~~

Tiki-tiki
125

~~

Surfing
136

~~

Drowning
150

~~

Inside Aeroflux
172

~ *VII*

~~

AeroFlux Presser
188

~~

Rock Traynter's Resort
204

~~

The Cave
219

~~

Climbing
226

~~

The Island at Night
238

~~

World Traveler
246

About the Author - 253

PROLOGUE

Conceived on an island universe

Imprisoned in SpireMine, Leonid Moriena spent his last days reflecting on his life and who he was. Still, the last action he took in life surprised him. He was an engineer and an activist. People who saw his life from the outside said he was self-sacrificing, but he saw it differently, he went to the forefront of action because that was his means of survival. It invigorated him. He had to act. The people who saw his life from the inside, his wife and daughter, saw it yet another way, as neglect, but theirs was an untenable point of view. The accolades he received for his service insulated him from their criticism, if not, in later years, their sorrow. Osana threw herself passionately against that barrier often early in their relationship asking for his time and his presence, but in later years she never raised her voice or shed tears or pressed her body tightly against his anymore. She had yielded.

His daughter, Kira, was another matter. His engineering team developed the aircraft, an AF-897, that led them to a new source of energy to power their world. She was unimpressed. As a child, she wanted her father close by, to hold his hand, as a teenager she punished him by pretending indifference, and as an adult she was simply distant. She never forgave him for putting his work ahead of holding her in his arms, so Leonid was startled when it was she who arrived to save him.

The AF-897 aircraft brought them to a small planet with a power source at its core. Tremors crossed the planet's surface, growing in intensity as the hastily assembled SpireMine operation inhaled the energy to fuel earth's needs. AeroFlux was unwilling to invest the time required to solve the engineering problem of how to extract the energy safely. When it became clear the company meant to use and discard the small planet, draining the core until it imploded, Leonid led his men to protest. He founded the Watchmen. In the planet's last days, the fallow mine became the dissidents' prison.

As the rumbling in the mine grew, the imprisoned men quieted, each entering the smaller cell of his own thoughts. They were like the planet now, silent on the surface, but in upheaval inside. The prison guards had gone, leaving the men in the mine. The catastrophe would happen quickly. No survivors were expected. They hadn't bothered to release the men so that they could die with their families. Leonid thought of his wife, Osana. The mourning in her eyes for the relationship they might have had weighed on him. When the choice had been his, he had so often left her. Now that it was beyond his control, he wanted only to be at home with her in her garden.

Then his daughter appeared at his cell door. He inhaled the faint trace of the outdoors on Kira's skin and touched her pregnant belly and forgot everything. He escaped with her. If he lived, he'd remember every detail; her white wrist smeared with soot, the sulfur stench of the steam-filled corridor, the soles of his shoes tacky on the hot stone, the steep incline and the grit stinging his eyes. She did not take him home, but instead brought him to the AF-897. They would try to leave the planet and get far enough away in time to live. Kira meant to save herself and her child and he was proud, for a moment, he'd given her the means to try.

Only after the silence of space enveloped them, and it looked as though there was a chance they might survive the implosion, did Leonid consider what he'd done. He'd left his men behind. If he lived, it would haunt him. He'd run past rows of his Watchmen every waking moment. They'd call out to him at night. Still, he willed the ship away, faster. He did not expect to survive, but he wanted to live to be a grandfather, guilt-ridden or not.

"It took time to come for me. Why risk it?" he asked.

Kira placed a hand over her husband's, splayed over the aircraft controls. "We're going to have a little girl. I wanted Doreena to know her grandfather."

Leonid had disapproved of Kira's marriage to the government-employed aerospace engineer and Nazar's passivity now did not impress him. Leonid would have put saving his family above every consideration. He would not have let his wife come to the prison mine and he wouldn't have taken his hands off the controls to hold Kira and comfort her the way Nazar was doing, not when it might take all his concentration to steer the craft and save them.

"The boy lacks passion," he'd complained.

But, of course, that's what had drawn Kira to Nazar. She didn't want a passionate personality. She'd seen the loneliness that had brought her mother.

"Your mother?" he asked.

"Still in her garden. She didn't think we'd even get this far," Kira said.

Of course, Osana would be placid through the end. He thought of her with her hands around a steaming cup of jasmine tea — no, she'd want to keep busy — he saw her patting mulch around her Sky-Blue Coronets. Either way, she was grounded on the planet. From space it looked peaceful, there was nothing to betray the cataclysm inside. After all the fighting he had done for it, she was the loyalist now while he would likely die off-planet.

Loyalty was a trait Kira owed to her mother. Osana had never left him even when he, consumed by his work and the Watchmen, had come to her so little. But Kira's passion to live was his contribution. They were one of only a few ships daring the attempt to escape into uncharted space. And that was Kira's doing, but they were still too close to the planet.

When the planet's gutted core collapsed and its husk crumbled into space, the ship tossed. Leonid lurched across the ship to the controls. "I'll take it."

Nazar had already unstrapped himself from the seat and Leonid saw, like a clear pool, the true reason Kira had delayed leaving to rescue him — why the mother would risk her child. Nazar knew the mechanics of the craft but he didn't have the confidence to fly it or the ferocity needed to save his family. Leonid took the controls. If the machine failed, he could not keep the craft aloft by sheer force of will, but he would try. He'd give everything to save his daughter and grandchild.

He kept the ship pointed outward as pieces of the planet battered its hull flinging them through space. When a glowing blue sphere appeared before them, he didn't hesitate. He directed the craft toward it taking their best chance. Inside the planet's atmosphere, peaks and valleys sparkled blue. The AF-897 whined as it spiraled down. Leonid pulled up and adjusted for a water landing, but the ship plunged through the blue and struck like a diver in shallow water.

Leonid awoke to whispering: "Water. Water. Water."

It was dark and cold and cramped in the smashed cockpit. Kira was still strapped into the chair next to him. The blood on her forehead had crusted into a black scar. Her lips were puckered, white and gaping. Her hands were folded over her belly. There was no blood there or pooled on the floor beneath her. He twisted around and pain shot up his spine. Nazar was crumpled on the floor behind him half of his head caved in, his arms outstretched and bent as though he'd tried to catch himself. The lips in Nazar's wrecked head moved, "Water."

"Water," Kira responded and Leonid moaned listening to the lovers pass the word between them. It reminded him of the way the Watchmen had whispered "Soon, soon, soon," up and down the rows of cells as the mine rumbled. Kira whispered "water" again and this time Nazar did not respond. They were dying in a slow, painful, predictable way like their home world with impotent protests. Leonid wished he hadn't woken up for this dying, but he fought to keep himself from going into shock as he moved his trembling hands to unclasp his belt. He slipped to the floor, crawled to Kira's side and lifted himself to her.

He heard her sigh and lost sensation. Numbness spread across his chest. He made one last exertion and stretched to lever open the hatch. The atmosphere would hasten their deaths and reduce their suffering, and he wanted to see where they had landed. He wished things had been different, that the planet he loved had been smaller, so that he might have had a chance of saving it. It had always been too big a task for one man no matter how many Watchmen he'd convinced to join the cause. He wished he had lived to see his granddaughter grow into a young woman and see what she would choose: loyalty or passion. The plank floated down into a swirl of soft blue. Behind him Nazar said, "Water," one last time.

"Doreena," he replied, the child deserved a chance at life.

He heard a splash and felt the ship roll before he died.

It took Leonid Moriena some time to puzzle out who and what he was. When he reappeared beside the spaceship, he floated alongside its warped shell in a blue haze. But on his next breath, his lungs filled with fluid. He flailed. Seeing light, he shot up. He surfaced gasping. His head and shoulders bobbed half out of the water like the ship beside him. He sucked in air. Blue light shimmered around him. Blue flakes floated on the water, a sparkling sea foam. He started to swim to the ship. He wanted to touch its cool surface and feel the pressure of it against his palm. He reached for it but heard splashing behind him.

"Help me."

He turned and saw Kira with her arm around Nazar's waist hauling him through the water. Nazar's shoulder stuck out like a fin. Water rippled around Kira, but she barely moved. He treaded to her, and grasped Nazar's waist while she held her husband's head.

"There." She pointed ahead at a shiny blue shore.

Leonid pulled Nazar's body tight against his and lugged his son-in-law through the water until he was able to drag him on shore. They sank up to their elbows in the soft blue. Had they crash-landed in the sea? But the blue did not feel wet. Instead, it tingled. It tasted salty-sweet.

"Get them off. Get them off."

He sat up shivering and turned to see Kira slapping at her arms and legs brushing billowing clouds of blue from her body. Nazar too was coated in the glittering film. It stuck to his face so that he looked metallic. When Kira knelt beside her husband and ran her hands over his face the flesh tones returned. Leonid ran his fingers through his beard. He peered into the blue powder that dropped into his hands. He blew and it puffed into the air and disappeared. Kira managed to clean herself and Nazar completely so not a sparkling trace of the alien matter remained on them. Leonid let the stuff rest on his skin and traced a finger through a skiff across the top of his hand. It tingled pleasantly. He sat for a long time trying to remember what had happened.

First, he remembered a photograph. When the international team of engineers had finished the aircraft, they had posed for a photo in front of it. He was the senior among them and they had put him at the center of it. They called him "chief." The South African called him, "*moriena*," which meant chief in his mother tongue.

"Father, are you ready to eat now?"

He looked up and Kira stood over him with her pregnant belly and handed down an open half of some orange fruit. He scooped out the smooth flesh with his fingers and ladled it into his mouth.

"Good?"

"So sweet. It tastes like home," he said.

Kira put an arm around him and he bowed his head. As a young man, he'd never cried. He took Kira's arm and let her help him to his feet. When he'd awakened beside the ship and seen its underwater wavering, he'd thought he was a ghost, but now his legs felt stiff from sitting. He had no idea how long he'd been on the beach. Except for Kira and the fruit everything was swirling blue. He ran his hands through his beard. It ended inches past his chin as usual.

He allowed Kira to lead him off the beach and continued to eat the fruit. Kira and Nazar had found a grove of trees and grasses — all kinds that he knew and could name— in the middle of the blue field. They'd made a lean-to out of palm fronds against the back of a green stone. There was water, food, and shelter everything they needed and Kira and Nazar busied themselves with the tasks of survival. They ate, drank, and slept. Leonid was neither hungry nor thirsty nor tired and his skin remained a constant temperature neither hot nor cold.

He pulled Kira aside, "Where are we? How did all of this get here?"

"All of what?"

"Home," Leonid said. "These plants that are just like home. How can everything be so familiar?"

Kira ignored him. Leonid knew his daughter and saw that she was annoyed with him the way she was whenever he'd left her either to work at AeroFlux, or to organize protests against it, or to be martyred in prison. She handed him a hollowed out gourd. "Here, Nazar and I do all the work while you ponder. Fetch us some water."

Filled with regret, for he knew he had been a terrible father, Leonid bowed his head, took the gourd and walked to the water with it dangling from his hand. When he got to the water, he dipped the gourd it in and water pooled in its yellow lining. He wet a finger in it and pressed it to his curled tongue. The water was clean. He drank from the shell and then directly from the lake raising it to his lips in a cupped hand. It was clean as a mountain spring, not salty-sweet as he recalled. And where was the ship? He peered out across the flat shimmering surface squinting into the brightness.

"Father, what are you doing?" Behind him Kira stood at a distance by the trees.

He had waded knee deep in the body of water. "I'm going to look. Wasn't that a sea? Wasn't our ship floating on the surface out there?"

"No, father," Kira said. The tremor in her voice sounded fearful, but there was nothing to be afraid of here: The weather was mild, the water and plants were safe.

"Something's wrong," he said.

"Don't expect trouble. It's a miracle we're here," she said.

He allowed her to call him back to the trees. Nazar met them outside the shelter. "Good news. I've found a spring. You won't have to go down to the lake anymore." He handed them cups of water in small gourds. "Taste. It's delicious."

Leonid put the cup to his lips. The water was cool and sweet and pure. He felt himself tearing again. "I miss your mother."

Kira took his hand and placed it on her belly. "I'm going to have a baby. You're going to be a grandfather."

The water in his cup spilled over the side. He couldn't keep his hand steady. "But we crashed."

He remembered the sulfur fumes and growing heat of SpireMine. In those final days of the planet, it had felt as though the prison walls were absorbing every joule of anger he and the Watchmen contained. For years, they'd warned against over-mining the planet. They had grown raspy with protest until they were silenced. When they were proven right, they were not released to their families. Kira had come to him smelling like her mother's medicinal plants and cultivated rings of Sky-Blue Coronets. He had forgotten his men in that moment. He had so wanted to live and be a grandfather. But he could not forget them now.

"But we died. All of us."

Beneath his hand, the baby swimming in Kira's womb stilled. Kira's taut belly softened and her flesh rose around his hand as it sank into her. With a hiss, she withdrew and turned her flattening belly away. Her elbows jutted to the sides as she massaged her stomach.

"Kira, the baby?" he asked drawing closer.

Nazar stepped between them and grabbed Leonid's shoulders. Leonid staggered back as Nazar plowed forward squeezing his upper arms. Nazar lowered his head until his forehead pressed Leonid's firm and cool.

"Stop. Don't think like that."

Leonid turned his head to the side, unable to bear the crushing closeness and Nazar's contorted expression. His legs bent and gave way beneath him. He stared through the trees as he tumbled to the ground clutching the sand. His knees ground through the smooth beige layer revealing the mysterious blue that shone just beneath. Leonid watched Nazar return to Kira and wrap his arms around her.

"She's fine. She's healthy," he said.

In moments, they turned to him. Kira looked ripe again. Her flight suit stretched around the oblong swell of her. Leonid rose to his knees, numb. Kira pressed her lips together and held her belly. "I'll have Doreena soon. Your granddaughter. This time, just let it be, daddy. Please. Not everything's a struggle."

He clenched his hand. He could still feel the swell and fall of her pregnancy in his palm. He understood that somehow, by thinking about death in this place, he had almost killed his grandchild. But he couldn't forget or ignore what he thought he knew.

"That was your mother's gift, not mine," he said. What was he, after all, without struggle?

He turned from Kira toward the body of water. It felt further away than he remembered. When he got to the beach, he sat with his head in his hands staring out across the lake, or the sea, where he thought he remembered they had landed.

One other time in his life, Leonid had felt like this: while working on the mining system, the team had hit a wall.

"Take a break," Leonid told them, "Just take a sit. Put your minds on auto pilot and it'll come to you."

Leonid couldn't remember the last time he'd eaten in the company atrium. There, among the glossy red anthurium lilies, an unexpected answer came to him: The mining system didn't matter. There wasn't time. AeroFlux didn't care about finding a solution, because they'd already declared the planet a cost of doing business.

Kira interrupted his thoughts, walking out of the trees to the water's edge. "We're leaving." She said pointing to the horizon. "There's a place for us to raise Doreena."

At first, peering out past the end of his daughter's fingertip toward the horizon, Leonid saw only a pale blue haze, but as he concentrated it clarified into distant dark spires. "A city?"

"Why not?" She placed her hand on his forearm. "If it scares you, couldn't you just not think about it?"

He looked at her helplessly and then turned back to the water. The ship had risen from the hidden depths. It was floating on the surface again. "You sound like the people who put me in prison."

The sand shifted as Kira turned. "All right. You know where we'll be. I wish mother were here."

"I wish I'd stayed with her," Leonid said.

He waded into the water. It lapped his ankles, calves, and thighs until he sank up to his neck in the warmth. Osana, she would have been happy just to be by Kira's side as she gave birth. She would not have questioned this, but it was not in his nature to leave a puzzle unsolved. He should have died on his planet where the rules made sense. He began swimming out to the ship with long smooth breaststrokes. He half-expected to find Osana there, now that he had thought of her, to find her sitting on the edge of the ship dangling her ankles into the water. Where the ship floated, the water became salty as expected. The body of water felt like it stretched far beneath him and extended around him. Yet, it was motionless, and the beach was always close. The ship's sides were scorched with black entry burns. Leonid placed his hands on its cool hull. He dove underwater and saw the yawning hatch through the clear water. He swam through.

The bodies were there: Kira and Nazar strapped into their chairs with waxy expressions. His body floated beside Kira's near the door. It occurred to him that the water was too clear and empty. The moment he thought it, it became murky. A movement caught his eye and a tiny silver fish darted by Kira's face picking at her cheek. He ducked back out of the ship and sidestroked to the shore.

When his feet hit bottom and he was standing upright, he heard waves rippling behind him. He froze in place, his first thought that he might turn to see one of the reanimated corpses behind him. Then he thought again of Osana. But did he really want her here, like Nazar and Kira were here, in some form masquerading as human? He did not. He had always wanted the truth. The ripples continued to play behind him until he found the courage to turn.

The woman resembled Osana. She had the same shape, but shimmered like the layer of powder that shone through the disturbed sand. She was the color of Sky-Blue Coronets. She held out a hand and, unable to stop himself, he took it in his. It felt like his own, the same temperature and dry, but tingling.

"This is not like you," the blue Osana said, her voice musically layered like a muted choir. "to come to a new place and see everything as it was in the place where you left. These shapes are tiring. We would rather flow."

They sat together on the beach; she with her legs bent like Kira used to sit as a young girl with her nightgown pulled over her knees. Leonid looked around at the trees, grass, shelter, fruit and tiny spring ahead of them, everything so familiar in this exotic place. He cried into his hands, grieving the loss of Osana, Kira, Nazar, tiny Doreena and himself as the woman stroked his back. When he was done crying, he dug through the sand and into the layer of blue. He scooped up handfuls of the powder and turned to her. "What is this? Help me understand."

"We are," she said, and did her best to explain. The blue particles that covered this planet were sentient inorganic helical plasma structures. Leonid, Kira, and Nazar were the first people they had ever experienced. Their ship had crashed through the soft blue layer and hit the hard rock of the planet. When the hatch opened, the particles were shaped by human thoughts. The plasma became the people and embraced their dying thoughts: water and Doreena. Leonid was made out of them and some of his own last memories.

As Leonid talked to the woman, the world lost the form imposed on it and began to flow naturally again. The beach and forest turned blue, the edges of objects became fuzzy until the unspoiled, shapeless haze returned. Exploring, Leonid let the glitter settle onto the surface of his skin, stick to the soles of his feet, and embed under his fingernails. It collected in the creases at the corners of his eyes and hung in flakes from the ends of his eyelashes. It got so that it coated the insides of his nostrils and he could taste it sweet on his tongue when he drew a deep breath. He slept within a warm blanket of blue. In time, he let the woman go, returning to her blue collective.

He realized he could rejoin them, too. His body would dissolve just as he'd watched the trees and fruits and water return to sparkling blue. He wanted to do this. But first, he needed to see his granddaughter; he'd died with that idea and it held fast within him.

Leonid stood and shook the blue from his hair. He began walking toward the city in the distance that Kira had pointed to some time ago. He stopped when he reached a slender line of reflective stone. The slick gray path stretched out across the swath of blue and wound toward the spires in the distance. Leonid reached down and touched it. They had no word for death. They knew only soft and hard, free and firm. The rock felt hard pressing them into the service of a single, solid form. They were trapped in it, imprisoned as Leonid and the Watchmen had been in SpireMine. Kira and Nazar were hardening this world, enslaving it to create the shapes they desired.

With each step along the stone to the city, Leonid grieved for the ones underfoot who had lost their fluidity and freedom to become the matter of Kira and Nazar's home. He understood that he and his daughter, and his son-in-law were a threat to this place. Their presence, their thoughts, harmed it. Therefore, they — himself, his daughter and son-in-law — must go. He would preserve this planet as he had fought, and failed, to preserve his own.

Leonid had never felt more of a responsibility to live according to his highest principles than now that he was a grandfather. He swung open the door and walked into his daughter's home. From floor to ceiling the room shone like water. On a dais at the end of the hall, his daughter and her husband sat enthroned. Their skin had a silver cast to it. They were no longer simple people at all. Kira held a shiny berry to her mouth. It looked like a metal bead, plucked off the silver tray beside her.

"Father," she said.

What must he look like to them with his fuzzy skin and his beard and hair dripping with blue? He could see his himself shimmering in the silver floor. A trail of blue dust lay behind him, tracked into the hall.

He loved his daughter. But she was not his daughter.

"He's come to see the baby. He's come to see Doreena," she said.

He wanted to see the child. And he did not. He wanted to do what was right, not want to fall in love with the idea of his granddaughter. Leonid hardened for the task ahead, and his hands grayed. He was himself, but not himself. He was only Leonid Moriena's last thoughts. Also, he was a new grandfather. He looked into Kira's hard, black glittering eyes. "You enslave them."

He lunged at Nazar first (he had never loved his son-in-law and this was not his son-in-law) and beat the boy's face with his harder hands until it shattered. It was easier then to pound into his torso until the man lay in chunks like coal at his feet. He was surprised at how easy it was, at how little resistance, until he remembered that the man was not a man, but merely thought hardened into submission.

When he looked up, Kira was gone. He went after her. The baby's wail gave her away. He heard its cry down a dark corridor and followed it in into a gray room. Kira stood there with the baby swaddled in a blue blanket. So soft. Where had she found it?

"Your granddaughter," she said.

He raised his hands and beat her away while she held the infant in her arms. Now that Nazar was gone, she would not fight.

"I already have what I wanted most, and I know you won't destroy her," she said, as he took the infant from her crumbling form.

He admired the child's perfect mouth, ears, nose, and the rosy tint of her flesh while he ground the mother's shell beneath his feet.

This child was Kira and Nazar and himself, the untainted parts and the destructive bits. If she stayed here with him, she would grow up hard, a black diamond girl, with the potential to pollute this soft blue world and turn it hard. What else would she know? He carried her out of the walls and across the scarred land. He returned with her to the soft blue loam. He held her to his chest. If she stayed here, if he lay down with her, she would return to the powder blue collective dissolving into soft waves. But as he lay down and the weight of her rested on him and her blanket became blue haze beneath his hands, he concentrated on her baby heartbeat, and her baby skin and the heat inside her dividing young cells. He could not help himself. He willed her to be, instead of letting her go.

He finally got up and walked to where the shelter had been and the beach, to the edge of the lake or sea, which had returned to waist deep fluffy blue. He waded through it to the ship, the solid, actual ship, where he removed the bones of the people (himself, Kira, and Nazar) and repaired the craft using the malleable blue to restore its hull. He created canisters and filled them with the plasma and placed them in the ship making no apology to the beings he sacrificed. Doreena would need them to grow, as she would need other people to give her form and hold her in place and help her become his grandchild. They would leave this place in peace. She was a fresh start, a seed. He would take her back to earth, to some small island. He would stay with her, keep her still, and be a grandfather.

***

Leonid Moriena loved Maui. The white sand beaches and cobalt waters sparkled as did the bright black eyes of the Hawaiians. It reminded him of home. Parts of it were better: the rustling palms, lapping water, and shifting sands. When lonely, he'd watch hummingbirds with nearly invisible wings flit between white hibiscus blossoms. Doreena was thriving. She was growing into a normal, healthy Hawaiian baby just as he cooed to her each night. When he carried her out onto the beach others coddled her, too. They called her *wahine*, a pretty girl. They liked the peach tint to her hair and the curls protruding from her bonnet of palm fronds and her broad cheeks. People pinched them until they became more and more pronounced and he had to make them stop. They lived off the coconut palms, selling weavings to tourists from a roadside stand and eating the fruits that dropped near their shack on the beach. People mistook them for natives.

But Doreena wasn't very old before she wrecked it, as he'd feared she might one day. He'd taken her to the beach at age three when she was walking and becoming more autonomous. He encouraged her to hold his hand but, lately, it would slip from his as she reached to touch the bark of the Hau tree or stroke the glossy red anthuriums. He was forever palpitating her hands in his, coaxing her digits back into fleshy, girlish fingers. One day after he'd climbed to the top of a coconut tree, hacked one open with a machete and shared the water with her, he lay back, his face shaded by his hat and let her wander towards the water on her own. Up and down the beach other children were doing the same, parading in the shallows and piling sand on the shore, unsupervised.

He woke from a doze and, at first, all seemed at peace past the pink-lined pohuehue vines sewn into the shore at the high tide line. Doreena lay on her stomach where the waves soaked the coral sands. Eyes open, she held her cheeks between her tiny hands and her curls swept across her forehead. A wave swirled up around her receding from her elbows and leaving a strand of seaweed stuck to her side. She giggled. He reached for his slim, silver camera. He loved this device, this miraculous compromise. It captured a moment and released it. The image was precise and permanent, but the picture did not tamper with reality. Everything continued as it was, unspoiled, leaving no residue of guilt. He did not own a computer to view the pictures with, but he had stacks and stacks of the square disks and had figured out how to use the drugstore kiosk to print the pictures onto paper. The snapshots wallpapered their hut.

He took a photo of Doreena and zoomed in on the image on screen. He'd captured her serene expression, an absolute sense of belonging. She was one with the sun on her face and back enjoying the rush of sea. She lay flat against the sand, her legs and feet behind her in the surf. He magnified her sea turtle green, *Honu*, eyes. Her gaze past him was absent. She was somewhere inside herself daydreaming. Then, he saw it behind her — the fin.

He leapt to his feet shouting. Lost in reverie, she did not respond. He looked at her, not entirely sure he could tell where her sides ended and the sand began. She had taken off her tiny bikini top. Her striped pink, brown and white briefs were nearly the same color as her skin. She blended into the sand. Down the beach, a *haole* mother and son were walking towards them hand in hand. Doreena's feet had spread and joined in one translucent sea green fan.

He caught her hand and yanked her up. Her green fin flexed against the sand. Her eyes focused on his and she shrieked. Sand clung to her round belly and sides. He kicked sand over her fin as the mother and son walked by. The woman pulled her son around to her other side and glared. He dragged Doreena up the beach yelling, "Stay out of the water!"

Doreena began to cry, another danger, too many tears and her flesh would start to flow away. It had been a mistake to bring her here.

"Selfish," Osana had said once under her breath during one of their fights. And he'd laughed at her. "Of all the things I've been accused of, Osana!"

But she'd been right about that too. It was selfish to want this child. But he could not stop.

He knelt and plugged Doreena's nose and mouth with his hand. "Stop." He half hoped she wouldn't remember the Breath Game, the way he'd taught her to breathe, but she flushed pink and her cheeks swelled. He held her puffed smile in his hand from corner to corner.

"Is everything all right here?"

The *haole* mother hovered over him. Her boy stood slightly behind, his hand hidden in hers. He couldn't see the woman's face just the sheen of light through her hair, but he could see the effort it cost her to confront him in the way her silhouette trembled. He released Doreena's face and her breath huffed out. She giggled.

"I'm her grandfather. She was playing too close to the water," he said.

Still, the woman stared down at him. Her shoulders shook. "You can't touch a child like that. That's not acceptable. Do you understand?" her voice trembled. "She's just a little girl."

He squeezed Doreena's shoulders. "Yes, that's right. She's just a little girl."

But the woman wasn't leaving. She should leave them alone. That was what these people did, left each other alone. He picked up his camera and machete. He didn't want to hurt the woman, but he didn't mind if he looked threatening. "Go away. Mind your own business."

The woman took a step back stumbling over her child. Then she was striding past him down the beach back towards the other people.

He whispered to Doreena, "Stay here, my little girl. Stay here."

Leonid held faint memories of these kinds of people from his former life, but they also confused him. They were separate from each other, distant. They did not share thoughts but, sometimes, like this woman, they formed sudden, random, one-sided connections. This unpredictable tendency and the woman's rigid certainty and focus on Doreena frightened him. How could Doreena live here among these people unaffected by their thoughts? How could he protect her?

He clutched the machete as he stared after the woman and then let it drop to his side. His shoulders slumped. He was capable of destruction. He could change that woman in an instant with the machete, remove her ability to shape the world with her heart. But he would not do it just because she threatened Doreena. He was sorry he had scared her, too. These people were not so easily shaped by emotion like Doreena or as interwoven in a universe of thought as himself, but he could not believe they were entirely unaffected by each other. It was still a harm to create fear needlessly on the gentle beach.

But in Doreena's case, it was necessary.

She pointed down the beach at the other children. "Why can't I go in the water?"

He knelt and whispered in her ear. "Sharks. Huge old beasts with mouths all teeth. They swim in packs like dogs," he lied.

As he walked Doreena back to their hut, he watched her feet skim the sand until her toes pinked. He bent every few steps and pocketed a stone or shell. He made her sit inside the rest of the day and count them. He stared at his photos and decided. He needed to take her away from the sun and sand and water — all the shifting, shiny lures. They needed to go somewhere inland, much more solid.

~ 1 ~

JUMP

On the island, Doreena Flora Moriena reaches a point of decision between two worlds and two men

On the island everything is tangled. Petals, tendrils and leaves entwine. Everything moves: the surf, the sand and the jungle vines. Even those island elements that seem most stationary shift. The stones shake: the miniscule ones that make up the red trail, the round ones collected at the bottom of the pool, the moss-coated planks up the walls of the cave and the two pillars that stand on the land's highest point.

Doreena Flora Moriena, who has lived her life as an amorphous person of shifting shapes easily influenced by the expectations of others, finally knows her ancestry. This question has needled her since childhood when the other children wondered why her skin was that color, and her hair so curly, and made fun of her accent, buzzing — *zza, zza, zza* — and said she came from somewhere illicitly off-continent, although they had no knowledge of geography. Eventually they left her alone, which was the way her grandfather wanted it and the reason why he did not tell her either the truth or a lie.

Now that she knows her parents, Doreena is in a quandary. She does not know where she belongs or how to be comfortable. She stands on the edge of a cliff contemplating jumping into the sea. The island shakes.

She's the only one still, and won't be for long.

In Doreena's last moment of indecision, the island blooms. Hibiscus trumpets, lily flutes, bird of paradise spears, jasmine bells ring, and waxy, red discs of anthurium charge through the jungle greens. The island contains an impossible combination of flora. Some of its wild botanic garden belongs in temperate climes, others in cooler ones. The plants grow naturally north or south of the equator. Yet, on the island, they grow in volume together like companion plants as if gaining benefit from each other's use of soil. Flowers arrange themselves down the slope of leaves, stalks, and stems to the sea. In miniature, they could wind nicely around a front reception desk. The confluence of their scents, musk-laden, fruit-sweet, and spice-tinged, carry up even to the jungle's edge and the mountain top. From here, from its highest point, the island threatens to erupt.

Through the sulfur plumes, Doreena catches a whiff of the floral tide and it poises her on the edge of the cliff where she's leaned out to watch her employers fall. The sales manager Marilyn's hands flap out in front of her like pink kerchiefs and the publisher, Rock, plummets after her. Months ago, Doreena would have jumped after them unthinking. But now an inlet of sand, a thumbprint of pink, at the base of the cinnabar-laced cliff distracts her. She knows the quality of that sand, the soft talc press of it against her skin. The little thumbprint idyll circled by white crests of waves on one side, and white blossoms on the other, looks calm like a remnant of the island she remembers from her first encounter with the magic place.

When she first came to the island, Doreena recognized the white Hawaiian hibiscus, *kokio keokeo*, her grandfather had planted around her childhood home and the tall palms from photographs of her infancy on Maui. The beach that had suddenly appeared around her had felt like childhood restored. Something in the air soothed her grief over the loss of her grandfather and quelled her anger at how he had left her abruptly with her questions unanswered.

On her own, she would have stayed on that beach. She would never have gone further than that first break of jungle with its grove of fruit. Behind her, the red mouth of the trail parts the jungle, but the tranquil beach at the end of it now has hurricane churned and sea-stained sand. There is no easy trail down to the new beach beckoning at the base of the cliff. From this height, were she to fall down to it, that pink sand, all the grains at once, would hit her body like stone.

Her employers, Rock and Marilyn Traynter, are speeding through the gray sky toward the reflective pane of sea with its white wave shards. Midway through the sky, the portal back to the city revolves. Its light inner rings look like rows of teeth. It draws Rock and Marilyn in, winks as they pass through, and then reappears over the sea. As soon as they are gone, Doreena, wind-pressed, and suddenly light, stumbles. Her bare feet hover above the pink sand, toes splayed, and then a hand catches her arm and pulls her back. Tom, *The Mirror's* number two advertising salesman, squeezes her upper arm, firm enough to get her attention, loose enough not to pinch, a father's practiced grip.

"Don't go unless you mean to. You're going to have to really jump."

Doreena envies Tom's children. She never knew her own father.

With Rock gone, the C-town City Fathers, *The Mirror's* sales force, and the people who love her look to Doreena Moriena. They examine her bare skin as though looking for a map in her blue veins.

"Is that how we get back?" Tom asks. He has a family to go back to and will surely jump.

Doreena admires his certainty. "Yes."

Tom releases her and returns to the sales force. The Stew, *The Mirror's* investigative reporter, pumps his arms. "That's all I need. I've seen enough." His eyes are wide behind his glasses. He jumps and lands in the fissures' center where he flashes through to C-town. For a moment, the green water of Lake Traynter shines through the opening. The City Fathers point down to Rock. They huddle in their black suits and prepare to jump. Following Rock has always been sound strategy. The circle of white heads unwinds into a line. Sand and sea spray streak their doughy faces. Just before they jump, the powerful old men clasp hands like schoolboys. The fathers fall, black specks, in a disordered migration. The fissure crackles as they enter it and plunge through to the man-made lake. Doreena's memory of all those heavy mornings, every day she's forced herself to get up and go into the city, lifts like fog as the fathers fall away.

Tom leads the sales force to the edge of the cliff. He points and bends his knees showing them how to make the jump. They leap one after the other off the edge. Even in casual dress, they look alike. She'd been one of them once, the best of them, actually — *The Mirror's* number one salesman. The drop of each one buoys her and she bobs on the edge of the cliff. The wind lifts her hair off the back of her neck crowning her face with curls. Tom turns back to her when he's seen the rest of the force over the edge.

"Are you coming?"

"I don't know."

He throws up his hands, jumps hard and speeds to the center. He can't wait for her; his children are home. However, much time has passed on the island, it's too much time to spend in a place that feels so far away.

Nine months ago, Doreena had been loved by her grandfather and then he had gone. Since then, other people had appeared who loved her, too. She has a best friend, Diane, a tribe of surfers who adore her, and two soul mates: Earnest, in his tweed jacket, and

Alonso, naked on the island like herself. Being with them now makes liquid shapes under her skin. The sudden swells of her body and the tremors of the island rock her. These people who love her come from C-town, so she has to consider going back.

The surfers in their wetsuits move to the edge of the cliff. Doreena wants to give them some token to remind them of this place, but her hands are empty. She kisses each of them and whispers their island names: Kyushu, Sri Lanka, Jamaica. They still have those places if they attempt to reach them. Doreena never took an island name, preferring to keep the name her grandfather gave her. It and the necklace are all she has left from him. Now even his ashes are gone.

The surfers, all except Alonso, turn their backs on paradise and dive off the cliff. When they leave the island, her breast and hips deflate and she's back in the compact virgin body she grew up in, a little stout and drooping toward the grassy lawn. Inside of her, the waves persist, however. Has this motion been inside her all along? Or was there a moment it began? She is unsure now.

Through the fissure, the City Fathers bob in the lake with their ties, the sales force paddle in billowing Hawaiian shirts and the AeroFlux union workers cling to their protest signs: "Maui forever." and "Jobs now!" Doreena stands between Earnest and Alonso knowing she must make a choice soon. If she jumps down into the cold lake, C-town will quell the watery sensations of which she has only recently become aware. A wave of heat rolls down the green lawn from the stone ruins, black and reflective as Traynter Tower, *The Mirror's* office. A jet of molten lava spews. Her island will soon be covered in heat and when that cools it will turn to black rock. Is this her fate as well? Now that she has lovers and heat flowing within, will she soon grow cold and hard again?

Diane grabs her hand. "Come with me." She pulls Doreena across the lawn until the cliff is just a green line across the gray sky. "Did I ever tell you I'm afraid of heights? It's easier for me if

I don't look down. I'm going to take a run at it from here. Are you coming?"

"I feel light," Doreena said.

"The wind."

"No, me."

"Look," Diane says, her red hair wind-flung into a tentacled headdress. "You can go back, pretend you don't know. Just don't think about it."

"Don't think about where I come from, what I am? How am I supposed to live like that?"

"You did before."

"But now I know. You don't understand. I feel them inside me."

Diane squeezes Doreena's hand and releases it. As she runs down the green lawn, her red hair sways. When she reaches the edge, she spreads her arms wide across the gray and her wingspan drops beneath the green line and disappears.

The watery feeling in Doreena rises. She is alone on the island with her two lovers. She approaches the edge of the cliff and stands by them; inside she flows between them. One side feels firm as a sandy shore and the other holds the openness of the sea. Clouds roil overhead and it is as close to night on the island as it has ever been. She listens to her lovers.

"I love you. Come back with me."

"I'll stay with you."

Doreena unclasps the necklace her grandfather gave her. She swings the empty vial on its silver chain. She sees the dark island through its clear glass. If her lovers leave her alone on the island, there will be no one's thoughts to hold her together. When she first came to the island and it warmed her, she wanted to meld with it. Now the heat of the lava rolls, ready to consume her. Or, she can jump away and forget this place. She can let the presence of her ancestors flow away and harden. The island stills. It has given her all the information it can — now she must move toward the sea or the jungle.

~ 2 ~

DOREENA

Once a solid citizen, Doreena loses her anchor and questions her ancestry

After work, on the day Doreena Flora Moriena received word of her grandfather's death, she could barely move. Her body, slowed to a molten pace when her grandfather left for vacation, began to stiffen. The paralysis crept over her as soon as she'd pulled out of the parking garage. Her hands hovered over the steering wheel and she ran the few streetlights on her way home afraid to come to a stop that might be permanent. When she was finally able to pull up to the curb in front of her home on Maple Street, Doreena failed, with her thick fingers, to turn the ignition completely off and the car stereo stayed on. Chapter 1 of *Stellar Sales*, "Mirroring Made Simple: The Persuasive Secrets of Body Language," continued. Looking at the house, Doreena felt the truth; that grandfather would not be coming back to it. It had been a chaotic day, but now she wasn't ready to admit it was over, enter the house and spend the night alone.

In the morning, she'd grabbed *The Mirror* on her way up to the sales office. The paper had been using the new silicon broadsheets for almost a year, but she still wasn't used to the jellied, flesh feel of them and the pink tint to the pages. She intended to flip through to the Entertainment & Food section to check her ads for registration errors, but the gross boldness of the 46-point headline drew her eye: Maui AeroFlux Flight Crashes. Beneath the header was a full-color shot of a mangled plane with emergency chute extended. Sliding down the chute was her boss, *The Mirror's* publisher, Rock Traynter, holding her other boss, sales manager, Marilyn Traynter, on his lap. Perfectly composed, the shot placed the Traynters in the bottom right corner of the frame, the place the eye naturally gravitates to when looking at a photo. The shooter had captured great expressions too. Rock looked oddly gleeful with the smoke rising behind him and a cluster of terrified passengers ahead and Marilyn, her face tilted up at Rock, looked awestruck. Doreena thought she had studied all Marilyn's expressions, but the one in the photo was new. This one photo could put an end to all the gossip about Marilyn's mercenary attachment to *The Mirror's* publisher. Obviously, she did love him, if only for the security. Positioned directly behind the couple was the maroon-winged AeroFlux logo framed by a black puff of smoke. It was a shot worthy of *The Mirror's* best eye, Andy Orson, but the photo credit read Stewart "The Stew" Holmes. *The Mirror's* investigative reporter didn't usually take pictures. Doreena could see how it could have happened though. Even as the plane plummeted, Rock would have had *The Mirror* in mind. He'd have called The Stew and ordered him out to the airport.

Beneath the masthead and the newspaper's tagline *Information is physical: C-town's daily source* read:

Seven die, 16 injured; Mirror publisher heroically lessens tragedy

In the early morning hours, AeroFlux flight 393 returning from Maui crashed on the landing strip killing seven returning vacationers and injuring 16 C-town citizens.

The Mirror's own publisher, Rock Traynter, and his wife, Marilyn, were on the flight returning from their honeymoon. Survivors of the wreck said Mr. Traynter's quick action aboard the plane saved lives.

"He's a hero," said stewardess Diane Wing. "As we were going down he got up and yelled, 'Come on, citizens.' And got everyone ready to evacuate. I was so glad someone took control."

Trouble began as the plane made its approach into C-town. It circled several times in the foggy morning before beginning its descent.

The story went on — AEROFLUX CRASH see back, A12 — offering little in the way of new information and ending, "*The Mirror* has opted not to list the names of the deceased passengers in this morning's edition in order to give AeroFlux time to notify their families." Doreena had already received her call early that morning, but from the Aloha Funeral Home, not AeroFlux.

Even before the physical stiffness had begun to set in, Doreena had felt grandfather's death in the wrong way. She'd had the wrong emotion, anger, and pushed it down and hurried to work even though she knew that was not what most people would do after learning of the death of a loved one. Doreena ran her finger over that last sentence on the back page, "notify their families."

Underneath the cool page of silicon, nubs rose. These quantum dots embedded in the paper had made her sales job easy and catapulted her into position as *The Mirror's* number one salesman. The dots embedded electrons in the paper, which relayed bits of information throughout the town. Sold in conjunction with a radio transmission of corresponding phosphorescent particles, the ads literally embedded a business' message in the fabric of C-town. In fact, it became impossible to compete without placing an ad in *The Mirror* and signing up for a corresponding package of phosphors. But since her grandfather had gone on vacation, Doreena hadn't been able to make a single sale. She wished she could see her grandfather's name in print and touch the rise of it. She could not believe he was gone.

A sidebar to the crash story confirmed the buzz in C-town. One of the City Fathers, Charlie Earl, had recently been dismissed (*The Mirror* couldn't bring itself to report "fired") from his job as CEO of AeroFlux and a successor had yet to be named. Word was the company was bringing in someone from outside of C-town, from back East. The double deck headline's rhetorical questions made *The Mirror's*, and therefore, C-town's opinions clear, "New AeroFlux CEO in trouble? What mistakes are behind the recent crash?"

Doreena, reading the paper as she walked into the pressroom, dropped it as the applause began. The pressroom, usually vacant by daybreak, was packed. The pressmen, in gray coveralls splashed with dried patches of pink plastic, leaned against the stainless-steel vats of silicon.

On a pallet of papers pulled into the center of the room, publisher Rock Traynter stood over them wearing his double-pair of sunglasses even in the dim blue lights used throughout *The Mirror's* offices. Standing beneath him were a few notepad-clutching reporters. The last time there'd been an all-staff stand-up at *The Mirror* the subject had been the new quantum information technology, what they all now called the dots. Warmed plastic and an electric sizzle had been introduced to the pressroom and Doreena remembered tucking her chin beneath her turtleneck to escape the stink. Now, it struck her as funny, how the colognes of the sales force stood out instead. They were all down here too, looking unusually at ease. There wasn't a single bright patch of color among them, no sign of Marilyn their manager at all.

"There we were circling for the third time," Rock said. "That was the best part of the whole trip for me being able to see all of C-town from that vantage point. We're an outpost in the middle of the Cascadian wilderness, but what we've built is so bright and so solid. I've never been more proud than I was looking down at our city, seeing Traynter Tower and knowing you were all here at *The Mirror*. The citizens of C-town are the best in the world. We're the only people who still know what it's like to live in America. We were the only ones able to preserve our way of life when everything else went to hell. That's what I was thinking when that hull began to shake. By that time, it was our third pass over the city, and we knew something was wrong. Marilyn had already joked that she wished we could go down over Pacifica for a softer landing, but I told her I'd take the firm ground over the ocean anytime. I said there's no place I'd rather crash than C-town and that's exactly what we did."

The way he said it made it sound like he'd brought the plane down in C-town on purpose instead of surviving an accident. He paused while the staff cheered. "Thank you. It's going to be a busy day."

The reporters and salesmen began to crowd toward the elevator. When Tom, *The Mirror's* number two salesman, spotted Doreena an expression of concern crossed his face and Doreena suddenly stiffened and began to topple. Something inside her lurched, an unfamiliar, unsettling motion. Tom caught her arm and held her steady.

"Are you ok?"

"I'm fine. I've never been sick a day in my life," Doreena said sounding so much like her grandfather that she wanted to scream, just like when she'd gotten the call. She clamped the anger down, but she could feel it, or something, roiling inside her underneath her thin, stiff shell.

"No," he shook her a little. "You look like you're about to faint, really gray. Should you be here? Do you need me to drive you home?"

"No." She couldn't explain how the idea of leaving made her panic and she wasn't sure which she was more afraid of, that she might freeze up completely or open into a flood of whatever was flowing around inside her. The only way to counteract it was to just keep on as usual which, of course, no one would understand. "It's my grandfather."

"Goodness," Tom said, more concerned than he sounded. He had three young children at home, so his language was always subdued. "Was he on that plane? Listen, you should get a look at the manifest. You work at *The Mirror.* We'll just ask The Stew for it. He went upstairs."

Doreena didn't want to tell Tom that she already knew her grandfather was dead but had come to work anyway as if it were no big deal. She liked his idea and wanted to see her grandfather's name in print. Maybe that's what was wrong with her, why she wasn't reacting appropriately, because she didn't really believe what she'd been told yet. She never did like conducting transactions over the phone. Things just felt more certain face-to-face. The paper wouldn't be embedded with the dots yet, but she could still see her grandfather's name in plain ink and run her finger over that.

In the stairwell, Doreena and Tom stopped just below the newsroom door when they heard Rock's voice and saw him talking on the landing. They knew better than to interrupt. Rock and The Stew had a tense alliance. The Stew had been the last reporter to come over from the *Post-Intelligencer.* The paper had folded shortly after he'd left, cementing Rock's grip on a one-newspaper town.

"Traveling at the speed of sound 1,000 feet per second over the ocean at the mercy of AeroFlux was a mistake," Rock said. "But this never would have happened on Charlie's watch. I want you to find out what went wrong with that plane."

"I'm on it," The Stew said.

"Damn fools. How dare they get rid of Charlie? Their new guy won't know the rules, the history, what holds C-town together."

"I've got a name," Stew said.

From the stairwell below, Doreena could see Rock get ready to do it. He reached up and lowered that top pair of glasses. Underneath were a second pair of dark shades. Behind these, people said, people who'd had the misfortune to get close enough, you could see the outlines of Rock's eyes through the green-tinted black panels. These same people (when they could be sure they were not in the same building as Rock) sometimes said they doubted Rock even had a light sensitivity. Maybe just wore the glasses to intimidate the hell out of people.

"How?" Rock said.

The Stew appeared able to hold Rock's gaze for a few seconds, but when he started talking again his words came faster. "I've got sources. The new CEO's Dalton Rees. And he's not just from back East. He came in off continent." When he's finished blurting this out. Rock stayed silent and The Stew spoke again, more slowly, "So, how was Maui?"

He made it sound off hand, but everyone knew Rock hadn't wanted to go on the honeymoon trip. Marilyn had had to work on him for almost a year.

"Gritty and hot," Rock said, and thumped up the stairs.

The Stew paused with his hand on the newsroom door. When Rock's footsteps faded, he called down, "Do I smell some salesmen down there trying their chops at snooping?"

"It's us," Tom said. "We're looking for the flight manifest."

"Ah, number one and number two." The Stew was now openly mocking, but he stopped when he looked at Doreena. His gold-rimmed glasses magnified his already large eyes. "Oh, you got someone on there. Yeah, sure." He handed over his green notebook. "Here's my list of the dead. It's short. But I guess if you know one name on it that's long enough."

Doreena looked over The Stew's scrawl of names.

"Nothing?" The Stew said. "Here's the manifest." The Stew handed her a roll of normal paper and flat type with an alphabetized list.

"He's not on this either." Had she imagined this morning's call? Except for her stiffness, nothing had seemed certain of late.

"Maybe he planned to stay a few more days," The Stew said. "That could be trouble enough. After what happened, I'm not sure how much longer we'll be seeing flights in and out of Maui."

"You think they'd cancel Maui service? Isolate us completely?" Tom said.

"Rumor has it," said The Stew. "The City Fathers were pissed about what happened to Charlie. Suspicious too. And now this crash. Bad timing for AeroFlux. It was bound to happen though, there's no mystery there, since C-town hasn't been letting them import the materials they need for maintenance. You won't be reading that story in the pages of *The Mirror* though."

Behind the door, they heard Vic Brown, *Mirror* editor, bellow. "We need tomorrow's headlines, people."

"Nope, screw Maui," The Stew said. "Rock's finally going to turn C-town into his own private island. That's today's headlines. Take that to the street and sell it." He grabbed his manifest from Doreena's hands and left them alone in the stairwell.

"I'm glad your grandfather's OK," Tom said when they reached the sales floor. "I know how much he means to you."

Tom, the family man, knew her grandfather was all she had. He'd hinted more than once it was a situation she should change. Doreena went to her desk and tried to keep her mind on work. Through the trodden gold carpet of the sales floor, she could feel the buzz of the newsroom below, the screech of phones, the roar of the editor and the rise and fall of the reporters from their desks. The last time Rock had had newsroom jumping like this was when C-town was separating from the United Government. *The Mirror* had been sparring headline to headline with the *P-I* whose editorial board favored unification. It was usually feature-story quiet. The sales force was excited too, but without Marilyn's oversight, their energy lacked direction. The guys kept popping up for coffee breaks and pacing the halls. Only Tom solidly made calls all morning and afternoon.

Doreena stayed close to her desk too, although she was useless on the phones. She did her best work on the street, in person with her irresistible Mirroring Technique, but she couldn't get herself to leave the office. She rode the elevator down a couple of times intending to head out, at least take a lunch break, but each time that stiffness set in. It settled over her like a heavy shell. And she wasn't hungry anyway. Her appetite had vanished with her grandfather. She'd tried to keep to regular meals like he'd told her to, "Stay healthy, have dinner." But she kept forgetting until she was already in bed, the same bed she'd slept in since she was four, staring up at the ceiling filled with her own imagined constellations in the uneven paint.

No one worked past six that night in sales, although the newsroom was still bustling below. As the office emptied out, that stiffness settled into Doreena's skin even in the sanctity of *The Mirror* office. She muttered the words from *Stellar Sales* as she drove home to distract herself. "To create a feeling of sympathy. Put your hands in the same position as the person across from you. Subconsciously, they will see you as like themselves."

Doreena was still sitting in her car in front of her house when her neighbor Mrs. Dammerung knocked on the window. "Honey, there's someone here to see you."

A man in uniform stood on her doorstep. He carried a clipboard and a small brown box. Mrs. Dammerung clung to Doreena's arm as she got out of the car and approached him. He wore a brown uniform with an orange and gold flower on the lapel. The embroidered script inside the blossom read, "Aloha Funeral Home."

"But I saw the manifest," Doreena protested. "I work at *The Mirror* and I've already seen the official record. His name wasn't on there. He wasn't on that plane."

Mrs. Dammerung squeezed her hand.

"Oh, I'm so sorry miss," the courier said. "Very sorry for your loss. He came back on that flight all right, but they wouldn't have listed him. Not like this," the man raised the brown box and stared off towards the house. "In cargo. It happened before on Maui, I'm sorry."

The courier angled his clipboard at her. Under cause of death the form read: drowning. Doreena took the pen the man proffered and signed, but her fingers stiffened around it and her signature came out sharp and angled, unlike her usual arching loops.

She took the box into her childhood home. Grandfather who had never been sick a day in his life, never missed a day at his job cleaning the halls of the elementary school, would not be returning. Doreena sunk onto the living room sofa. At some point, Mrs. Dammerung left a plate of cookies on the table. They sat side-by-side with the brown box stamped with the maroon-winged AeroFlux logo. Mrs. Dammerung's pfeffernusse were a proud family recipe passed down from her German grandmother. Doreena bit into one, tasteless dry crumbles, and the powdered sugar flaked onto her black slacks. Grandfather was gone and he'd left without answering any of her questions, ever. He hadn't answered her when she'd hinted or when she'd confronted him and now he could never tell about her parents. He'd left her for Maui, left her alone, and left her heritage a mystery.

When she looked up again, Mrs. Dammerung was gone, the carpet held a spray of powdered sugar, and cookies dotted the floor. Doreena clasped her hands to her chest. Had she done that; thrown those and yelled at her neighbor? She hadn't meant to, now she'd have to find some way to apologize.

She reached for the box. Inside was a copper canister the courier had said now contained her grandfather. When she lifted it out, it was surprisingly light.

At the bottom of the box was an envelope. She touched the letters across the front. They were nearly smooth except for the press of plain ink into the pulped wood. There was a little of her grandfather in the letters, Doreena thought, as she touched her own name written in his hand — the enormous D devolving into a scrawl. Beneath her name was the bump and lift of something enclosed. Whatever the object was in the envelope, she hoped it contained answers.

~ 3 ~

MOVING

New people, new places and new ideas; Doreena dislodges

Doreena did not get a chance to open the envelope right away. The other piece of mail she received along with her grandfather's ashes was a final eviction notice. She had to move out of her childhood home to make way for the White Spires condominium project, immediately. Apparently, the city's acquisition of the neighborhood had been going on for some time. Her grandfather had mentioned it, but it still blindsided her. She'd never expected moving to be her sole responsibility, or that she'd be going anywhere without him. But not even *The Mirror's* top salesman could persuade C-Town's city planners at this late date that it was a bad idea to replace the historic homes on Maple Street with condos. The homes were too near the lucrative downtown core, and C-town, with its tight borders, needed density to grow. It was a losing battle, especially since the developer was Mark Traynter, Rock's older brother.

Doreena thrust her hands down on the counter of the C-town Planning Office and squared off with the urban growth director in a classic gesture of power. The urban growth guy held his arms out and his palms up and Doreena easily read his body language. He respected her position at *The Mirror*, and he'd like to pacify her, but, honestly, there was nothing he could do.

"At least include some low-income housing," Doreena said, thinking of Mrs. Dammerung. "Some of my neighbors have lived in those houses for years. They can't afford a new condo. Maybe on the top floor."

"The top floor is for the penthouses," the planner said.

"Well, maybe the floor beneath that."

Doreena packed her possessions while the chainsaws buzzed. The trees shading the block fell. A black Traynter bulldozer plowed into the first home on the block as she stacked boxes in the back seat of her car.

"You're glad you didn't have to see this," she said to her grandfather as she placed him, in his copper urn, beside her on the passenger seat. She placed the envelope on her lap as she drove away tracing her name with her finger again. In her rearview mirror, the bulldozer reached the middle of the block and rolled over grandfather's hibiscus. Each spring, he'd filled vases with bouquets of the blooms and placed them on her bedroom dresser so that she saw them first thing when she awoke. He told her that although the fragrance of hibiscus was renowned, in fact, only the white one had scent and the plant had once been nearly extinct until the Hawaiian people had created a special preserve to save their native flower. In her memory, her childhood on Maui was all fertile beach and lush jungle, the only aspects of the past her grandfather mentioned freely.

She kept hearing Mrs. Dammerung's parting words, "Poor child, left alone." The words made her feel exactly that: poor and alone. Fighting sluggishness, Doreena stepped on the gas, before the bulldozer could scrape through the soft fir floor of the house, which held her childhood in its grooves and stains. She left the downtown core, with its sparkling high-rise condos, of which White Spires was soon to be the latest, and centennial homes outfitted with third bedrooms, and took Burrows overpass to the low rent district. As soon as she entered the unfamiliar territory near the outskirts of C-town, she began to tremble. Her hands gripped the steering wheel, but inside, they shook. Across from the Aeroflux Industrial Complex, stood a pre-Revolution era brick building, The Narborough Apartments, her new home.

On her way into the building, staggering from queasiness as well as the weight of her largest box filled with photographs, Doreena stopped and stared at Hawaii. A tear ran through the top of the poster and red, block letters stretched across the bottom quarter of the page — HAWAII. Between those two spaces lay paradise. A pearly white shell cupped a swath of blue in a shade lacking a good Pantone match. On the right a palm tree leaned in, its fringed fronds falling green over blue. The box began to slide down the front of her flannel shirt, but she didn't look away. When the door in front of her clanked and swung open, Doreena stumbled back still staring at the poster.

"I'm closed," a woman said. "Moving in? You want that glass door, there, up to the apartments."

The box slipped. It landed on its side with a clatter of frames and a cascade of photos, which began immediately to melt into the wet pavement. The woman reached for them with wrinkled hands ringed with large stones.

"No, I've got it," Doreena said. Hands flat, she swept the photos back into the box, but when she hefted it up to the shelf of her hip the bottom sagged.

"Just a moment. I've got what you need," the woman said.

"Never mind." Doreena turned to go, but the envelope with grandfather's letter, which had been on the top of the pile was gone. The glass door the woman passed through was locked. It clanked when Doreena pulled on the brass handle. She peered after the woman into a dark, cluttered space. A light appeared in the back and a body moved into it. The woman, probably as tall as Rock

Traynter, walked with a strange spread-legged gait. She returned with a crisp cardboard box imprinted with the AeroFlux logo.

"My letter?" Doreena said.

The woman patted the front of her sweatshirt pocket. A fringe of silver hair peaked out from under her hood.

"Let's get these things into a firm box. I don't blame you for getting distracted by Hawaii. She used to be one of my favorites, every bit as lovely and close, too. But you've been." She picked up one of the photos. "Did you grow up there? Off-continent?"

Doreena could see the rest of the question, "Where are you from?" crinkled in the corners of the woman's eyes. The picture the woman was holding was one of Doreena's favorites. It was taken of her on a Maui beach. She was a toddler grinning in the sand and holding her chin in cupped hands. Her legs and feet were hidden somewhere behind her in the surf. Her curly hair, which now even the stiffest gels and hairsprays could not wrangle into a professional look to meet Marilyn's approval, framed her child's face adorably and her matte brown hair shone with glints of copper in the island sun. But as much as she loved this picture, Doreena had been disappointed to find it tucked into the back of an end table while cleaning out the house. She'd mistaken this moment on Maui for an actual memory, but all she'd remembered was a photograph. It explained why she'd seen herself with the eye of an amateur photographer looking out and perfectly placed in the center of things. All she knew of her life before C-town was what her grandfather had given her, a flat, incomplete picture with MAUI running along the bottom in red letters.

Doreena grabbed the picture. She did not like this woman's acquisitive touch. "We moved to C-town when I was three. That photo is all I know of it."

"Well, keep it close. You'll want warm dreams. It gets very cold in an old building like this."

"Of course, it does," Doreena said bitterly. "Seems like I get cold in October and stay that way through March."

"Makes sense if you grew up on Maui. The body sets its internal thermometer early. You always carry the weather of your childhood with you," the woman said lifting handfuls of Doreena's things and moving them quickly from one box to another in the rain. The woman nodded across the street at the AeroFlux complex. "There've been more people moving out than moving in with all the layoffs. You an engineer?"

"Oh, no, I work at *The Mirror.*" Doreena said. Just mentioning *The Mirror* made her feel more solid and certain. Her grandfather's death wouldn't change anything about her job; there would still be ads to sell.

The woman dropped a handful of photos into the box. "Don't be asking questions here. This is a haven. None of them engineers can afford Hawaii, but they can dream. A lot of them wish they could leave." Underneath her sweatshirt hood, the slits of her eyes were a shadowed blue.

"Don't you dare quote me."

"I'm not a reporter. I'm on your side. I'm in sales."

Speaking of sales, she was behind on hers. Her manager, Marilyn, would be after her soon. She could hear the pep talk; "You've got to produce if you want to stay number one." She nodded toward the Hawaii poster in the store window. "You know, you put something like that in *The Mirror* and you'd get a whole new clientele. They'd drive out here. It would only have to run six months and they'd never forget you." As soon as she said it, Doreena could see the poster scaled in full color on an inside page in the entertainment section.

"I'll stop by on my way out tomorrow. What is it you sell here?"

But she was alone on the street. The envelope was back on top of her box, and the silver-haired woman with the odd way of walking was gone.

Marimbas greeted Doreena when she entered The Narborough apartments. Maracas and steel drums sounded up the stairway. On the third-floor landing, an easy guitar and mellow male vocalist joined in the music muffled behind one in the row of black doors. A sepia haze of smoke held the scent of burnt salt. Doreena strained to keep her arm pressed around the AeroFlux box. She knelt on the stairway, afraid if she set the box down now she wouldn't be able to heft it again. Her arms were limp from unaccustomed use. Puddles on the landing and a skiff of black sand led down the hallway fading into the trail of brown carpet. The music and the mess, she guessed, came from behind the same door. She continued up to her apartment. The tarnished plate read C-4. She went up and down the stairwell freighting her things, until she'd stacked boxes so high in the entryway, she couldn't see into the living room. She didn't remember what it looked like back there. Her only impression of the place had been, "small," but she'd signed the lease in a hurry. There weren't many decent places to live in the industrial part of town. This one, cramped and cold, was all she could afford.

After moving all her stuff, Doreena managed to hang her work clothes before sprawling spent on her bed hugging her grandfather in his urn and the letter to her chest. The warmth of moving dissipated as she lay in the mildewed room beneath the tinged blue ceiling. She placed the copper urn beside her on the floor, down by the tremor of marimbas, and read grandfather's letter. His rolling script matched the voice she heard in her head. The letter was typically terse and directive but lacked his usual logic. In absence, he'd become vague:

Dear Doreena,

Hold me. Do not bury me. Do not release me unless your life begins to shift. Keep me with you until you feel transient. Then release me. Please not in C-Town. Never there. And carry some of me with you at all times.

Love,

Grandfather

It was baffling. What did he mean, "transient"? Why "not in C-town"? Where else? And where, where was mention of her parents? He knew that what she wanted most from him, any information about who she was and where she came from, but he'd left her no clues. He'd carried all her hope away with him. Accompanying this short missive was a long list of his usual directives and one bizarre request. She was ashamed to note she had not been doing most of the instructions including the one at the top of the list: Eat regular meals.

The bizarre request concerned the necklace coiled in the bottom of the envelope. She swung the glass vial capped with a swirling silver plug on its knotted chain. Grandfather disapproved of "flashy" things: "Draws too much attention of the wrong kinds." This would be her first piece of jewelry and it was beautiful, but as she read what he wanted her to do with it, she didn't want it anymore. His instructions said to fill it with some of his ashes. She imagined wearing grandfather's ashes around her neck his death resting always on her chest. She already felt the weight of his loss. She didn't want to do it. Worse, she didn't want to figure out how to do it, how to get some of the ashes from the urn into the slim-lipped vial. Even opening the urn terrified her. She'd never seen cremated human remains. The urn was small, but somehow, she kept picturing organs. As a child, her grandfather had read to her from illustrated anatomy books. "And this is where your heart is for pumping blood," he would say touching the picture and then her chest. "And your kidneys, and your liver and your pancreas."

She'd thought he'd wanted her to become a doctor, but he'd stopped when she was older. And he had a phobia of hospitals: "Stay out of them, Doreena. You'll be better off. Those are places where people go to be sick and then die. Just be a happy, healthy girl and you'll always be well." As a child, she had crawled into his lap after a long day of teasing at school to hear him croon and pet her, "Healthy girl." As a teenager, she'd no longer been comforted. They had argued. Everyone was deciding what to do with their lives and he wasn't helping her make choices. He never pushed her toward anything.

"You are fine where you are," he said. "Don't let them get to you."

"I can't just be *happy*," she said. "I have to do *something.* That's the way it works."

He could have expected more of her. Then what would her life have been like? Mrs. Dammerung was right. Grandfather had left her hopelessly handicapped, poor, and alone and unsure of her place in the world without him, and now he'd left her with the task of taking his ashes and fulfilling his wishes. In the morning she knew, somehow, she'd manage to do what he asked. Afraid her thoughts of ash and organs would bring on the nightmare that she'd been having again, Doreena resisted sleep, finally getting up and taking two blue sleeping pills so that she wouldn't be useless tomorrow at work. In the nightmare, her hands were missing. She was sure she could find them within *The Mirror's* pages, but there was no way to turn the silicon sheets with her blunt wrists.

On Monday morning, the cold woke Doreena. The apartment was still, the pulsing marimbas gone. She hunched naked in the shower shivering while she figured out how to adjust the faucet. Finally, the pipes groaned and she angled her stiff, aching shoulders into the slim stream of heat. She used up all the hot water and then carried grandfather to the bathroom and twisted the urn's cool lid.

Her hands slipped around it. She imagined the lid flying loose and grandfather spilling onto the tile and mixing with the previous occupant's debris. But on her next try the lid came off cleanly in her hand. Inside, grandfather was sealed in clear plastic. His powder was chalky brown with a hint of pink like a pasty cheek. There were chunks, but they didn't look like bone. She pressed a finger into the baggie and a cakey clump gave way. She snipped off a corner of the bag and looked for some small implement. She eventually used the end of a make-up brush to guide traces of grandfather into the necklace vial. Grandfather disapproved of make-up, a showy way to draw attention to oneself, but she'd started wearing it when she began work at *The Mirror.* Marilyn said it was part of a professional sales appearance and grandfather couldn't argue with that. She's made her first trip to Denrigger's make-up counter and come away with an expensive collection of color-filled tubes she could easily afford at the time.

Once filled, Doreena capped the vial and hung it around her neck. The necklace felt lighter on her chest than it looked. Grandfather's ashes were nearly the same as pink-brown shade as her skin. Now that she had it on, it seemed somehow less grotesque, so long as she kept it hidden and no one ever asked what was inside. One she grew accustomed to the oddity, it actually felt comforting. For the first time since grandfather had left, Doreena thought about breakfast. But transferring the ashes had taken time and now she was late for work. As she raced downstairs, she bumped to a halt on the third-floor landing and her face slapped up against cold, wet rubber.

The man she ran into on the stairs of the Narborough was wearing a wet suit and carrying a surfboard nearly as long and wide as the hall. "Hey sorry. I didn't mean to snag your *da kine.*"

Whatever that was it sounded lewd. Cold water dripped off the end of his board and soaked through the shoulder of her rust-colored sweater. He smelled dank, fishy, and seasoned like one of the seafood restaurants downtown, Watertown or The Dungeness.

He swung the board around to the side holding it under one arm. "Oh, hey. Well, I can see the sharks circling. We can meet and greet another time."

His wet suit ended at the knees exposing his taut brown calves. Muck colored sand dusted the backs of them.

"Your music is too loud," she said.

"The Steelheads," he called back. "Everybody loves them. Give it time."

The street outside the Narborough was dark. There were no phosphors here along the street or across the highway at the AeroFlux industrial complex. It was even blankly dark across the awning where the business name should have glowed. Doreena hadn't gotten the impression from the woman that it was a new business. New business owners were quick to identify themselves. But if she didn't have any phosphors yet, she must be new. Really new. Fantastic, that meant big sales, Doreena would get this place lit up in no time. The woman would need print ads and radio, dots and phosphors, to work her way into the hearts and minds of C-town. This find was pure luck and great timing; just what Doreena needed to lift herself out of a downer month.

The door to the business opened with a chime. There was a decidedly un-C-town spice to the shop's mustiness. Variants of the Hawaii poster in the window covered most of the brick walls. The posters showed random sets of sky, water, sand, and foliage in shades of blue, white, and green cocked at various angles. They could all have been the same place except for the names stretched beneath them in block red: Tahiti, Jamaica, Sri Lanka, Trinidad, Tobago, Belize. The store was a jumbled collection of bric-a-brac, too cluttered for browsing. The owner appeared to have no retail sense. Many of the objects were vaguely familiar in shape but made out of strange materials. There were dolls and sculptures, tapestries and baskets, hats and brooms, and stones, seeds, powders, coins, and grasses. Whatever kind of business this was, it definitely needed *Mirror* advertising. Doreena would suggest a huge discount sale to get rid of inventory.

The woman came down a hall from the back toting two industrial-sized thermoses from which the spicy scent wafted. She was wearing that same gray hooded sweatshirt, and some kind of sarong tied around her waist over leggings. Her silver hair was slicked wet to her forehead. She didn't exactly look ready to greet customers.

"You," the woman said.

Doreena patted her bag. "I've brought my things for you, the rate sheet and contracts. I'm sorry I was distracted yesterday. I could have got you set up right away. I didn't realize this was a new business. I'm sure you're anxious to start."

She looked for a counter, but seeing none set her bag on top of a table that lurched to the side as she did so. She removed a sheaf of papers. "I bet we can get you running in print tomorrow and the radio up this week. We're quick like that."

The woman dropped the thermoses and the table rocked. "Not interested. Get out."

"I'm sorry," Doreena pressed her palm down on top of the sliding papers. "I didn't mean to rush you. I'm just trying to help. When did you open?"

"I've been here awhile," the woman said.

"But I've never heard of you."

"Just leave, please. I don't need any."

Doreena noted the woman's crossed arms, a defensive gesture indicating resistance. She extended her hand; a move designed to break through the woman's psychologically erected barrier. "Let me start over. I'm Doreena Moriena."

The woman didn't budge.

"Listen, you can't run a business in C-town and not be in *The Mirror*. No one will know you are here. You need some nice phosphors."

"The people who need to know; they know. Besides I live here. These are just my things."

"But this is a retail space. You can't have a residence here. That's against city ordinance. And you can't run a business in the dark. That's illegal."

"There isn't really any business. It's a museum. You know, a place to keep old things." The woman smirked, as she did so her lips and eyes nearly disappeared in deep folds of skin.

"I know what a museum is." Doreena said, thinking of grandfather again.

On weekends as a child, grandfather had often taken her often to the C-town museum. He had read to her off the placards beneath aerial photographs of what had been farmland before the construction of C-town's condos, offices and Traynter Tower. He'd showed her the old farm and logging equipment with jutting metal teeth. They'd walked down the hall with the photographs of the Traynter's ancestors and mannequins dressed like Rock's great-grandmother in long dresses with buttons down the front and high-necked collars carrying babes in trailing white lace. Every time they went, Doreena asked her grandfather about her own ancestors, but he always evaded: "We're here to learn about the Traynters. They built this town." Even so, she'd persisted. She'd been sure one day he must tell her about her own parents. She didn't even know what they looked like. She had pictures of hibiscus shrubs, coconut palms and pineapple plants, but none of them.

This place didn't look anything like C-town's official museum. It was too small and disorganized to contain a history. The photos were in color and the many little objects lacked weight and permanence. "What kind of a museum is this? These things don't look very old."

"No, just out of date. You can't get them anymore so that makes them history. My what an unusual necklace," the woman said pointing at Doreena's chest.

Doreena had taken the necklace out and absent-mindedly begun to stroke it while thinking about her grandfather. She tucked it quickly back under her cowl-necked sweater. "Just something my grandfather left for me."

The woman stepped forward and enfolded Doreena's hands in hers. Her hands, like the rest of her, were very long and she wore rings of polished stones. Doreena wondered if her grandmother's hands had looked anything like these.

"I'm sorry. Listen, I'm Hobart. It's always nice to meet the neighbors, but I'm not having anything to do with your *Mirror*. We're not hurting anything here. It's OK for people to dream."

"Dream about what?"

"Leaving C-town," the woman said. "Yes, yes, these are all things from off continent back before the borders closed. People come here to think of other places. It's natural. When times are stressful, people want to go look for a place where the food's plentiful. That's the drive that pulled us across continents."

"Who?"

"I mean people in the broad sense. Eons ago. Humankind. Kind as we can be. That's all it is an evolutionary drive. You can't stamp it down. Me and mine never tried to. Somebody starts getting antsy it's best to let him go search for higher ground. That's all it is. No harm."

"Except that it's irresponsible." Doreena said. "You leave people alone with bills to pay."

"So, you know something about that? Listen, it's better to be left in the lurch than kept company by someone who's staying around just to share their misery. Going through the motions doesn't do anyone any good. So, I doubt Rock Traynter would be happy having The Travel Museum in his paper anyway."

He wouldn't be very happy knowing that you weren't in it either."

"Well, maybe he's not a very happy person and there's nothing you or I can do about it. I'd appreciate it if you'd let us be. We're out of the way and not trying to attract undue attention. Now, I've got to take the boys their tea." Hobart hoisted the thermoses and swung them towards the street. "Get out of my shop."

"So, it is a shop." Doreena said. She couldn't remember the last time she'd failed to make a sale in person. As she left the museum, Doreena cast a backward glance at the posters: St. Martin, Dominique, Costa Rica, New Zealand, Aruba, Galapagos. She could still see them as six months of ads: full-page, full-color. She could see the awning lit up in tropical phosphors - pink, turquoise, yellow - lettered in avant-garde Tiki-Tiki font: The Travel Museum.

"Those posters would look great as a section in the C-town style pages."

"Honey, I hope that's not your car."

The driver's side window of her car was busted. Glass littered the sidewalk. There were scratch marks around the face of the radio where the thieves had tried to dislodge it, probably before deciding it was too much trouble for such a cheap system. They should have known from looking at the car that there wasn't anything good in it. Like all the cars in C-town it was an old model, but not old enough to be classic. The punks must have been lured by the pile of CDs on the passenger seat, and then disappointed by the selection.

Hobart put a hand on her shoulder. "I'm sorry. This is a bad neighborhood for petty crime. You never want it to look like you have things worth taking."

"Apparently, I don't." Doreena said.

"Could be worse." Hobart tilted her chin at the AeroFlux engineers gathering on the sidewalk in green union sweatshirts. "You've still got your job."

"Not for much longer if I don't make any sales."

Doreena lifted the lock on her door. Getting a replacement window for her car was going to be trouble but Hobart was right, she'd rather that than spending the day circling a burn barrel. The chill wind whipped Doreena's curls into her eyes as she headed for the overpass to downtown. She blasted the heat but only managed to singe her fingers where they curled around the steering wheel.

Channels of fog lay beneath the freeway blanketing the swamps around Lake Traynter. Downtown, the fog lifted. Pink sun lit the cityscape and the smell of fried dough from the city's bakeries sweetened the freeway exhaust.

Doreena fished around in her CDs, inserted *Stellar Sales*, and skipped to track 2 "Redefining Your Place in the World" and repeated with the narrator, "The secret to the irresistible pitch: stay positive. Your sales destiny depends on commitment."

A paycheck was never a certainty in sales. The top seller today could be on the street tomorrow. It all depended on effort. She was already wondering if she would be able to make rent and whether she ought to report the illegal business she had discovered to Marilyn this morning or wait a little longer and see if she could bully Hobart into a sale.

~ 4 ~

MANGO

Mirror Island arrives

Arriving at the reflective, black Traynter tower, Doreena cast a longing look back across the street at The Lofts, the condos overlooking Broad Street where the Traynters lived. Once a year, Rock and Marilyn invited the entire *Mirror* staff up to watch the C-Town Founder's Day parade from the balcony. Everyone looked forward to the yearly procession of floats and city services, police cars and fire trucks. The reporters, pressmen and sales force competed to predict which of the floats in honor of the Traynters' ancestors would earn the Grand Prize. The reporters usually won. Rock gave a speech reminding them how an independent C-town had persevered despite the collapse of the United Government. They all left bloated with pride and blackberry punch. Doreena wished she could afford to live in The Lofts. How easy it would be to cross the street and come to work each morning. She tallied how many full-page, full-color ads she'd need to land each month to live there. The entire entertainment section wouldn't cover the rent.

She grabbed a paper off a stack of slicks on her way into *The Mirror* and skimmed the front page on her way up. It was a mass of dueling headlines partitioned into an acceptable layout of boxes and sidebars. The reporters had made a busy night of it. The biggest headlines read: Rees Named New AeroFlux CEO, AeroFlux Fires 300 Union Workers, and Who Needs Maui? City Fathers Question Flight Risks.

The sales office smelled like the fish fertilizer her grandfather sprayed around his hibiscus. They'd cleaned the carpets over the weekend again. Across the room, Tom was already pounding the phones. He had the best phone sales of any of the force and many of the lucrative categories: automotive, banks, real estate. But Doreena bested him on volume with retail and restaurants. No one was a better closer than her on the streets and while Tom left at 5 to get home to his family Doreena worked late. She hadn't taken any time off to mourn her grandfather, but it still felt too long since she'd been in the office at her routine and focused on sales. Tom waved her over as she passed by his cubicle. He had his arm around a petite woman whose head barely reached his shoulder.

"Meet Diane," he said. "She's new; just got back from her first ride around with Marilyn."

The woman looked up at Doreena with tiny, black eyes. Above them she'd painted seven lines of metallic eyeshadow in shades from pale green to gray. Everything else about the woman was acceptably professional. She wore a tailored suit and crème scarf. Her hair was a wild, feathered red, but so lacquered in place it barely moved.

"It's hard at first," Doreena said. "But if you stick with it, Marilyn's strategy works every time."

"Don't worry," Tom said. "She'll cut you loose as soon as she's broken you in."

"She said my make-up was unprofessional," Diane said. "I like my make-up."

"Marilyn's on a tear," Tom said. "She's got a special assignment for us, Doreena. Top priority."

Doreena tensed. Special assignments took time away from commissioned sales.

"Heads up. Put on a happy face," Tom said, looking past her.

Marilyn rounded the corner and stood between them, monochromatic as always. The color of the day was red: lips, nails, shoes. It was a real patriotic red too, like the C-town fire trucks, and could not be mistaken for the deeper AeroFlux maroon.

"Stop sniveling, Diane," Marilyn said. "You're part of our winning team. I want you to feel like a winner, look like a winner, act like a winner, sell like a winner."

Diane slunk off to her cubicle, her desk still bare and unadorned.

"So, what's the target?" Tom asked.

"The publisher wants AeroFlux," Marilyn said. She always called Rock, "the publisher" at the office. "And this absolutely has to happen. Whatever it takes. Top priority. It's now or never. We could lose them."

"Lose them?" Tom asked.

"Yes. You don't read your own paper? This morning's headlines. The City Fathers are talking about revoking AeroFlux's permit to operate. That means no more imports. No more flights to Maui. We'll be completely isolated from the outside world. I want you to reel them in, put them in the pages of *The Mirror*."

Doreena exchanged a glance with Tom. Neither of them could afford imports or vacations to Maui. So, if C-town evicted AeroFlux it wouldn't make a huge difference to them. However, the idea of an isolated C-town clearly panicked Marilyn, and it was big news that C-town wanted to bring AeroFlux into its connections of dots and phosphors — and potentially a huge commission, even if they split it. Before the plane crash, AeroFlux had been off limits to the force. Rock hadn't wanted to give the company too much access to his town. This was an important sale. An enormous get for *The Mirror*.

"We're on it," Tom said.

"If you can't get an appointment today, let me know," Marilyn said. "I promised the publisher we'd get this done, ASAP." Marilyn turned to go and then trained her eye on Doreena. "Stop fidgeting. What's that? A little gaudy, isn't it?"

Doreena shuffled nervously. As Marilyn hustled back to her office, she tucked the vial of grandfather's ashes back under her sweater. She had to stop playing with it before it became habit. Wearing human remains probably wasn't even legal.

"Relax." Tom said. "We'll get it done. Hey, you see my latest?" From a desk filled with family photos, he picked up a picture of his wife and kids, this one in a hand-painted frame, and held it out to her. In this photo, too, the family was all pink-cheeked smiles. "We were out at Lake Traynter this weekend. There's actually a nice patch of green there, if you can believe it. The lake reeks, but the kids had fun and Bonnie packs a mean picnic. We had a great time. Saw some guy actually trying to surf on it."

"Surf?" Doreena recalled the smack of the wetsuit against her face this morning. "Um, pathetic. I mean, are there even any waves?"

"It was weird, yeah, but he sorta got upright a few times. Gotta admire that."

"Admire what?"

"Someone who knows what he needs to be happy and goes for it. That's talent."

Doreena frowned. Here it goes. Tom had that look: the married person's default concern for singles. Even though she hadn't told him about her grandfather's death, he pitied her just like Mrs. Dammerung. He should worry more about his own sales.

"So, you're thinking of taking up surfing?"

"No, I've got my family." Tom said. "I'm just saying it's important to have something in your life that makes you feel that way."

"Yeah, like a big commission," she said, tired of the lecture. "You better call AeroFlux and see if they'll even see us after we sicced The Stew on them and slammed them in the headlines."

"Don't worry, if they want to keep doing business, they'll see us," Tom said.

If she hadn't been loyal to *The Mirror* and in need of a big sale, Doreena would have wished AeroFlux would refuse them and give the City Fathers another reason to send them packing. Without AeroFlux, her grandfather couldn't have left her.

By late afternoon, Doreena and Tom were headed out to AeroFlux in the drizzle. Red brake lights — circles, triangles, squares — burned through the fog still thick beneath the overpass. Cold air rushed in through Doreena's open window. Tom, pressed up against the passenger door, caught her glance.

"It's not you. I'm just trying to preserve my hair."

"Sorry. It got busted out last night."

"Expensive. It's hard to get replacement glass. I had a customer once said it ran him a couple weeks pay."

Doreena imagined a long winter ahead of driving around with an open window.

"So, where'd the new girl come from," she asked. "She looked a little fragile."

"Ah, that's interesting," Tom said. "She was a flight attendant on Rock's flight. One of the people he helped save. He hired her, I think, to make a point to AeroFlux. They may be C-town's biggest employer, but *The Mirror's* the best steady work in town. Not likely to kill you in a crash anyway. I'm curious to meet this new guy, Dalton Rees." Tom lowered his voice. "Even Rock hasn't met him." He picked up a stray CD at his feet and smirked turning it over. "This looks like Marilyn's handiwork." He peered around at the back-seat. "A lot of it. Do you really listen to this stuff?"

Tom pushed the CD into the player and a man's voice began to lecture, "to get people on your side a highly motivated seller creates connection."

"That one's not the best," Doreena said.

At the next light, she turned and pawed through the collection of cases behind her until she found *Stellar Sales.* She fumbled with the CD case in her lap as they exited the freeway. When they stopped at the turn lane into the AeroFlux plant, Doreena leaned forward to switch out the CD.

"Oh man, we have to cross the picket line," Tom said.

Hundreds of striking workers lined the street in front of the AeroFlux plant. In their matching green union sweatshirts they looked like a row of arborvitae hastily planted to meet some C-town building code requirement. Just like this morning, the same huddle of 10 or so circled the burn barrels in front of the AeroFlux landmark sign, with its maroon-winged logo.

"They won't be happy," Tom warned.

When the light changed, Doreena directed the car around the corner. *Stellar Sales* piped up, a woman's voice, "Say no? They won't want to."

"Nope, not happy. They're glaring." Tom said. "Tell you what, if I was out of work I'd be at home with my kids for a few days while I looked for another job. I wouldn't spend my time standing around. You?"

Doreena looked from the AeroFlux protesters to the low rectangular plant in front of her to Tom sitting beside her and imagined what she would do with a few uninterrupted days off. She sat on the sofa staring at the remains of her grandfather in the copper urn on the coffee table in the empty, still house until the bulldozers tore in or, updating her vision, sitting in her cold, dark and cramped apartment, silent except for the occasional marimba vibrating beneath her feet. Tom seemed to be baiting her again, trying to get her talk about, well, she didn't even know what his point was anymore. She didn't appear happy enough for him. What difference did that make? What business did he have making her feel inadequate? She was *The Mirror's* number one salesman.

"Not everybody wants to have a family, Tom," she said as a blue haze spread across her vision. It was as if an advertising designer had leveled out all the magenta and black and placed a cyan filter on the world. Doreena blinked hard and clutched the steering wheel. She saw her hands in a blue haze around it, but also felt her palms fold into fists. Her fingernails dug into her palms. The draft from her open window disappeared and the canned heat blasting her fingertips dispersed.

Real warmth permeated her skin. It created an instant thaw as if she'd burst through time to August instead of beginning to warm in March and slowly adapting to the onset of spring. Blue sky, white sand, and blue sea spread out in front of her. The planes of color met in sharp lines. It looked as though she'd stepped directly into the surface of the HAWAII poster except the colors moved. Prisms of sunlight glinted along the crystalline sand and the sea shimmered. Doreena squinted and held her hands before her eyes. She twisted around and a wave of green leaves rolled ahead of her. Green skeins brushed her hands and face. She lifted her buttocks searching for solid ground to stop the undulating sensation. Her hips shifted against sand. She placed her hands on her bare thighs to steady herself. The world rocked and her clothes were gone. Ahead of her a spicy froth of decomposing and blooming vegetation wafted from the verdant shadows. From behind her the scent of salt-soaked flora and fauna rose. The air thrummed a sound like hummingbird wings. A flash of white drew her eyes into the jungle. A hibiscus blossom stretched five-petaled fingers to her. Thin crimson veins ran into its center. She recalled its name: *kokio keokeo*. It was the only hibiscus flower that held scent her grandfather had told her. And with that rising scent, she felt his presence.

"Grandfather?" she said.

A woman's voice, layered like a muted choir, answered. "Pretty girl," it said or, maybe, "Big kitty."

A tumble of red and green churned down through the branches and landed in her lap. Its smooth skin nested against her thigh. She reached for it with both hands and heard a squeal like a wild pig — no — tires.

"Doreena!" Tom shouted.

She remembered she had been driving and rammed her foot forward. Her shoeless heel ground into sand. She was naked on a beach and then the headrest slammed the back of her neck. The cowl of her sweater scratched. Her hands curled around the steering wheel as she wrenched it around. The car spun toward the AeroFlux sign and the union workers in a blur of green and red. Metal crashed, and the car thudded to a halt. Maroon-wings splayed over the splintered windshield. The car had smashed to a stop in the AeroFlux sign. Doreena exhaled; head bowed. In her lap lay an oval fruit, a mango, with its red and green skin intact and a sheen of soft blue on its surface. It tumbled between her knees, leaving a trail of powdery glitter like the dust from a moth's wings across her lap, and plopped into the purse at her feet as the door beside her opened. A man leaned in and touched her shoulder.

"Are you OK? Are you OK?"

He kept shouting and she realized he expected her to answer. She didn't know how. There was tightness all around her. The rocking had stopped, and she was being held, stiff, in her own dry, cracked skin. It ached. It hurt. She tried to nod.

"Don't move. Just sit still."

She couldn't at first, move at all, and then her body began to shake, head, chest, and limbs. She was colder than she'd ever been, and her skin felt scraped and sore.

"Anyone have..." the man said, and then turned so that she didn't hear the rest of it. The reddish ring of his hair was shorn around a balding patch. In the sun, she imagined, the core of each hair would shine like the ripe inside of the mango in her purse.

The man took off his jacket and tucked the tweed around her. The fabric held workshop smells — must, oil, cleansers. The hibiscus scent was far away now, and the name of the flower escaped her.

"K, K, Ko, Ko," she said trying to remember.

"She's in shock," the man said.

Sirens blared outside. Ambulances sped toward her in a line like a Founder's Day parade. The passenger door opened, and she looked to the side and saw Tom slumped in his seat, blood on his face, a medic leaning in beside him. She stopped shivering and unbuckled her seat belt. A police officer stopped her.

"Help him," she said. "He has a family."

"We will. Tell me what happened. That man says you were rounding the turn and then started veering. He swerved, grazed the side of your car and then you jerked the car straight into the sign almost like on purpose. You on some kind of medication?"

She shook her head. "My vision. Something went wrong. Everything went blue."

"Black?"

"Blue."

The cop looked at her like he thought she didn't know her colors.

They put Tom onto a stretcher, hoisting it to their shoulders and moving towards the ambulance. The medics made the lift look easy, the way Tom probably, on weekends, swung his kids onto his shoulders, effortlessly. Then the medics came for her, easing her into their arms. She stared at the mangled intersection of her green car and the red AeroFlux sign. The man who had given her his jacket stood a ways off clutching his bare arms. A barricade of union workers hovered behind him hissing, "Scab."

"This is not the time for that!" a cop yelled.

They lifted her into the ambulance. The man came forward with her purse and placed it in front of her. What was the word she'd been trying to remember? "Kio, Kio?"

"Did she just say cuckoo?" a policeman asked.

The medics shrugged and slammed the ambulance door.

"Wait!" she yelled, remembering. "I can't go. Don't take me."

The sirens began again, this time with her inside them. She was going to the hospital afraid because her grandfather had told her never to go there, and afraid because for the first time in her life she did feel out of sorts, even sick, stiff, and palsied. Doreena stared into her purse at the undeniable mango with its shimmer blue rind. She wanted very much to take it out and hold it and press its soothing skin to hers, but she did not know what the paramedics would make of that and thought it somehow safer to keep the fruit secret.

~ 5 ~

RETINA

Under the island influence, Doreena cannot see clearly

In the commotion of the emergency room, Doreena lost track of Tom wheeled away behind one of the sets of swinging double-doors. She hoped his family would come for him quickly. As her grandfather had warned, once inside the hospital Doreena sickened. "They'll imagine that there's something wrong with you, and the next thing you know there will be," grandfather had said, and he was right. As the doctors, nurses and interns guessed what could be wrong with her, their speculations flowed alternately over her body. Doreena's blood surged red into the test tubes as expected. They tested for epileptic seizures, diabetic shock and multiple sclerosis and Doreena felt faint, lightheaded, and stiff.

The description of MS seemed most apt: the slow way the stiffness settled into the joints. The brief interlude of ocean had showed her how bright and painless the world could be and how her limbs could loosen. She felt dull and tight here by comparison. But if she admitted this, and let the hospital diagnose her with one lifelong disease, what was to stop them from giving her another?

"You'll get sick and eventually you'll die there in one of their hospital beds," grandfather had said.

"Don't worry," one of the nurses said patting her hand. "Adult onset for these illnesses is uncommon. You are probably fine. We are just being cautious."

Most people outside the hospital in C-town were fine. It was only when they entered the hospital, and admitted some weakness or susceptibility, that they became sick. Doreena wanted to get back to her work at *The Mirror* where everyone was well.

"I'm perfectly healthy. I've never been sick," she said. Doreena would no more disobey the doctors' authority than she would argue with Marilyn at *The Mirror*, but she could try to sell them on her health. The medical team was annoyed that she had no records, did not know if she had any allergies, and had never been to a doctor before. "It was my eyes. I saw things," she said, trying again to distract them from their mission of fitting an illness to her.

Finally, they brought her to the ophthalmic surgeon and placed her in front of a machine that shone harsh beams like blue sunlight into each of her eyes blinding her temporarily. They guided her to a small room and left her alone waiting for the doctor and her vision to return.

"Dr. O will be with you shortly," the nurse said.

After a while, a man in a lab coat with small, black eyes entered.

"Luckily, there was an opening in the OR tonight. We should be able to save your vision," said Dr. O.

"But I can see," Doreena said.

"Not for much longer if we don't operate."

He tapped at a console and two images appeared on a screen behind him. They were nebulous midnight blue globes shot with dark, wavy, and off-center yellow blotches like errant rivers and yolks. Waves of blue like sheer drapes hung down the globe on the right.

"You have very healthy veins," Dr. O said. "Those spots are your optic nerves, part of your brain. Your retina detached there in your left eye. You can see the outlines of it slipping off. That's what's causing those yellow bubbles you're seeing. The floaters."

The blue waves did remind her of the haze she had seen just before the beach appeared. But those yellow splotches, was that all it had been: the beach, the water, the sun, the sky, the jungle and the hibiscus? Floaters? The diagnosis was inarguable. Her name was printed in the bottom right corner of each image in ultra-bold, condensed. It reminded Doreena of the way she drew up large sales contracts in advance penning in the business owner's name so that it seemed inevitable. All they had to do was sign. She should do that for AeroFlux.

"The retina is delicate like wet tissue paper. We'll reattach it with a laser," Dr. O said, pointing at the diaphanous blue waves flowing through the left image.

"I can't miss work," Doreena said, she wondered if Tom would be back to work tomorrow and whether they'd be able to get another appointment with the AeroFlux CEO. "I have to make a big sale."

"Don't worry," Dr. O said. "It's a short procedure. We'll send you home tonight."

They propped her eyelid open in a steel clamp in front of a buzzing laser. Her eyelid strained. Her eye teared and then the laser seared it dry. Wisps of smoke rose in her peripheral vision. She tasted charcoal and disinfectant in the back of her throat. Once this was over, if it ever ended, there would be medical bills and car repairs. She would return to *The Mirror* without interruption or accidental arrivals of beach.

"Will I still be able to see color?" Doreena asked.

"Oh yes," Dr. O said. "This doesn't touch the rods and cones. That's more a function of the optic nerve. This isn't brain surgery exactly. It just comes close. Were you worried we were turning you into Rock Traynter? It takes more than a simple operation like this my dear to become head chief of C-town. Yes, it takes a special vision; indeed, the man is more than merely colorblind. But you, you'll still see all the colors you want: AeroFlux red and New West green."

Doreena stayed quiet for the rest of the operation. She hadn't meant to begin a political discussion.

The man could have his opinions but as a *Mirror* employee she had no interest in hearing any criticism of her publisher. Not everyone appreciated the way Rock and the City Fathers had preserved C-town's way of life, but her family, she and her grandfather, had always been staunch supporters.

"This is the best place for us. We wouldn't leave if we could," grandfather had repeatedly said. "And we've got Rock Traynter to thank for it." He'd been so happy, at first, when she'd told him she'd taken a job at *The Mirror*. It was only in the past few years that he'd become strange about it and they'd started to argue over dinner.

"Enough about that place, Doreena. I've had it," he would say.

"But I'm *The Mirror's* number one now."

"Yes, yes, you are. I know. But what else? What else is there?" He sounded like Tom when he talked like this. She could feel him pressuring her to be unhappy, to be restless, and it frustrated her. If he'd wanted her to do something different with her life, he could have told her, he could have taught her. He had always been all she had. She'd always done what he wanted. He could have shaped her into anything, but it was too late for him to change his mind now. She had her job at *The Mirror*, and she loved it every day. She was part of the operation that kept C-town stable and solid. She was content and secure, and he couldn't convince her to feel otherwise.

"Well, we could talk about my family. Why don't we talk about that?" she said, and that always ended the discussion. It used to make him apologetic.

"I'm sorry, Dori," he'd say. "Tell me again about how you upsold The Watertown."

More recently, he'd grown silent and pushed his plate away. She'd begun working later to avoid him. But they always ended up having dinner together whenever she got home.

After the surgery, Doreena was in a cab outside of the Narborough building with a bandage over her left eye trying to locate her wallet in the recesses of her purse. Beneath the bandage her numb eye bulged and throbbed. She didn't remember getting into the cab, but she remembered them asking if there was anyone she could call for a ride home. There wasn't. Tom was in the hospital, too, and she wasn't ready to face Marilyn's disappointment over AeroFlux. She'd suggested the cab and was glad they'd let her go. She feared staying overnight in the hospital and finding out she required more surgeries. Now, if only she had enough cash to pay the driver. Impatient, he reached back and flipped on the overhead light. Inside her purse, Doreena's fingers slid over silkiness, the fruit. It was still there. Somehow, she'd expected it to disappear along with the hanging drape in her eye, but the fleshy oval thing remained.

The driver stared at her in the rearview mirror. She pushed the fruit aside and found some bills behind it, enough to pay for two curries at Raja's. She stumbled out of the cab, head down. For the next few weeks, she had to keep her head down so that her eye would heal correctly. "The gas we use now absorbs back into the eye much faster," Dr. O had said. "But you have to keep your head down to hold the shape of the retina."

On her way up to her apartment, Doreena clutched the smooth stair rail. Grey-brown sand dusted the second-floor landing, but the surfer's marimbas were silent. On the worn wood floor of her apartment, just under the door lay a sheet of sherbert paper. Next to a hand-drawn picture of a palm tree, someone had gotten carried away with tiki font. Tomorrow night, The Surfers, — Was that a club, a support group, a band? The flyer neglected to explain. — were meeting 7:30 p.m. at the Labor Temple. She tucked the flyer into her purse beside the smooth mango.

Before bed, Doreena emptied the baggy the hospital had given her. There was a tube of ointment, a vial of eye drops, a bottle of codeine, and a doughnut-shaped plastic air pillow. She took two pills and sprawled across her bed face down in the blow-up ring inhaling plastic fumes. She hoped Tom was OK. She imagined his wife and children sleeping beside him in the hospital chairs.

As she fell asleep, a wash of blue swept over her. Her right eye opened wide to a blue haze. She jerked awake into a crush of in-flated plastic. She was afraid to see floaters and that her retina was detaching in her other eye now. She'd be blind. She flailed, her arms swimming through the bedspread, remembering the car crash, and afraid she was about to strike something ahead of her. But the bed stayed firm beneath her belly. She stretched her arms ahead of her and saw her body below her in a glassy blue shell. She rode the tingling haze into a sunlit land.

This time, when she arrived on the beach, she lay like a seal on the sand. The water lapped her toes. She propped her head up on her elbows and rested her chin in her hands. The bandage over her eye had disappeared along with her pajamas. Her back grew warm in the sun. She could see clearly with both eyes in vivid color. She looked up the white beach to the wall of jungle green. In the shady vines, she could see a flutter of white, the hibiscus petals. Doreena brushed her curls out of her eyes. She lay as she had as a toddler on the Maui beach. When she'd found the photo, her grandfather had told her a little of that time. Grandfather loved photos and she could always get him to talk about them.

"I like the way they capture a moment. They make it something solid that you can hold in your hand, but it isn't really caught. The people in the photographs they go on. They stay fluid."

They had lived together in a hut by the roadside selling coconut palm weavings to tourists.

"Everyone thought we were native," he said. "We looked like we were. Especially you."

They'd eaten pineapple and coconut. He'd bought a camera and decorated the entire hut with photos of her. They'd spent their days walking the beach, sleeping under palms, Doreena had climbed trees and he'd taught her to count using seashells and stones.

"It sounds so wonderful," she said. "Why did we leave?"

He laughed once. "You were too hard for me to keep track of in that wild place all by myself. You were climbing trees like a monkey and scuttling along the sand like a crab and always wanting to go in the water like a fish. It was too much, too much."

Another time he'd been serious. "It wasn't safe," he said. She'd thought he'd meant politically, but later, when she'd caught him in a reflective mood after a dinner in which he hardly eaten anything, he'd elaborated, "The water, the sand everything constantly shifting. It wasn't safe for you. We needed to go inland, somewhere much more solid." She'd known that he wasn't talking about politics or the United Government, but about them, something unique and dangerous about herself that she didn't understand and which he refused to explain.

She remembered her grandfather telling her about the little lemon-yellow fishes she'd played with as a child. She stood and turned toward the ocean. It was clear blue all the way out to the skyline. Palms waved at either end of the bay. She waded into the water. In the shallows the fishes were there, tiny flashes like darts of sunlight above the wavy sand. Tiny mouths puckered over her toes, tasting. Up the beach, a forked red mouth of a trail cut into the jungle green. Beyond it, coconut palms waved and pineapple plants bristled. She bent and touched the purple flowering pohue-hue vine winding through the sand and reached for a mango resting in its coils. She peeled away some of its red-green skin with her teeth. Juice sprayed her cheeks as she bit in, dipped her tongue into the hole and gnawed toward the seed.

She heard the woman's voice again, "Look up."

Doreena threw her head back. The sun scorched her eyes through a blind of palm fronds. She panicked, suddenly remembering the doctor's words, "Keep your head down or you'll damage your eyes."

She was looking up into puffy white clouds, and then she was face down in the inflated plastic pillow, feeling the flannel of her pajamas and her bare toes brushing the cotton bedspread. She lay in a lingering palsy and sweat as though awakening from a nightmare, but a ripe, green fruit peel scent competed with the plastic surrounding her nose and mouth. Whether it was real or not, the disorienting motion of her travel to the beach lingered.

In the bathroom, the bandage covered her left eye again, but the throbbing had stopped. She wanted to look and see if it was healed. Nothing in ALL CAPS on the sheets of aftercare instructions said she couldn't. She unwound the bandage and lifted the patch of gauze. Beneath it her eyelid swelled around her scraped eyeball. Red speckled the white. Her brown iris bled like an unfertilized egg. Her vision through the eye was cloudy with translucent edges. It looked painful and as she looked it did begin to throb. She put in the eyedrops as directed and the stinging released blood-spattered tears. The beach seemed more distant now, more dreamlike.

Her feet grew numb on the icy tile, and she noticed a sparkle of sand between her toes. She bent to examine it rolling a few grains around in her palm under a finger. The grains were delicate white, not the course gray-brown skiff on the stairwell. When she went to brush her teeth, she plucked a sinewy strand of orange, a bit of mango, from between the gap in her two front teeth. She was afraid to think what this all meant. She felt debauched and hungover, as if she'd done something sinful, and she thought she'd better get to work.

It took her a long time to get there. She ended up head down waiting for the C-town center bus. In the relative light of dawn, she'd managed to spot her car, the mangled hood collapsed into the guts of the engine, where the AeroFlux workers had pushed it across the street. It looked irreparable. As she waited for the bus, the slow wend of passing cars made her self-conscious of standing alone on the street like a hooker or a transient outsider living on the abandoned Freeway outside of C-Town. She imagined a long winter of standing in the dark like this unless she could sell enough to afford repairs. She relaxed when she saw the leg of wetsuit come up beside her and recognized her surfer neighbor.

"You're not taking your surfboard onto the bus?" she asked.

"I'm heading out to Lake Traynter."

"Isn't it early?"

"Always do the best thing first thing. Then the rest of your day is golden," he said. He bent down to peer up at her with one green eye. The other was covered by a matte of dirty-gray curls. "What happened to you?"

"Eye surgery," she said. "And I totaled my car."

"So, you're going to work?"

Until he said it, it hadn't occurred to Doreena that she could have called in sick and spent the day lying in bed with her head down in plastic worrying about her declining commissions while the union workers across the street began another day of protest. Her scorn was guilt fueled. The beach dream had left her with lingering shame, even though she was now rightfully in her stiff scratchy suit headed to work and this guy was in a rubbery wetsuit about to waste the day on a waste-filled lake.

"Yeah dude," she said. "I guess I could try to surf on a man-made lake. Are there even any waves?"

"Not really," he said. "But you gotta get stoked about something."

His head disappeared from her view of the pavement as the bus wheezed to a stop in front of them. On the bus, he placed his board across the aisle from her. It was covered with stickers, SEXWAX, STOKED and REEF, and decals of tiny islands sprouting palms and clusters of Hawaiian blossoms. Instead of taking the direct route into town across Burrows overpass, the bus wound along the industrial strip and then through the marshlands.

"Nice mango," the surfer said.

"Mango?" she asked.

"Yeah, there."

She looked down at the fruit — the mango, with its glazed sugar sheen, which was still in her purse. She put it on the other side of her, away from him, to hide it.

"Where'd you get that?"

"It's a long story. I was listening to a motivational tape. I had a car accident. It appeared. I work at *The Mirror*."

"Ah, that makes sense. Mangoes, motivation. Sounds like transference, a psychological thing."

"I'm not crazy. That's a real mango."

"Yeah, I saw, a real motivation manifest."

"But how did it get here?" Doreena muttered. It was hard to take the surfer seriously, hard to care what she said to him, or what he thought. He was wearing a wetsuit on a bus in C-town and he seemed to take the mango in stride. "It's not like I carry fruit around with me."

"You don't?"

"Not usually. I mean, tropical fruit, where would I get that?"

"Good question. And even then, why carry it around? Fruit's for eating."

"I've eaten some."

"So, there's more where that came from? I'd be interested to meet your source, Betty."

"Not Betty. Doreena," she said.

He bent down again so she got a flash of green eye, muck-colored curl and a bit of tooth. "I'm Alonso."

The bus stopped. The surfer disappeared from her view and lifted his board.

"You can explain your fruit fetish tonight," he reached across her legs and pointed at the sherbet paper about The Surfers in her purse beside the mango. She shoved the flyer deeper into her purse and snapped it shut.

"You gave this to me?" she asked.

"Nope."

"Who then?"

He gave an easy shrug and hopped off the bus. It left him standing on the gravel roadside piercing the gray sky with his board. His curly hair flopped across his forehead in a tangle a lot like her own lay naturally, but it looked right on him.

Once the surfer was gone, Doreena thought of an explanation for the mango. Maybe The Traynters had brought them back from Maui for each of *The Mirror* employees. By the time the bus pulled up a few blocks from Traynter Tower, Doreena expected to see mangoes on each of the salesman's desks. If she was going to sell AeroFlux today, they could all do with some mango motivation. Satisfied with the explanation, Doreena couldn't wait to get to work and leave her woozy, guilt-trippy hallucinations behind. She was *The Mirror's* steady number one not some surfing derelict. At work, Marilyn immediately called Doreena into her office.

"I've been looking for you all morning," she said. She did not sound pleased.

~ 6 ~

MARILYN

A sense of stiffening

Doreena's eye surged rhythmically beneath its bandage as she peered up at Marilyn with her one good eye. Marilyn's color of the day was scarlet: lips, nails, suit, and shoes. Doreena sat in her inferior position in the low cushy chair forced to peer up at Marilyn, prominent on the edge of her desk framed by the display of gold embossed awards behind her.

"Tom's out, broken clavicle," Marilyn said. "You and I will be going to AeroFlux this morning. It's critical we get them on board. Are you ready to corral Dalton Rees?"

Doreena nodded and suppressed a wince, which she hoped Marilyn would attribute to her injured eye. It had been a long time since she'd gone out on a call with her boss. Ride-a-longs with Marilyn had been frequent Doreena's first year at *The Mirror* and the intense scrutiny had been exhausting. Under Marilyn's tutelage, Doreena had changed aspects of herself she had thought were ingrained.

"You're blinking too much," Marilyn had observed after one of those early sales calls. "Liars blink a lot. You need to slow it down."

"But it's a reflex. I can't control it?" Doreena said.

Marilyn had waved her protest aside. "Of course, you can. It's easy. There's nothing about yourself you can't control. Someone like our publisher doesn't even stop there. He controls the world beyond himself, even his own environment. Listen, reflexes are only useful for people who aren't paying attention. Maybe they'll save you in a pinch if you just want to breath and keep your eyes wet. I'm teaching you to have heightened awareness, to operate at a very high level. I want you to use everything other people take for granted to your advantage."

There were ways Marilyn liked sales done and those were the ways Doreena had learned to do them.

"Our publisher tells people that the paper is called *The Mirror* because it reflects everything that's happening in C-town," Marilyn said. "But *The Mirror* means something else to The Force. Mirroring is our most powerful sales technique. Closely observe the body language of your prospect. Reflect their gestures back to them. Subconsciously, they will begin to see you as like them, and that's when you've got them. Mirror neurons in the brain fire in response to these gestures. You can impose your will on someone from the outside effecting them at an internal level. You know they won't refuse to advertise in *The Mirror,* but I want you to dig deeper. Create that lasting connection. Upsell."

After that first year, Doreena became a honed sales professional, a sharp instrument of *The Mirror* sales team Marilyn called The Force. The mirroring technique came, although she'd never express it like this to Marilyn, almost reflexively. Doreena outsold everyone on the force mirroring the position of clients' hands and guiding those hands to sign bigger and bigger contracts: full-color, full-page, placement in the Entertainment pullout section.

Now she laid her hands on her knees, awkwardly, palms up. She'd become an expert at the mirroring technique, but she was afraid to use it with Marilyn who would know what she was doing. She never knew what to do with her hands when Marilyn was watching her closely. She worked to keep her postures open and receptive. The mirroring was so ingrained, she fought to keep her fingers splayed and not mimic Marilyn's hammer fist.

"Let's go over this play by play," Marilyn said. "I'll start off with positioning and branding. You make the sale. I'll finish with pricing and placement. You get them to sign."

After the lecture, they headed out. Marilyn drove them across the overpass in Rock's infamous Ford, a stunningly restored vintage car with a pea soup paint job that only a colorblind man could have overlooked. The car had been a classic even before the revolution, but it smelled new. As they drove past the picket line onto the AeroFlux complex, Doreena slumped to avoid the glaring men in green. Crumbled bits of the landmark sign poked through the lawn.

"No worries. Tinted windows," Marilyn said. "You really did a number on that sign."

From the parking lot to the building, they walked under metal curved liked the hull of plane. Marilyn appraised Doreena. "I don't suppose there's anything you can do about the bandage. It's clean anyway. Try to look up during the presentation at least."

The AeroFlux lobby was a silo with black screened walls. In the center was the base of a red sculpture that Doreena knew without looking up was a giant pair of wings. Inlaid in the marble floor was a map of the old United Government. Arching stripes of crisscrossing gold indicated AeroFlux's old flight patterns joining the raised bronze cities. C-town lay on the edge of the Northwest, a bronze island, with one thin strand of gold crossing the Pacific Ocean to Maui.

"Please have a seat and watch our film," the receptionist said. "Mr. Rees will be with you shortly."

Doreena and Marilyn sat on the low bench that ringed the room and the black walls flashed blue as the film began. The United Government promo encircled them. The movie family, three beaming generations, set out from The Capitol, a flag adorned temple. They piled into a small electric car, a modern kind not available in C-town, and embarked on a road trip to visit long lost relatives spread across the once united land. They headed southwest across the continent and visited with homogeneously friendly folk in the bayous, grain fields and deserts. This was the supposed expanse of the UG. So far, Doreena could not find any specific fault with the film's portrayal of the UG. Aside from the suspiciously well-chosen lighting and the steady cheeriness of the traveling family she could not pinpoint any factual errors.

Then the fictional family drove up the West Coast. They passed through redwood forests and along the lighthouse dotted beaches. They sped down an empty evergreen-lined freeway into mountainous, forested Cascadia and sallied along to the flat sea-level meadows of Island County. This part of the film was blatant falsehood. In real life, on their way north, the family would be driving over scores of squatters encamped on the Freeway. And the island areas of Pacifica, depicted in shining blue, were already largely underwater as the Rust Red Seas with their poisonous and choking algae-packed waters were rising. Only those with no other place to go attempted to live there on the remaining peaks. It was no place for a holiday and any relatives who'd once lived there were likely dead. Still, the UG family continued their fantastical jaunt entering what the film referred to, in pre-revolutionary terms, as the Great Pacific Northwest and its capital New West.

Marilyn groaned. She turned to Doreena. "They were showing this propaganda when the plane crashed. Rock was furious. It's one thing when they use this kind of thing overseas to keep up the façade, but to use it on our own people. You see how they set New West up as the capitol with no mention of C-town at all. We're completely off the UG's radar and AeroFlux is in bed with them. We've got our work cut out for us."

Doreena's eye throbbed. She searched her purse for her pain pills, but all she had in there was that weird mango. The rest of the film was basically an AeroFlux commercial. The little blond boy and his spry grandfather toured the plant with awestruck faces and ended up staring at the enormous metal wings in the lobby repeating the company's motto, "Traveling all ways into the future." The film ended when the well-traveled family returned to the UG capitol for a hug beneath the old flag. It fluttered through the final frames.

As the screens faded to black, a man approached them. Everything about him had an off-continent look. There were foreign angles to the cut of his hair and suit and even an odd tilt to his facial features. Doreena rose to greet the CEO.

"I'm Dalton Rees," he confirmed extending his hand.

Doreena left his hand extended, untouched, deferring to Marilyn's lead. His hand remained empty an uncomfortably long time until she looked down and saw Marilyn sitting with her head in her hands and hunched shoulders trembling. She was crying. Seemingly, overwrought with emotion. Doreena completed the handshake with the executive.

"I'm Doreena Moriena with *The Mirror,*" she said. "And this is Marilyn Traynter."

At last, Marilyn stood her eyes wet with tears. If the emotional display was a sales strategy, Doreena wished Marilyn had given her a heads up.

"Could it be there is a little patriotism left even in C-town's most stalwart supporters?" Rees said. "It is nothing to be ashamed of Mrs. Traynter. The film, as it was designed to do, affects many."

Marilyn flushed.

"This room. It reminded me of the plane, before the crash. They say the lack of control, the womb-like environment on a plane makes people more emotional," Marilyn said. "The UG and its partners are excellent at manipulation."

"Mrs. Traynter," Rees said. "I am so sorry for the unfortunate incident on our jetliner."

Rees led them into a small conference room decorated at intervals with black and white photographs and left them while he collected his associate. Once they were alone Marilyn, still weeping, pulled her aside.

"The presentation. You''ll have to handle it, Doreena. I can't. That film. It reminded me of my grandmother. She lives in the southeast and I haven't seen her in years," Marilyn said. "Please, let me collect myself."

In fact, Doreena felt perfectly capable of giving the presentation on her own. If anything, it made her less nervous to have Marilyn watching her than to have to stand beside her jumping in at random moments and knowing that Marilyn was judging her every word and nuance. The best would have been to give the presentation on her own. But she also felt guilty, Marilyn was so broken up by the fact that she hadn't seen her grandmother in years that she was unable to speak, but Doreena was able to carry on even though she'd lost her grandfather days ago.

"That's fine," Doreena said. "I've got it."

Rees returned with the man who had given Doreena his tweed jacket at the accident. He was wearing another jacket identical to it.

"This is one of our engineers, Earnest Wilde," he said.

To remove awkwardness about her eye patch, Doreena quickly explained about her recent eye surgery before beginning. Then she started in on her pitch. She watched both men's analytical and authoritative posturing and instead of glossing over the technical part of the presentation she gave them a more detailed description.

"The City Fathers strive to keep everything available to the citizens of C-town just as it was. We drive the same cars, communicate the same ways, and eat the same foods as we did before the economic collapse. Our quality of life has not diminished. We've been insulated from the effects of the economic collapse of the United Government. However, in recent years there is one great innovation we have come to depend upon. Advancements in quantum information theory allow citizens of C-town to share greater unified thought. Quantum dots, bits of information and ideas, are embedded into the silicon sheets of *The Mirror*. The information is then not only read in the normal fashion by newspaper readers, a circulation of more than 100,000, but also absorbed into their mindset and into the collective group of C-town. This process is enhanced by the polarized photons that transmit quantum information in radio waves to the phosphorescent lights that shine throughout C-town. Every business that uses *The Mirror's* day and night system, print and radio, dot and phosphors, becomes part of the fabric of C-town on a quantum level an indissoluble part of the collective working for our fair city. Truly, information is physical, and *The Mirror* is C-town's daily source."

Repeating the tagline left Doreena flush with excitement, as did the men's engaged and interested reactions. They were both leaning forward, now, and nodding slightly. They'd begun the presentation, both of them, with hands clasped and fingers interwoven and pointed up in displays of confidence. But her words had toppled those steeples and their fingers now pointed towards her. That was important because confident leaders were less receptive to new ideas. Now, she'd gotten their attention. They were ready for her pitch. Marilyn had started off the presentation leaning back in her chair with her arms crossed, closed into herself, trying to regain her control, but even she was leaning forward now. Her arms were folded on the table in front of her, she was looking up and watching Rees.

"Your company's aim has always been flight, traveling. Traveling all ways into our future. You look at any means to connect people geographically. *The Mirror's* mission has always been information. We look for any means to connect people by information sharing and by thought. Advertising in *The Mirror* is not just a way to strengthen your brand or to advertise your message. Being in *The Mirror* means becoming a part of the fabric of C-town and entering the hearts and minds of its citizens."

Doreena could see Marilyn nodding now. She knew she liked the way she'd worked the AeroFlux mission into her pitch. Her eye was throbbing, but she thought she had them. She explained the terms and conditions. She laid the rate sheets, the mock-up and contracts in front of them. She could see Rees signing the bottom of a yearlong full-page, full-color contract. At the end of her presentation, she paused and then asked Rees to sign.

"No," he said. "For the same reason we never have. AeroFlux is a monopoly. We have an established brand and we operate outside of C-town."

Surprised, Doreena looked at Marilyn. Her fists betrayed her anger. She gave Doreena a curt nod. Doreena felt the stiffness of Rees refusal, but she had to go on with the next assault. She hated this part, attempting to batter through another's will. His hands were splayed fingers wide on top of the table, in forceful refusal. She mirrored the position and cleared her throat.

Marilyn jumped in.

"Mr. Rees, you're new, from off-continent. You aren't familiar with how C-town does business. So, may I remind you that you've never refused to advertise in *The Mirror*? We've never invited you. But things aren't looking good for AeroFlux now. It looks like your faulty maintenance is to blame for that crash and now you've gone and laid off 300 workers. You need an image campaign."

"We wouldn't need an image campaign if we were allowed to import the goods we needed to properly maintain our fleet. We wouldn't be laying off workers if we were allowed to look for new revenue streams and export goods. We can't employ people to build planes when there's nowhere to fly," Rees retorted.

Doreena glanced at the engineer in the tweed jacket. He was leaning back with his arms crossed now. He gave her an apologetic little smile. Now that their bosses were fighting there was no chance of a sale. Uncomfortably standing in the center of the room, Doreena drifted to the side and began to look at the photographs. Most were aerial shots. There were sweeping views of inland Island County taken before the perfect circle of Lake Traynter had been dredged inside the C-town city limits. Vineyards surrounded hourglass-shaped Silver Lake; the county's only natural body of water. Farmlands spread around the small, flat speck of C-town before the AeroFlux industrial complex had sprawled to the forest and Traynter Tower rose to dwarf even the old growth firs.

She heard Marilyn's voice go from shrill to dulcet pleading behind her.

"Don't do this. You know what Rock's planning to do? Cancel that last flight out to Maui. He says we won't need it anymore."

"What?" Rees said.

Then another photo caught Doreena's eye. It was a photo of men assembled in baggy metallic flight suits. They had UG badges affixed to their shoulders. In the center of them, a man who looked just like her grandfather held his helmet under one arm and saluted with the other. Even in the shadow of his salute, she recognized the three furrowed lines across his brow and the dark mole on his cheekbone beneath his left eye. At the bottom ran the caption, Captain Leonid "The Chief" Moriena and the crew of the AF-896 bound for SPIREMine (Soviet-Prussian Interstellar Resource Excavation Misson).

Earnest, the man in tweed, approached her. "What is it?"

"My grandfather, that's him."

"Hardly," he laughed. "That's a historical photo. It'd have to be your great, great, grandfather maybe. That's one of the crews heading out to mine the energy source, back when we thought we had discovered an unlimited supply of power — before the destruction of that planet resulted in the collapse."

Then, he asked, "But which one did you think?"

"The one in the center, "the chief". His name was Leonid Moriena. He died last week. But he was just a school janitor."

"A family name perhaps," Earnest said.

"I don't know much about my family history, and I've always been curious," Doreena said. "He never mentioned a connection to AeroFlux."

They turned and saw that Marilyn and Dalton were standing, shaking hands. They'd seemed to reach some kind of agreement although the contract was still unsigned. Doreena caught the end of their conversation.

"I'm serious, he means to do it, turn this place into a real island. He'll freeze the flights out to Maui. He says if C-town has a real vacation spot we won't need to travel. We just need some kind of a getaway."

Dalton laughed. "In C-Town? What's he going to do build a resort on Traynter Lake?"

His eyes lingered a bit too long on Marilyn's scarlet chest.

Marilyn raised her eyebrows. "Good guess."

"No, really," he said, incredulous. "Well, if anyone can do it."

Before they left Earnest asked Doreena for her phone number.

"I'd like to get my jacket back," he said. "And I'll see if I can find out more about this Leonid Moriena for you."

Back at *The Mirror*, Marilyn brought Doreena into her office and closed the door behind them. Closed-door meetings signaled failure to the entire Force. Doreena was on edge the moment it snipped shut. She stood holding her hands behind her back as Marilyn started in on her about the lost sale.

"You were doing well until he said no and then you just dropped it. I had to jump in. The problem is you lack follow through. You don't commit. Rejection ought to energize you, not demoralize you. You just don't get the thrill of the hunt. I understand it with Tom. He's good, but he'll never be great. For him it's all about his family. He's just doing what it takes to support them. But you, Doreena, you could go all the way. You are sales. You could really be the best, but you lack passion."

Doreena wanted to protest. She was the best, usually. Her sales had only recently slipped, and she was still on Tom's tail even if he did have the more lucrative categories. But Marilyn was right. Demoralized. The word stuck with her. It rang true. It wasn't the first time she'd heard that other criticism either: lack of passion. Wasn't that what Tom was always going on about? Her grandfather had accused her of it during one of their last big arguments. At least it seemed now that's what he'd been getting at. She'd been cooking large ethnic dinners, too much food for the two of them especially when they were upset and barely picking at the meals. It was her way of hinting, trying to get him to open up about her family history.

"Do you like this dish?" She would say. "Maybe it's part of our tradition."

On Founder's Day she'd made dishes of mashed root vegetables: red, orange, and yellow. The sodden steaming mounds filled the house with an earthy scent. Her grandfather sucked sullenly at the tines of his fork while she talked about *The Mirror.* He'd interrupted by flinging his fork across the room.

"That's enough!" he said. The fork had stuck into the wall, breaking the illusion of solidity. The handle had vibrated as he yelled. "Enough about Founder's Day. I'm done paying homage to Rock Traynter and his perfectly preserved town. Would a little change be so bad?"

"You've always thought so!" she said. "I'm sorry. I didn't mean to go on. It's just been a great week with all the Founder's Day specials and then the party watching the parade."

"It's the same every year. Don't you ever get tired of it?"

"The loft has a fantastic view," she said.

"No, not the party. The whole thing, *The Mirror.* That hard place."

"Well, it's my job. It's not so hard." Doreena got up to serve him some of the mashed potatoes. "I thought maybe this was something mom would have made. I was imagining it, anyway."

Grandfather lowered his head. "Never mind. I'm a hypocrite. I'm as bad as Rock Traynter. I've done the same thing to you."

"Done what?" As she said it, she felt her entire body stiffen. It was as if her clothes were wrapping more securely around her; the zipper on her pants wrenching closed, the buttons on her blouse a notch tighter, the apron tie cinching and even the elastic around her underwear and bra squeezing closed. She felt heavy and over-stuffed, as though it were the end of the meal. She clutched the bowl of potatoes to her chest.

Her grandfather looked up at her and shook his head sorrowfully. This relieved the pressure, and she began to move again.

"She didn't cook," he said.

She stopped with the spoon over his plate, this time of her own volition, waiting for more. He knew she savored every tidbit about her origins, especially her mother, but he just spooned the dish into his mouth and chewed silently.

"Your grandmother would have liked this. She had her own garden. She liked to garden." He got up from the table and lifted the rolltop desk. He handed her the red notice. "I'm sorry. I'm not in the mood to celebrate the Traynters. This is the last Founder's Day we'll have in this house."

She took the red eviction notice. The city had sold all of Maple Street to Traynter Construction to develop condos.

"Oh, grandfather I'm sorry," Doreena said. "But we can move, all right. Maybe even buy one of the new condos."

"I don't have the energy to move." He looked out the window, his gaze lingering on the hibiscus. "It's been so long since I've seen any hummingbirds."

"It's just the wrong time of the year," she said.

She could see he was sad that he wouldn't see it bloom again and that's when he'd said it. "Doreena are you happy? Isn't there something you've always wanted to do?"

And now his words had the opposite effect on her. She swooned with a sudden lightness. The zipper, the buttons, the tie and the elastic bindings around her loosened. She touched the window-pane to steady herself afraid that she might topple through, smashing on top of the hibiscus shrub. "Like what?"

"Do you ever imagine things are different?" he asked. "I just want you to live, be passionate, be happy."

Her hand was light on the thin glass window. It wavered beneath her touch. Light shimmered in the pane. She thought for a moment, her hand might pass through. This tremulous nature of her body disturbed her much more than the onset of stiff, heavy, awkwardness. That felt safer and more familiar.

"Grandfather," she pleaded. "I don't know."

"Look, never mind. It's just me just getting old. You're fine, Doreena, you're fine just the way you are. I don't mean to be critical."

Now both of the odd feelings were passing and she was returning to her usual state-of-being. The way she felt most of the time at home and at *The Mirror*. But Doreena wasn't ready to forget the strange sensations. They were part of something she needed to know.

"There is something I've always wanted. That would make me happy," she said. "To know about my mother."

She waited. But he said nothing. And she felt no different now than she had always felt, like anyone who'd lived in C-town all their life. They returned to the table and finished their meal in silence. Afterward, he'd come to the kitchen.

"I won't always be here," he'd said, and left her alone to wash the dishes, so startled she'd forgotten to serve her homemade pies. Months later he'd told her he would retire and travel to Maui. When she'd asked when they would leave (she'd have to give *The Mirror* notice) he'd said, "No, just me. You can't leave C-town, but I have to go."

Never mind he'd said. Her grandfather had told her never mind about being happy and then he'd told her nothing.

Doreena looked at Marilyn standing behind her desk. There was a new photo perched on the edge, a personal one. It showed Marilyn on a Maui beach in a broad brimmed hat. Her face was covered in shadow. The photo had been printed in black and white, the way Rock Traynter would see it. The bright sun destroyed any delicacies of shading so that the sand, sea, and sky melded into a gray sheen. She could see why Rock preferred C-town. The overcast days would be easier on his light-sensitive eyes and the textures of its buildings more visually appealing than the flat sand and sea.

Doreena did not know what these people meant: Marilyn, Tom, her grandfather. She thought she was performing up to expectations. What more did they want from her?

"I'm committed. I'm passionate. I'm happy," she said.

"I almost believe you," Marilyn replied.

"You're the one who was crying. I've never cried," Doreena said. She knew better than to draw attention to her lack of tears. It was an oddity about her, an unfair advantage, like how she'd never been sick. But she was angry, and letting it get the better of her, or she wouldn't have tried to argue with Marilyn at all. "Not so much that I couldn't make a sale. What about your happiness? Worry about that."

Marilyn's response frightened her. She'd been holding her hands with her thumb on top of her clenched fists in her usual hammer fist lecturing style. But now her fists dropped. Her hands opened, palms up in a receptive posture, onto her desk. Some of the meaner pressmen took pellet guns to the flocks of pigeons that dripped white onto *The Mirror's* reflective black surfaces. Marilyn's hands looked felled and limp like those downed, pellet-stung birds. She moved to the door and opened it.

"Maybe I will," she said as Doreena walked through.

That night it was silent on Doreena's way up the stairs to the Narborough. She felt heavy and stiff, but empty. She looked in the cupboard, but she wasn't hungry for anything in there, any quick thing she could eat alone on her couch. No, not even that, she wasn't hungry at all. She hadn't been since grandfather had left. She knew she should eat regular meals, but she was tired of taking orders especially from someone who was no longer with her.

She thought of Tom in the hospital and felt guilty because she hadn't gone with the rest of the Force to visit him. But she wouldn't go back to that place. She called him instead. She told him about the AeroFlux failure and apologized for the accident.

"It's OK. We'll bring them around," he said. "And it's nothing serious. I'm healing. I'll be back in soon."

His words were innocuous enough. He hadn't accused her, but the phone call left her feeling angrier. It wasn't serious for him. She was the one alone, with Marilyn mad about the AeroFlux failure, and the wrecked car and the sinking sales. Anger thickened and stiffened her like a shell. If it settled in, she'd soon be immobile beneath its weight.

~ 7 ~

ALONSO

Mirror Island returns

In the morning, those stiff, angry feelings weighed even more heavily across Doreena and her eye still throbbed as she boarded the bus to work. Her need to escape those feelings would soon cause her to make an unusual choice, a deviation. Doreena was going to follow the surfer off the bus, although at the moment she worried about her sales and her bills, the usual motivations. With her good eye, Doreena watched the sun spilling pink over C-town's marshlands. The bus' slow detour around town gave her plenty of time to plan her sales strategy for the day. Sell more; that was her strategy. She needed new clients, quickly, before her year-end review. She couldn't afford another zero day. *The Mirror* didn't float zeros and she needed commission for car repairs and rent. Doreena stared at her knees inches in front of her eyes. Her head still ached with the pressure of sleep, but even with the smelling salt offensiveness of bus, she could barely lift it.

"You OK?" Alonso, the surfer from her apartment building, swayed over her. Again, she envied his mussed curls.

"Just cold," she said. She pictured Alonso later in the day. He'd be standing on this same bus, dripping wet, going back to the Narborough. Then he'd flop down on his bed in his smoky sandalwood and clanging marimba apartment. He'd stare at the ceiling and daydream.

"So, what do you do the rest of the day?"

He shrugged. "This is the part that matters."

The bus slowed and he hefted his board. The assault of colors — yellow, turquoise, pink — pained her one eye. "See for yourself. It's something you have to experience."

Doreena knew that was wrong. Bad experiences were just bad. Everyone did not have to have them individually. Her grandfather had taught her that. "There's no sense following folly," he'd said. It was possible to benefit from the experience of others. This was why she'd had so few bad experiences: she'd escaped the random traumas — accidents and illness — that occasionally befell her co-workers.

But Grandfather was gone, and with him his insulating, protecting influence. Since then, she'd experienced both. But she now wondered as she never had before, hadn't he kept her away from some good experiences, too? Her co-workers celebrated engagements, marriages, and births. She hadn't even dated. Maybe it was time to experiment with her life.

"You think I'm the kind of person that blows off work?" Doreena said.

"You're more than your job," he said. "It's just a job."

"Just?" she said. "You know I work at *The Mirror*, right?"

As the bus stopped, Doreena surprised herself by rising from her seat and following Alonso down the aisle. Their brief exchange had left her feeling a bit more fluid. It was a relief to feel the easy movement of her limbs as she descended the short set of stairs. Alonso looked weird enough on his own, a surfer in a swamp, but she added to the oddity squat beside him in her scratchy suit. Even the bus driver, who must have seen everything, smirked as he pulled away. The dawn lit the frizz of her bangs framing her face and pinked Alonso's curls. As the cold air filled her lungs,

Doreena's head cleared. She felt more awake, and alarmed. This was not what she was supposed to be doing.

"Excellent," Alonso said.

"The other salesmen do this all the time. I'm sure," Doreena said.

"I've never seen any surfing salesmen."

'This kind of thing: slacking. It was going to be a zero day anyway."

She justified avoiding work. Only a new sale could save her figures and what hope was there of landing a new client in C-town, where there was, by design, never anything new? She was part of the system that kept it that way.

Doreena's gray pumps crunched into the gravel and Alonso flip flopped beside her until they reached the dirt path down to the park. It cut through a blind of chirruping cattails hiding a marsh full of birds and amphibians. Even with the heels of her pumps sinking into the mud, Doreena could keep pace with Alonso's easy stroll to the water.

She'd been to Traynter Lake twice. Once with her grandfather when she was in elementary school. She remembered the long bus ride, lobbing hard bits of bread at hissing geese and the reflective black surface of the lake. Grandfather had squeezed her hand hard, crippling her fingers, when she'd reached for the water. He hadn't let her touch it. When she'd asked to go again, Grandfather had said, "No, it's too cold and those birds are mean." He preferred to keep her in town. Her high school graduation picnic had been there, but Doreena had been too anxious that day to enjoy it. People kept asking her what she was going to do next and she didn't have a plan. Besides, graduation hadn't seemed like much to celebrate. They'd all only done what they'd been told to do, she more than most. As it turned out, it wasn't a big deal. Afterward she'd gone to work for *The Mirror* and continued to live at home with her grandfather. Change was optional.

As they approached the brown sludge of Lake Traynter rimmed with gray sand, Doreena heard her grandfather's disapproval "People are always doing silly things. That doesn't mean you have to. My sensible girl." Doreena was already beginning to blame Alonso for her plummeting numbers and her unpaid bills. The geese, still holding sentry on the lawn, hissed at him as he stopped in front of a sign posted by the C-town Planning Department: Construction Scheduled.

"Rock's really going to do it," Doreena said. "He's going to turn this into a resort. Imagine hotels and restaurants, here."

"Damn. They're taking this too. We have got to go."

"Go where?"

"Away. Anywhere we can get to."

Alonso jumped down the rocky bank. The smooth sludge surface of the lake steamed with the digestive stench of cannibalistic algae and angry goose innards. It promised an icy entry. Swimming in there was the last thing Doreena would want to do, especially first thing in the morning.

"You get cold?"

In response, Alonso plucked at his wet suit.

"Even so."

"When I get out there, I'm in my zone."

He splashed in up to his waist holding the board high before he slid vertically into the water and crawled on top of it. He paddled out to almost the middle of the lake where gray-green water fell from a ringed metal spillway. Doreena sat on the lone bench near the water. She pulled the sides of her suit around her and crossed her arms. She could hear Marilyn critiquing, "Open postures, open postures. Closed body language is bad for sales."

"I'm just cold," she said, aloud to no one, except the geese.

Out on the lake, Alonso managed to stand up and surf the effluent a few feet before crashing. The water had a greasy sheen to it like the stretch of a lower order salesman's pants. On his way home, Alonso would drip red algae onto the bus, grimy lake water into the Narborough and trail brown sand up the stairs and into his bed. The gunk he picked up in the lake would mat in his hair and reek. The thick clouds of incense he burned would barely masque the stench. Maybe he'd shower first, strip out of his rubbery skin, before he could begin the rest of his long do-nothing day.

In the middle of this sudden, imagined stretch of Alonso's bared torso, a blue haze washed over Doreena's vision turning the pink sky violet. A tug across her skin accompanied the haze. She associated the feeling with swerving toward the union protesters, the vulnerable men, and the impact of the car into the AeroFlux landmark sign and shied away from the pinching sensation, the lift and pucker of her skin. For a moment, she hovered over the translucent watery outline of herself sitting on the bench, long enough to see that there was no harm in disappearing here. She was reluctant to leave her cares in C-town completely behind, but she could already feel herself irresistibly warming. She stilled in the grip of the haze. The pinch softened to suction. Warmth embraced her. Waves rose and fell in front of her.

She was sitting on the sand, hugging her bare knees, feeling the sun on her rounded spine and watching the ocean rise and fall. It occurred to her that she should have been scared, or at the very least startled to be pulled out of her expected reality into this one. But everything about this place soothed her. Even her nudity was a comfort. It had been easier to come here than it had been to step off the bus. The place seemed to ask and expect nothing of her and she didn't feel a twinge of guilt about anything she had left behind. Her only concern was that she might not be here long enough to get all the way warm. She stayed still as long as possible so as not to break the spell. When she felt absolutely warm, as though the sun's rays pinioned her, and her legs cramped, she finally rose. She looked from one end of the beach to the other. Palms swayed at either end of the bay. Behind her lay a wall of green. Flowered pohuehue vines grew through the sand below them. A sweet scent drew her toward the jungle. She pressed her face into a cluster of five-petaled hibiscus and inhaled. The bandage over her eye was gone again, along with her wool suit. She squinted with one eye and then the other watching the red tipped stamen of the flower jump side to side. It was dusted with beady pollen that reminded her of the newspaper's quantum dots. The colors of Alonso's surfboard were here, but set in motion: the yellow sun shimmered, the turquoise sea rippled and the hibiscus blossoms, large enough cup her breasts, fluttered in the breeze. The liquid intensity of the colors filled both Doreena's eyes. She looked up.

Through the leaves, velvety yellow triangles or waxy emerald rounds, a path cut up a hill. She took a few steps onto the exposed red soil as it curved into the jungle. Fruits grew here in a clearing: hanging green guava and mango overhead and pineapples sprouting at her feet. She picked up a fallen smooth-skinned mango. Ahead, the path continued up a short steep hill and disappeared. The leaves rustled. A woman's voice trilled from far away. "Calm sea meat," it said or sounded. Leaves whispered across Doreena's face. She clutched her necklace in one hand, the mango in the other, and turned to run back to the beach. She tripped on a vine and fell forward, falling face down, into the dirt.

The vermilion path turned black. Rubbery arms clamped around her and pressed her into a cool, wet torso. Alonso dripped onto her wool suit. The stench of the man-made lake on him was unmistakable. She'd left the magic beach behind. Gray sky framed Alonso's muck-colored curls. The creases around his eyes and mouth glowed with the dawn. He looked older this close up, even her own age. His hands were on her shoulders.

"Where are you running to?"

"Did you see? Did you see me go?"

He shook his head. "You were sitting there." He pointed round at the bench. "And then you were running up the path."

She'd brought back another fruit. She palmed the mango and hid it behind her back. It tingled in her hands. "I've got to go."

He pointed. "There's your bus."

She squeezed the mango. Her fingernails slid through the soft, trembling rind, under the thin, smooth skin and into the slippery, wet fruit.

"Wait." He grabbed her shoulders. He reached down and pulled at a white flap between the buttons of her blouse. A piece of petal, with a soft blue sheen, tore off in his hands. A faint sweetness went up with it. The rest of the blossom slid down Doreena's shirt and lodged at the waistband of her scratchy skirt.

"What's this?" He slid the petal between his fingers. Did he feel the slight vibration of its powdery surface? "What else are you hiding in there?"

All the fear that had eluded Doreena on the beach, caught up with her now. The place, the island, that had seemed so serene before now felt dangerous. It had come and gone, captured her, in ways she could not control. It was because she hadn't gone to work. If she kept to her routine the island couldn't come. It couldn't take her unwillingly. She'd given it an opening. The bus wheezed as it accelerated toward the park. Doreena turned. She dropped the new mango into her purse beside the first one and began to run up the hill. Her skirt bunched around her thighs catching on her thick stockings. Her pumps slipped. Stepping sideways onto the grasses for traction, she sank in mud up to her ankles and lost her shoes in it. She yanked her heels out of the mud and they came up with a sucking sound. Ahead, the bus had stopped. She hurried toward it in muddy stocking feet, with a goose-like waddle, sweating through the frizz of curls on her forehead. Clumps of mud fell from her shoes.

A group of surfers got off the bus: among them were two blond twins, younger, stockier versions of Alonso; the older woman, Hobart, from The Travel Museum; and a dark-haired seal-faced man who was nearly as tall as Hobart. They stared down Doreena.

"She's cool," Alonso said. "Come see the damage. They're building a resort."

Doreena climbed on board the bus and sat on the edge of the disabled passengers' seat. She wiped her brow and brushed her eye bandage. Through the window she saw the surfers standing statuesque around the C-town planning department sign. On the way into work, the cold seeped back into Doreena's skin along with the accompanying stiffness. Just before she reached her stop, she reached into her purse for one of the mangoes. It vibrated in her hands. She squinted into the gloss of its faint blue rind and saw a reminder of the glint of island sun across the ocean. She lifted it carefully to her lips and touched the outer layer with the tip of her tongue. It was light and tingly with the faint taste of saltwater taffy. With the taste of it on her tongue the stiffness vanished, but the island consumed her thoughts.

In *The Mirror's* office, the island receded. Her being seemed to settle into place, neither too stiff nor too fluid, but exactly as she needed to be. The idea that she could suddenly shift into some warm, foreign realm was ludicrous here. She took the back way up to the sales office detouring through the pressroom which stank of beryllium and silicon as the sheets for that day's run curled onto the cement floor. Today's headlines were: "Who needs Maui? One last flight" and "Resort planned for Traynter Lake." Doreena stopped off in the basement bathroom to bathe her stocking feet in the sink and wash off her pumps. She squished them back onto her feet, toweled flecks of mud off her suit and dabbed at a brown smear across her bandage until only a yellowish splotch remained. Her eye throbbed beneath it. She was relieved to be back at work, but aware she would not make a great sales impression.

On her way up the stairs, she heard Rock yelling at The Stew outside the newsroom. "Keep the pressure on. Keep digging. I want those headlines."

"I'm on the outside of this 'cause that's where *The Mirror* is," The Stew said.

"Then get in. That's an easy fix. Everyone knows I'm temperamental."

It made her glad that in sales they only had to answer directly to Marilyn, not the even more intimidating publisher who was stern and tumultuous as an avalanche. Lacking a car, Doreena's sales ability was severely handicapped. She zeroed out on cold calls, while listening to Tom, back at his post, nailing call after call. In desperation, she left in the afternoon to see what was in walking distance of *The Mirror*. The owner of The Watertown held up his hands, "You've got all I can do. What happened to your eye?" Doreena left quickly. She usually softened up the restaurant owners by having lunch, but she couldn't afford it and besides she hadn't been hungry in weeks. Doreena kept waiting for her skirts to loosen, but they were binding around her waist as usual.

She walked the rest of the block in a daze when she passed the words "Coming Soon," scrawled across butcher paper in a front window. A vacant shop? What was coming? A new business of the right kind meant opportunity — if it was in her category. Doreena tried to see in around the edges of the paper. What had been here before? A vacuum repair business, an auto shop? There had been some kind of a fire, she remembered. She tried the door. A red and blue animatronic bird squawked as she entered. Ukulele and accordion music played somewhere behind a collage of wicker tables and chairs. The bird's head jerked to train one plastic eye on her.

There wasn't a trace of smoke left inside. The only smell was new carpet. The tables and chairs gave her hope. A new restaurant? A man stepped out from behind them in checked pants wiping his hands on an apron. He twitched with the unmistakable energy of a new business owner, but there was something else familiar about him in the way he stood, the way he moved.

"My first customer. C'mon back."

She followed him past a back counter stacked with fishbowls through a swinging door.

"Yeah, I've got a lot to do on the décor. But it's the food I love," he said.

The kitchen smelled of baked salt. He reached over a tray lined with white blobs and scooped one onto a cracker. "So, it's lacking presentation. You gonna tell me it doesn't taste good?"

Doreena bit in. Cod. Her hope ebbed. "Seafood?"

The man frowned. "Yeah. We open in a couple of weeks. I expect to see you back. But you don't look very excited."

"No, it's good. A new restaurant. I'm just the person you want to see." She'd start him off with a quarter page, two colors. He'd need a big splash. Restaurants were tough. He'd be lucky to last a few months. She'd have to maximize her commission meantime.

He smiled. "I thought you were. Listen, it'll be better than you think. I've got a connection. We'll serve Silver Lake wines."

Again, there was something familiar. This time in the confident curve of his lip. But Doreena felt sorry for the guy. All the restaurants had Silver Lake wines and all the owners thought they'd finagled something special. C-town didn't allow imports, but the winemaker, just outside of town, was an unofficial exception. Doreena reached into her briefcase for her broadsheets to begin her pitch.

"So, when will I hear from the city about the liquor permit?"

Doreena held out *The Mirror*. "I'm not with the city."

The man's lips tightened, and his fists clenched. The only other time *The Mirror* had gotten that reaction was that woman, Hobart, at The Travel Museum. But if Hobart disliked the paper, this guy loathed it. He looked ready to pull it out of her hands and tear it into shreds. He looked ready to tear into her, too. Normally, her association with *The Mirror* was a source of pride. It was her job, her place. Recently, though selling for *The Mirror* had begun to feel unpleasant and possibly even dangerous. What was it with these new businesses? Didn't they believe in advertising?

"I thought you were with public health," he said.

Doreena backed into one of the tall refrigerators. As the cold seeped through the lining of her wool jacket, it clicked. This location had been the plasma center before the fire. All this stainless steel had been used to store blood. He must have gotten this space cheap.

His eyes narrowed. "Yeah, yeah. I'll buy an ad. Fuck him. You got a contract on you. I'll sign it now."

She wanted to leave, but she needed the sale. And no matter what this guy thought, she owed everything to *The Mirror*, everything she was for the past nine years. A new business had to be in *The Mirror* and it was her job to make it happen. Doreena reached into her briefcase and extracted a contract and rate sheet. The guy glowered, grabbed and slammed both documents down on the counter. The edges dipped into fishy waters. "I'll take a half page to announce the grand opening, full color and then I'll sign a six month, no, make it a year, for a quarter. Tell him I'm going to stick around. And I want radio, too. I want this place lit up, phosphors everywhere, the brightest spot on the street. Gimme a pen."

Doreena reached into her purse, where her hand brushed the cool-skinned mangoes, and handed him her gold closer pen. Too quickly, the guy scrawled his name at the bottom of the contract. Doreena could already hear Marilyn, "You only get commission on qualified buyers." A too good to be true contract smacked of desperation. It usually meant the business would go under before they could collect. But what was she going to do, argue? At least she didn't have to go back to the office empty-handed. Doreena thought of the mangoes and suddenly wished she didn't have to go back to the office at all. A little blue haze, a little suction and she wouldn't have to worry about *The Mirror.*

"And tell him, I don't want any deals. I'll pay it," he said.

He? Doreena read the signature Gavin Traynter and, suddenly, she got it, the swagger in his step, the curve of his lip — this was Rock's little brother. They were marked with the same pallor capped by dark hair, Rock's shorn close and Gavin's swept across his forehead. Gavin's eyes were a pale gray. Everyone wondered what color Rock's eyes were under his redundant shades. Could they be this dove color, too? This was the ingrate son who hadn't wanted anything to do with either family business: Traynter Construction or *The Mirror.* He'd wanted to make his own way. No wonder it irked him, trying to do his own thing and still beholden, as they all were, to *The Mirror.* Doreena stuffed the contract in her briefcase. He'd advertise alright, but Doreena wouldn't get to keep commission on any contract signed Traynter. Today was another big zero. No commission. No rent. No other way to spin it for the boss.

How had the island come earlier? Had she been doing anything special? No, it had just happened. She couldn't will the island to come, but she tried.

"You don't think I can make a go of it do you?" Gavin said, misreading her look of concentration.

"No, it's just, well, seafood." Doreena said, then she sighed. There was no use trying to bluster a Traynter. "No, I don't. You won't last three months."

"You know I'm a bartender, right?"

"Everyone does."

"Well, I can cook too. People like seafood."

"Yeah, but there's The Watertown, The Dungeness and Surf n' Turf. It's all seafood. You need a hook. Something more exotic."

"In C-town, exotic, right. What would you recommend?"

Doreena had her hands in her purse, stroking the mangoes, as though that would bring the island near. "How about an island theme? Do this place up in Tiki font."

"A Tiki Lounge? That's a nice schtick. But I'd still be serving the C-town usuals and that means fish."

Without thought, Doreena held up the mangoes one in each hand. "What about these?"

Gavin turned the fruits red over green in his hand. Then he held them up to his nose and inhaled. The shimmery blue flowed into his nostrils. His nose twitched. He pulled it away and stared at the red and green skins with the soft blue glow.

"What is this some kind of fruit-based phosphorescence?"

Doreena shrugged, reminding herself as she did so, of Alonso.

"And it's edible? Is it safe?" He pressed two fingers into the stuff, tasted it and smiled.

When he finally held the swinging door open for her, his apron was splattered orange. They were both smiling like kids building sandcastles on the beach.

"Where did you get this? Does Rock know about this? No, never mind. I'm a Traynter. I can keep secrets. Just, can you get more? This is exactly what I need."

"I'll let you know," she said. "And I'll tell you where you can get some authentic décor too. And what's with the fishbowls?"

"Those, you'll see. You know I'm a bartender, right?"

"Everyone does."

On her way out, she touched her tongue to the lingering sweet at the edge of her lip. It was 5 p.m. on a Friday, the perfect time to get fired. But back at the office, no one noticed her or her deficient sales. Instead, the hammer had fallen on The Stew. He was gone. Rock had canned him.

"You should have heard them shouting," Tom said.

"I'm next, I know it," said Diane. She'd yet to log even one sale.

Even Marilyn looked shaken and her odd color of the day, a casual rosebud pink, most unprofessional really, made her appear unusually fragile.

~ 8 ~

SALES MEETING

Doreena entangled, exists on Mirror Island and in C-town

On a Monday morning, Marilyn called Doreena into her office and announced that she was going on maternity leave. As *The Mirror's* number one salesman Doreena was now in charge of the sales floor. Doreena had known she was in for a bad day as soon as she arrived at work after another arduous bus trip so long it felt like an actual journey. It surprised her when she arrived at Traynter Tower instead of somewhere different. "See me!" had been scrawled in red beside her desk.

In Marilyn's office, the color of the day was pink again like the inside of an island fruit. Pink flowed at the cuffs of Marilyn's billowing blouse and rippled down her front. It made the double-strand of pearls at Marilyn's neck blush. It shone on her cheeks and lips and even in the highlights of her black hair. Around her, the glass furniture and shelves of sales awards met the pastel rays with an icy glare. The florescent light overhead dulled the cake-frosting color to cooked-salmon at the tops of Marilyn's shoulders. Marilyn, in pink, no longer looked like she belonged although she told Doreena what to do with her usual primary color directness.

"You'll manage in my absence," she said.

When she was done, she struggled to rise from her chair, the wheels slipping forward under her pregnant center, and Doreena had to position herself beside it so Marilyn could use her as a hoist.

"Just a wave of nausea," Marilyn said. When she had collected her breath, she made a giggly dressing room sound. "I forgot; I made an appointment to check out the birthing suite. There's so much I need to do to get ready."

Her tone was conspiratorial, and although the meaning of it was lost on Doreena, she was drawn into a conversation about room service and whirlpool tubs as if Marilyn were planning some kind of exotic getaway rather than the grueling procedure of giving birth. Marilyn carried on as though Doreena were one of her sisters (she was rumored to have a large family somewhere outside the UG). It was as though Marilyn were suddenly having a conversation with someone completely different.

She began talking faster with a trace of some off-continent accent. Her hands punctuated her gestures and Doreena could not have mirrored the movements subtly, or kept up with them, if she'd tried.

Doreena wondered who she was now, or who she was supposed to be, in Marilyn's mind. It was disorienting, but she liked the conversation they were having. The fluid energy of it put them on equal footing. They could even have had a friendly argument. She wanted it to continue and expand to other subjects. She could talk to Marilyn about how she lived at home, and never dated, about how strict her grandfather had always been and how he left her for Maui and returned as ashes. She wanted to share everything. This is what it would be like to have a sister. She especially wanted to tell Marilyn how it felt not to know her family or her people. This seemed like something Marilyn would especially understand. She might even be able to help her, somehow.

Then Marilyn stopped abruptly. She seemed to remember herself and who and what and where they really were.

"Well, you're in charge," she said, speaking the way she usually did at *The Mirror.*

Doreena looked at pink Marilyn who was leaving work early to run some personal errand. Her face stiffened into a familiar scornful expression, a borrowed expression, one Marilyn usually directed at her. Doreena recognized it from the inside out. It was the look Marilyn used on her when she lost a client or wore the wrong thing to work. The look meant, "How unprofessional!" Doreena expected Marilyn to react to the look in a shrinking way, as she did. But nothing about Marilyn appeared to diminish. She seemed oblivious to the How Unprofessional look. Doreena thought that was a weakness. As sales manager, Marilyn, did not have to share her figures. Now Doreena wondered what they were. Her own sensitivity to nuance had propelled her to number one. It was her greatest asset and the reason she excelled at face-to-face sales.

As acting sales manager, Doreena's first task was the weekly motivational sales meeting. She did not have a successful attitude about it. Everyone dreaded the Monday morning meetings in the conference room so cold they called it The Meat Locker. The Force hated how they took time away from sales and openly griped, but Marilyn considered them an essential part of her management strategy.

"I'm motivating you, like it or not," she always said.

Doreena waited with her hand on the icy door handle watching the salesmen make their way towards her through the glass corridors. She anxiously looked around before pushing her way in.

"Our publisher is really concerned about sales. So, he'll be at the meeting," Marilyn had said, last thing before she left. "Listen, put on a good show. Don't let Rock bully you."

Rock was waiting for her inside. In minutes, the rest of the Force filed in stopping short when they saw Rock and shoring the edges of their cups from the rise of coffee tsunamis with their hands. They exchanged grim looks behind the publisher's back.

Last in, Tom, and the new girl, Diane, went back out in search of chairs. No matter how many people were expected at a meeting, there were never enough chairs. Doreena avoided looking into the mirrored shades covering the publisher's eyes instead watching her wisps of breath rise.

"That's why we call this The Meat Locker. You'll learn," Tom said to Diane who was shivering in a sheer floral blouse.

Doreena tucked her chin into her turtleneck. Through the tinted glass of the conference table, she could just make out the hatch marks on her watch: 9:56 a.m.

When Rock began to speak, his voice boomed steely gray. "Don't worry I won't take up much of your time. I can't. Sales are down. We're the only newspaper in town and our numbers aren't good."

To a man, The Force mirrored Rock's posture leaning forward with their hands clasped on the glass surface in front of them. The exception was Diane. The new girl was holding her arms. The closed off posture communicated inattention, but she was probably just cold. Under the table though, the salesmen's feet began to relax. They held wide stances, their legs twitching and feet shuffling. This movement suggested an ease and impatience, which agreed with what Doreena had observed herself after Rock had been speaking awhile. They'd heard this before. Rock was giving them a variation on, "The Higher-Calling Speech." Marilyn began most meetings with this speech where she reminded them that they weren't just selling ads; they were selling thoughts at a quantum level. These thoughts shaped the reality of C-town and were what kept the town intact, preserved its economic stability, and made it a tranquil predictable place to live. The alternative was the chaos and deprivation outside. There was no governance, social order or commerce in most of the rest of the UG. It wasn't even possible to get basic commodities. Rock's Higher-Calling Speech was nearly identical to Marilyn's. She'd probably gotten the gist of it from him, but there were slight differences. Where Marilyn used "security" and "stability" Rock went on about "loyalty" and "tradition".

The speech was supposed to make them all feel part of something bigger. It usually worked on Doreena. This calling tied her to *The Mirror* and strengthened her commitment. The speech made her feel a certain way. In thrall of it, her spine straightened, and her mind fastened on *The Mirror* as she planned her sales attack for the day. But today was different. She was distracted thinking about how she was going to handle being sales manager and what she would say when it was her turn to motivate. The jumpiness of the Force below the table indicated they were thinking about their own commissions and just wanted to get back to sales. Was this the way it always was? Was she the only one the speech affected?

"So, if you haven't been fearful for the state of your city, it's time to begin," Rock continued. His words clanged. He stopped and reached for his shades, a sure sign that no one would like what he was about to say next. The salesmen glanced to the side trying to look away, but the room held no distractions. Unlike the AeroFlux conference room with its historical photographs, the walls here were bare. Each man ended up staring down into the table, where they could see Rock reflected. He removed a layer of shades and revealed the second shinier pair underneath. These smaller circles still hid the outer corners of his eyes and the tiny array of muscles that Doreena always looked to distinguish a real smile from a false one: crinkled meant genuine smoothness meant false. Rock's shades disguised the difference. The Force had a running pool as to the color of the publisher's eyes. So far, no one had been able to claim it. The list of possible colors had become increasingly creative as the obvious choices were taken. Diane had added cerulean to the blue category that included lapis lazuli, azure, turquoise and aquamarine. Having seen his brother's eyes Doreena guessed one of the grays would fit: flint, steel, or granite. Her early choice, if she remembered, back when the pool was new had been a simple combo: gray-green like the surface of Lake Traynter.

"We're not tolerating dissidents anymore," Rock continued. "The fabric of this city is stretched thin. It's been difficult keeping this town together and operating insulated from all the chaos outside and we can't afford to be lenient. People who don't have C-town's interests in mind won't be a part of this organization."

Above the table, the salesmen looked the same, hands pressed together on the tabletop, but, below the table, legs were crossing. It was a classic defensive reaction. They were literally protecting their genitals as though they were about to be kicked. Diane's arms still clenched her upper body, but her feet crossed at the ankles indicated it wasn't just the cold twisting her body into knots. They all knew Rock was talking about how he'd fired The Stew, once his favorite reporter, and telling them they could be next.

"Businesses who don't have C-town's interest in mind will be marginalized." He meant AeroFlux and the cessation of the Maui flights, but what Rock said next was new. "Some businesses we've been selling to have been trying to use *The Mirror* to dissent from within C-town. We'll continue to sell to those businesses because we'd rather have them in our pages than out, the City Fathers will work to bring them into the fold, but meanwhile if I catch anyone on my staff patronizing any rogue businesses, if I hear of any involvement, I'll fire you on the spot."

Doreena immediately thought of The Travel Museum and Gavin Traynter's new restaurant, but a wave of puzzled glances passed among the salesmen. This was apparently news to most of them. Rock turned his head her way. She could feel his gaze on her beneath those opaque shades and saw herself reflected in them as a metallic shadow. Where would she be without *The Mirror*? Everyone she knew was here. All she had without it was a small, apartment in a dark part of town.

Then, he unclasped his hands and leaned back in his chair. "Marilyn is on maternity leave. Doreena Moriena who has been our number one is taking over in her absence and it's time I turned this over to her, our motivational speaker."

Doreena caught Rock's use of the past tense. Already, he knew her sales were slipping. How far had she fallen? She stood. The chill of the leather seat clung to her skin through her wool skirt. She positioned herself at the front of the room, an elongated closet, and looked down the table at the sales staff wedged around it.

Around the room, the Force turned their attention to her and, in the transition, when they stopped mirroring Rock and waited for her to begin their gestures revealed their emotions. Some leaned back. They touched their mouths and faces. They propped their chins in their hands. Diane made swirling circles with purple pen on her notepad. Didn't she know *The Mirror* hated doodlers? They were impatient, bored, and leaderless. She saw this all in a flash and knew that once she began this individual dissension would dissolve into a unified image. When she started to move, they would move with her. She would be the mirror and they the reflection. The prospect terrified and exhilarated her.

"Maybe Doreena needs a round of applause to get started," Rock said.

Leaden clapping followed. The Force wanted to get this over with. The best she could do would be to keep it short. Doreena ran her hands down the sides of her wool skirt wishing for pockets. By the time she readjusted the bandage over her left eye, the room was silent again. The Force hung waiting in front of her like slabs of frozen beef. She clasped her hands in front of her and watched them do the same up and down the table in rows of white knuckles and wedding rings. It was almost the gesture Rock had used but his fingers had extended confidently out towards the center of the table, whereas hers were closed, holding something in, hiding an intention. She was the sales manager, a stiff, solid role, but a fluid feeling of leadership also rushed over her. They were under her direction. Would they follow? Where did she want to go?

Doreena launched into a few safe lines from Stellar Sales, but the words sounded flat and strangely uninspiring in her own voice. "What should we, as sales professionals, say? What motivates the buyer to come to the point of purchase?"

Mangoes, Doreena thought, and as soon as she did, she knew it was dangerous, but once she started, she could not stop thinking island thoughts. Motivation mangoes, mango motivation like the surfer, Alonso, had said on the bus. This time, when the blue haze began to wash over Doreena's vision, she recognized it. The island was coming. Even in an undercurrent of relief and desire to leave the cold conference room and the cold stare of the salesmen and flow to the warm place, she fought it. It was wrong to disappear and a terrible precedent. If the island could take her from here, from the certainty of *The Mirror* office and the routine of the Monday morning meeting then it might lift her from anywhere at any time. She would never be entirely sure where she was or where she belonged. As the soft suction pulled at her skin, Doreena flung her arms wide grasping handles of air. The blue rushed her like a wave. As she flowed back with it, she looked through a translucent backless version of herself into the still bored faces of the sales force. She watched them mirror her gesture. They unclasped their hands on the table. Their palms opened up into that most encouraging sales sign, a gesture that meant they were receptive to experience. Doreena thought if she could just clench her hands into fists, she could prevent the rush away to the island, but she could already feel a little of the warmth rising, soothing her skin and lessening her resolve to stay. In the peripheries, her fingers stretched. She heard herself say, "I'm motivating you like it or not." The Force laughed. Then, they were gone.

So much for her leadership skills. No one came with her to the beach. She arrived on the island alone. She stopped struggling and listened to the waves. The haze squeezed her and released. The clench of heat and spiced saline reminded her of stepping into C-Town Dry Cleaners at first. Then a fresh wind blew off the ocean. She faced turquoise waves and wiggled her bare toes in pink sand. The bandage over her eye was gone again. She stood in a surround of bright light and walked into the surf. Sand scrunched underfoot. She squatted and shuffled forward. Her tailbone dipped into the warm water, and she pushed her fingers into the smooth wet sand. She squinted into the translucent blue at sparkling white shells and darting lemon-yellow fishes.

In the back of her mind, she remembered vaguely that she'd been afraid come here. The island's sudden arrival or her sudden departure, she wasn't sure which, was wrong. It wasn't supposed to be possible, but that didn't seem important now. She was happy to have the place to herself and glad the sales force wasn't around to spoil it. All her personal concerns: moving, falling sales, car accidents, her eye, money trouble with rent, car repair and medical bills melted away. Even the bigger anxieties placed on her by *The Mirror:* responsibility to manage The Force, rogue businesses, AeroFlux, The Travel Museum, Gavin Traynter's restaurant, plummeting sales threatening the stability of C-town eased. She relaxed into a perfect, comfortable, tranquil release. It seemed impolite to worry about work here. She remembered grandfather tiring of her talk about *The Mirror*. It was like that. She could almost hear him as if her were sitting across from her at the dinner table, "Just be quiet a moment. Eat, eat."

Doreena looked back over her shoulder at the waving jungle greens hiding mangoes and other fruit behind them. She was almost hungry now, or at least the sensation of sweet, juicy pulps would feel good on her lips and down her throat. She heard the voice call and understood it this time, not "calm sea meat," but

"Come see me." But she didn't want to leave the beach. This one place seemed perfectly safe and pleasurable. So why go? Not that the island wasn't safe, but all safe places had boundaries. Within the UG, there were enclaves: Maui, D.C., and Cascadia. Island County, Cascadia was safe within the borders of C-town or New West and unsafe without, all around Silver Lake and down the long stretch of Freeway. Even C-town was only safe in those certain neighborhoods Mapleton, Denrigger Hill, and Rosemont brightly lit by phosphors. Dangerous unknowns lay on certain streets, in the industrial part of town across Burrows overpass, in Lakeside and Marsh Creek and out by the border along the forest. On the island, the line between the white sand and the green jungle seemed a likely barrier, as impassable as the one between the sea and the sky. Besides there was something, she thought, she wanted to do here, now.

Grandfather's ashes dangled from the chain on her neck over the low waves. They sparkled pink like Marilyn today or a blush wine and the glass vial glinted in the sun. She looked past the ashes at her bare knees, and then up and down the beach. It was a long curve with palms at the ends of the arch and empty. There were no sails in the water, no ships in the bay. Along with all her other worries, her anger about grandfather's death and the loss of her family mostly faded. A sadness lingered. Her wistful feelings in harmony with the island's nature grew. It wasn't just that she'd lost grandfather. There was more she was missing. A desire to move, to do, built and became a physical pressure that expanded her skin. Doreena stood suddenly and raised her arms to the island sun. Her torso stretched. She arched her back and the sun's rays warmed the length of her body in a long slow glide. "Come see me," the voice sang again from somewhere in the jungle behind the hibiscus.

Then she heard the sound of popping hungry fish mouths — no — applause. Hearty, lively applause like waves slapping a board filled the air. She caught a glimpse of her translucent blue form in front of her before she snapped back into it like a shell. She stood before the sales force. Her arms dropped to her sides. The Force smiled and applauded. Afraid she was naked she hunched forward clasping her hands in front of her and twisting like a jungle vine. But the bandage over her eye was back along with her wool suit. The Meat Locker cold began to seep in through her clothes. The light was so dim she could hardly see. She made her way back to her seat feeling along the tops of the chairs. The salesmen began to rise and make for the door. Doreena turned to Tom and Diane.

"I'm sorry," she said. The words came out in a whisper. Her throat was dry. "What happened?"

"No, don't worry about it. You did great," Tom said. "And I'm not upset Marilyn tapped you to manage instead of me. It was a good choice. Besides I don't envy the time it'll take away from your commissions." Tom dropped his voice and looked up at Rock talking to a couple of the Force by the door. "Hey, did you get that bit about rogue businesses?"

Doreena nodded. She was searching Tom and Diane's faces for clues, but they were acting like nothing unusual had happened. "His brother Gavin's opening a restaurant. He signed a contract the other day, but he's no fan of *The Mirror*."

"Hmm. Well, where is it? So I can stay the hell away," Tom said.

"Just around the corner, seafood."

"Oh, no worries. No one's going to risk their job for a seafood joint," Diane laughed and her rainbow of eyeshadows shimmered like the sides of a fish.

"I ran into another one, too. A business that wouldn't buy in. Near my apartment."

"Well, get them in, Doreena," Tom said. "Rock sounded serious. He fired The Stew. No one's safe."

They stood. Doreena turned back to Diane.

"I did great?" Doreena asked.

"Yeah, I think you even motivated a couple of us," Diane smiled. "Me for sure. I'm ready to give it a try again."

As they passed by Rock, even without seeing his eyes, Doreena could tell his attention was on her. He turned toward her, but all he said was, "You surprised me. I didn't know you had it in you. Marilyn's doing a very good job with you."

Then he turned his ominous attention to Diane, "See me in my office."

Tom and Doreena exchanged a look. Neither of them had ever been in Rock's office.

Back at her desk Doreena opened her bottom drawer and looked for a mango in her purse. She was thirsty deep down and felt dry inside like a stale crust. Her search was fruitless. She'd given both mangoes to Gavin Traynter. While she was rummaging, a few salesmen stopped by to tell her what a great speech she'd given. She wondered what she had said. No one had noticed her disappearance. Doreena reached for her coat. It was time to get out and sell, even if she had to walk around the same oversold blocks, she didn't think she could handle hearing anymore how good she'd been in her role as sales manager, how surprisingly so. When she looked up, Diane was beside her, her face streaked with the cascading green and yellow shimmer of her eyeshadow.

"He fired me," she said. "I'm leaving now."

"Oh, Diane," Doreena said. "I'm sorry. I'll go down with you."

"I'm OK with it. I guess I can try that new restaurant now," Diane said. As they walked toward the elevator, she flung her long red hair back over her shoulders. "Have you ever noticed there are no windows?"

"What?"

Diane spun pointing around the office. "No windows. Not by our cubes or in the conference room or even in Marilyn's office."

Doreena shook her head. When they arrived on street level. Diane pointed up. "Look at the outside, see how the building looks from the street."

The outside of Traynter Tower was a pillar of black reflection. It was all windows. "I see what you mean. But that's usual for office buildings, isn't it?"

"You ever been in Rock's office?" Diane asked.

Doreena shook her head. Like all of the Force, she hoped never to be asked in there. Rumor had it the only person who'd ever enjoyed their time alone in Rock's office was Marilyn.

"That's where they are," Diane said. "The windows. His office goes all the way around the outside of this entire floor. He can walk all the way around the city. He can see everything."

Doreena imagined Rock looking down and seeing C-town around him in shades of gray. "Did you see his eyes?"

Diane shivered. "No. You can have my guess in the pool if you want: cerulean."

"Well, good luck. You'll be looking for a new job?"

"Yeah," Diane said. "I'm thinking something with windows."

Doreena watched Diane walk towards the parking garage as she headed the other way aimlessly. She felt sad that Diane was leaving. She'd thought, from their brief conversation, that they could have been friends. That would have been something new, a friend at work. Marilyn and Diane were both free of *The Mirror*. How could she escape? There were ways: sick days, maternity leave, and windows. But the easiest way was the island. It just came for her and *The Mirror* went on as always.

As she walked the downtown district, she began looking for the blue haze, waiting for the suction pull and thinking about when she would go back. Once she allowed herself to think about it, she could not stop thinking about when the island would come. The very effective, motivating ocean view remained ahead of her as she walked the streets. She remembered the feeling of wanting to rise up on her toes and reach her arms up into the worshipful gesture on the island. Her sun stretch was a posture she couldn't even catalog. She did not know what it meant because it was not something people did in C-town. But her desire to do it, the way she'd wanted it, struck a chord. Was that the feeling that Marilyn and Tom and her grandfather had been talking about all along in all those many conversations where they'd asked her: What drives you? What are you passionate about? Isn't there something you want to do? Doreena wanted to raise her arms and stand under the island sun. She wanted it, a way out. Now if she could only figure out how to get back and how to control it.

It occurred to Doreena that it wasn't just locations that were safe or unsafe. Thoughts had borders, too. That was what *The Mirror* was all about, gathering the right thoughts together and using them to protect C-town. *The Mirror* advertisers, the full-page, full-color spreads taken out by the City Fathers were the safe thoughts, those outside of *The Mirror* like AeroFlux and The Travel Museum were not. Now Gavin Traynter with his rogue business was trying to blur the lines. Within her own thoughts, concentrating on her sales and her income was safe. Island thinking was dangerous and unknown. But she could not stop thinking of it; how she wanted to go back, and how, after all, there was no reason not to if she could find a way. She'd apparently been better in absence, than she'd ever been trying. She could spend her time motivating the sales force by remote while living on the island if she could only control getting there again.

~ 9 ~

SURFERS

A growing island addiction

Doreena wandered the blocks around Traynter Tower going through the motions of work while waiting for the island as she always did now. Although she'd never gone further into it than the grove of fruit, she was sure it was an island. There were no traces of other people on the land or water so it must be out of the way and it had that insular feel that reminded her C-town, actually, a place that existed on its own where everything that happened boiled up from the inside. Doreena found that she went to the island about once a day, every day, always in short bursts, never at the same time, either morning, noon, or night. The timing of the island departures each held its own tortures. Longing for the island came with a particular kind of dryness, a stale, toasted feeling deep within. It was strongest when she returned from the island, faded as she tried to go about her routine and then ached like a phantom limb as the island subsumed all her other thoughts. Her need for it was like thirst. Never had she been so conscious of her insides before: she didn't get sick to her stomach and her menstrual cycles were mild. It was easier to tell when Marilyn's menses began, marked by increased pressure at work, than to take note of her own period which always began quietly a

98

few days later. But for some reason, the island focused her attention on her gut, and a series of unseen internal events.

If Doreena went to the island just as she was waking, she arrived at work warm and content. The feeling faded by midday leaving her restless and distracted. She was in agonies by evening fairly crackling inside with the dry feeling and "island, island, island" her every thought. Returning to her apartment after work, she went immediately to bed, to bring the island sooner. When she went midday, at her desk or while talking to a client, it divided the day into two equally trying sections: waiting to go and longing to return. If the island eluded her until nighttime, she would wait for it the entire day and sit up far into the night and could not sleep unless it came. Of all the unpleasant patterns, Doreena had decided that going to the island in the morning was least agonizing and it was worst when it waited until night because she worried that it would elude her all together and a long island-less day would pass. She'd start to think she had only imagined it and worry it would never come again. The island occupied her thoughts especially when she was at work, at *The Mirror* office, trying hard not to concentrate on her sales. She looked for the blue haze and felt for the soft suck around her skin. The island retreat never took her when she most wanted it, which was most of the time. It always appeared to surprise her.

Today was shaping up to be the worst kind of day when there was no island until night. Doreena walked around Traynter Tower passing the same storefronts pretending to herself that she was still trying to make sales. She needed her island. Even in her wool overcoat and scarf, the cold numbed her. Still, she didn't go. Steam fogged the windows at Raja's. She wished she could afford a five-star curry to warm her from the inside, even if she wasn't hungry. Her hand crooked to open the door. Her fingers were so stiff, from the outside in with cold, and from the inside out with the crisp island desire. Inside, the restaurant was hot and moist as boiled potato. A strong marsala tinged the steam yellow. As much as Doreena wanted to join the few diners inside, she waived the menu away and asked to speak to Mr. Elitamby instead. The owner came right out wringing his hands on his yellowed apron.

"I didn't want to neglect my favorite client," she said.

"I'm glad you've come. We've missed you, Dori. And I've been putting off a call. I wanted to tell you in person. You've been so good to us," he said. "We have to close. It's no good without the Maui flight. We can't get anything. We're into our last stores, all the spices we squirreled away during the collapse."

"Oh, Mr. Elitamby."

In her mind, Doreena struck a line through Raja's on her dwindling sales sheet.

This would be her fourth cancellation this month. That was bad, but almost as bad was the thought of no more curries, the only heat that cut through her cold.

"My dear, it's a tough spot." Mr. Elitamby hung his head. "The City Fathers, they used to make sure we businessmen could get everything we needed to keep things running as they were, one way or another. But things have changed with that new AeroFlux CEO. They don't like him, so they'll turn us into New West where we can only get local goods. What I wouldn't give for cardamom."

Mr. Elitamby held Doreena's fingers as he spoke, an extended handshake, as was his custom. Doreena thought of the mango in her purse. She bet there were spices on her island if she knew where to look. But there was no guarantee she'd see it again.

Around the block, Doreena looked back over her shoulder while passing in front of Gavin Traynter's restaurant. He'd named it the Tiki-Tiki Lounge, but inside and on the menu, it was just a smaller version of every other seafood joint in town. The restaurant looked empty, unsurprisingly, since Rock had refused to run his brother's ads after all and threatened to fire any *Mirror* staff he caught inside. Doreena had overheard some of the lower ranked salesman wasting valuable time gossiping about the new rules.

"Can he do that?" one of them had asked.

"Hell, yeah, he can. If you're that stupid, maybe Rock should just fire you now," another had responded. "This is at will employment. Means he can fire you at will."

Doreena ducked down the next alley and knocked on one of the gray metal doors. After a while, an aproned Gavin Traynter opened. He waved her into the Tiki-Tiki Lounge kitchen. Doreena reached into her purse and handed Gavin a couple of mangoes. "I know it's not enough to make a difference."

Gavin smiled at her and took the fruit. "Thanks, though, I appreciate the thought," he said. Reaching for a small paring knife, he began to slice through the red and green skin. "And these are delicious. I've been dreaming up recipes: Mango Salsa, Mango Martinis, Mango Spritzers, Mahi-Mahi with Mango Butter Sauce."

He held out a bit of the melty orange fruit to her on the end of the knife. Doreena took the slice of mango and rolled the wet slip of it around in her mouth. The liquid comforted her and a soft, fluid feeling washed over her when Gavin looked at her.

"You know, it's not like I'm Rock's enemy," he said. "I'm a Traynter, too. I love C-town as much as anyone. I've never wanted to go anywhere else. I'm perfectly happy here. I just wasn't interested in the family businesses: construction or *The Mirror*. They're all about controlling the town. Seems to me like too much work."

Doreena stiffened and responded instinctively. "It is a lot of work," she said, the Higher-Calling speech leaping to mind. "C-town couldn't be what it is without Rock and *The Mirror*. It would have fallen apart with everything else."

"Well, we could relax the control a little bit. Some free trade. Some imports," he said.

"It's a slippery slope," Doreena said, glancing at the slices of mango sliding off the side of the cutting board and beginning to feel ashamed. "I have to go."

"Yeah, right," Gavin turned away. "Well, if you find a way to get more imports. Let me know."

Doreena left the kitchen with sweetness on her lips but returned to the office guilty about her lackluster sales and traitorous visit. She worked late leaving phone message after phone message and missed the early bus. She sat at the stop as the phosphors for the boutiques flickered out at 6:30 p.m. and the ones for the bars flared to life. A layer of grime covered the street. Soggy scraps of silicon newspaper lay in the gutters like pink algae. Her body was stiff with cold, her muscles tight with a feeling she was beginning to associate with C-town. It trapped her. She wanted her beach, to walk the length of its salt-washed, pure, unspoiled sand. On the bus ride home, she imagined circling her island. The ride was so slow, she could have walked all the way around it she supposed if not for its palm-edged ends. Instead, she trudged up the stairs to her apartment.

Inside she took a mango off the top of the pyramid of tropical fruit accumulating from her morning island visits. She pressed its smooth skin to her cheek. She imagined she could feel island warmth pulsating inside it. Instead, she went to the window. She stood still in her wool coat and scarf massaging the mango. For a moment, she felt the island coming. She held her breath and wrapped her arms tight around herself to keep from gasping and reaching and wanting the beach to come too much and breaking the spell. She willed the suction to grip her and pull her free of her wool trappings and finally released the day's tension and discomfort. What she wouldn't do for just a moment, it was usually just a moment, warm and naked, on the beach. The sun would be high overhead as always. No matter when went she went it was always, always into the bright light of noon. The weather was the same, hot and balmy. Hibiscus and pikake, Hawaiian jasmine, infused the air. The fruit was so sweet, and mostly water; it didn't require an appetite. She would peel back the green skin of a fresh guava with her teeth and dug into it up to her gums lolling her tongue into its pink flesh. The juice would drip from her chin soaking the sand.

The mercurial island didn't come. In the industrial section of C-town below, she could make out the tar-covered rooftops and the brick edges of the buildings. Then there was the open darkness of the swamp and the lake beyond. Far away, downtown, phosphors glowed violet. A long night of longing stretched out in front of her alone. She squinted and imagined the glow as the blue haze. Rock Traynter would stand like this in his windowed *Mirror* office looking out at his gray city. The difference was that he controlled what he saw. If she could, would she want to see her island like that stretched out below in front of her? The idea frightened her. As it was it was, the island stayed hidden up in the jungle behind her. But she did want to control it, to be able to make it appear when she needed it. The pressure of not being sure of something as essential as her location was stacking up inside of her like her pyramid of mangoes. An idea came to her, and Doreena rummaged in the bottom of her purse. She came out pinching a soaked and mealy scrap of flyer between fingers coated in a brownish-orange rotten mango mush. The surfers were meeting tonight. They had traveled. Maybe they would know about the island and give her a clue about how to control it. Doreena filled her purse with mangoes and headed out into the night.

In the rain, without phosphors to guide her and unused to dark streets, Doreena searched for the Labor Temple. Her hair dripped in wet curls by the time she found the square, brick building with pale orange illuminating "bor Tem" over the locked double doors. A man approached, a moving piece of night, except for the beige bag slung across his back. She recognized Alonso when he whispered, "This way, you here for the meeting, right? Round back."

She followed the algae-musk that clung to him behind the building and down a stairwell into the temple's winding corridors. Dim fluorescent bulbs flickered across Alonso's wetsuit. Mold blackened the chips in the walls. Icy water dripped onto her coat through cracks in the ceiling. The carpet released a fetid odor as it sank beneath her feet. They entered an unmarked room where men sat in a circle of folding chairs with wet suits peeled down to their waists and drums poised between their knees. The building's pipes creaked and groaned, and warm air hissed down on them from the Reznor box overhead.

A pile of canvas bags lay in one corner. The men, the blond surfer twins and the seal-faced man from the lake among them, looked up at her as she entered.

"What's with the *malihini*?" one said.

"She's alright," Alonso said. "I invited her. Let's get started."

He shut the door behind them, sat down and swung the bag between his legs. He unzipped it revealing the taut hide tops of a pair of Congo drums. One by one, the men reached for their bags. They flicked the tops of their drums with their fingers. In the drumming, Doreena began to be able to tell the blond surfer twins apart. Both of their hands moved fluidly across the drums, but one of them had a lighter touch and the other a thin scar on his right hand. A rhythm emerged and intensified, widening the room with its echoing waves.

After a while, Alonso rose and gestured to Doreena to sit in front of his drum.

"I don't know how," she said.

"Just tap it," he said. "When it feels right."

Doreena joined the rhythm with hesitant touches of the drumhead. After a while it was like she'd been doing this forever and could go on doing it forever. The drum sound reverberated through the small room as if it were trying to escape. A bead of sweat slipped through the fringe of her drying hair. She soaked it up with the rust-colored cowl of her sweater. The drums dropped into a low steady tapping. The men began to chant strings of strange words interspersed with a few she did know: Easter, Cat, Destruction, Fire. A fluid feeling rippled through Doreena until the chanting trailed off into a low hum, the drumming stopped, and she realized she hadn't longed for island since she'd seen Alonso. Now the stiffness of wanting it returned. She wrung her hands over the drum.

"Welcome to the surfers. Those are the names of the islands we love," Alonso said.

He pointed around the circle of men and began rattling off foreign words. He'd gotten halfway around when she realized he was introducing her to the surfers. She was usually good with names, her sales training had armed her with mnemonic devices to remember introductions, but she couldn't keep track of these ones: Ehukai, Hapitit, and Barritz. The men, alike in their wetsuits, didn't offer much in the way of distinguishing guideposts. The twins were easy though: A-Bay of the light touch and J-Bay, with the scar.

"Those are our names, also some of our favorite surf spots," Alonso said.

Doreena was sure these surfers who held drum circles in the basement of the Labor Temple and called each other by made-up names, were the kind of people her grandfather had been keeping her away from her whole life. "The odd ones," he'd forbidden her to befriend. The first girl she'd met when she'd started school had been one. "Stay away from her, she's an odd one," her grandfather had said. Since he worked at her school, he always knew who the "odd ones" were. The other kids, the not odd, never approached Doreena. She'd gotten used to being mostly alone, but she'd never learned to identify the odd ones for herself or understood what grandfather really meant. Now she thought she understood the difference between them and most of the people she interacted with in C-town. It wasn't something she knew but something she felt, not only emotionally, but as an actual physical reaction. The surfers, came with that unsettling, but rather pleasant fluid-feeling that reminded her of the island.

"I'm Doreena Flora Moriena, nice to meet you," she said, in the stilted, distant tone she'd use with any of her clients, but then a wave of feeling swept over her and the next words rushed out. Her voice stayed low, but there was a new vibrato quality to it. "Did you say islands? Do you know how to go?"

He shook his head. "We got holed up here coming out of a surf meet in Westport on the coast. We were heading south when everything went to hell and the freeway clogged. We've been saving up for a Maui run, but so long as we're here we're trying to loosen things up adding our ideas to the mix. Eventually, we'll hit the road again, but it's gnarly out there. Meantime, we'll hunker down."

"What do you mean loosen things up?"

Before he could answer, the door swung open and a surfer giantess taller than all the men entered. Her silver cap of hair took on a blue tint in the dim light near the ceiling. It was Hobart from The Travel Museum. The woman's odd name must be a beach somewhere.

"What's the hold up?" Hobart spotted Doreena, trained eyes on her, grabbed her elbow and torqued her around. "You know she's with *The Mirror,* right?"

"She's cool. I'll vouch," Alonso said.

"Not good enough." Hobart's grip tightened. "Rock sent her to spy on us."

"No," Doreena said. She tugged her arm free and dumped her purse, so the mangoes rolled over the concrete floor. "I'm here on my own."

The surfers stared down until Hobart picked one of the fruits up, then the rest of them followed suit.

They faced Doreena in a ring, mangoes in hand.

"Where did you get these?" Hobart said.

"I have a connection," she said.

"Who are you working with? Who's your importer?"

"It's just me, now."

"You? You can get in and out?"

Doreena shrugged. "Sometimes, it's kind of unreliable."

"I bet. I don't believe it." Hobart said, but she was staring at the fruit in her hand. "We may be able to help."

"Help?" Doreena said. "Help me what?"

"Move product," Hobart said. "For AeroFlux."

"Mangoes, motivation. Motivation, mangoes," Alonso said. He'd bit into one of the fruits and a drop of juice gleamed in the corner of his mouth.

"Don't look so surprised. I know what you're doing. You're not the only one. A lot of people aren't happy with the way things are. We're working to change all that. See there," Hobart pointed up to a large vent near the ceiling above pyramid shaped structures that jutted into the room. "Those are for acoustics. *The Mirror* works on a quantum level embedding dots in the fabric of the paper, spreading the ideas throughout C-town and infiltrating people's consciousness. It's the same way any communication works except *The Mirror* purposefully creates particles of thoughts with a specific intention, keep C-town insulated and uniform. Our drumming works the same way, but we put the message in the music. We want to counteract *The Mirror* with free form openness and flowing thought."

"Flowing," Doreena said. "Loosening things up."

"Yeah, Rock's got us all constipated," A-Bay, the light-touch twin said.

"Like a kidney stone. Let's show her the new product," J-Bay added.

A group of the surfers stayed behind and resumed drumming while Hobart, Alonso, and the twins, led her down the hall through swinging double doors into a large room with a concrete floor. The phosphor lit room was moist and hot and the walls lined with banks of computers and audio recording equipment. Faders glowed. Spools of blank pink silicon were stacked in one corner and a river of broadsheet flowed across a press covered with a fresh array of pale blue dots. Fleshy blobs of silicon bubbled in vats beside tubs of phosphorescence. It was an eighth the size of the equipment in *The Mirror,* but there was no mistaking the setup of the press or the smell. She'd stopped noticing the chemical burn in *The Mirror* office, but now the warm silicon reminded her distinctly of her childhood. Her bedroom had been on side of the house that caught the afternoon sun along with grandfather's hibiscus. Her windowsills were lined with invisible women, anatomy dolls, the only kind grandfather allowed.

"These dolls show what real human bodies are like inside. Those others are just plastic. They don't look like real people. There's nothing inside them. They're hollow. You look like a real person," he'd said.

She'd thought maybe he wanted her to be a doctor, but he'd discouraged this. "Don't be around sick people. Be healthy," he'd said.

She had seven dolls in various stages of exposure: skinless, lacking major organs and utterly skeletal.

In the heat of summer, they melted a little and the hot plastic smelled a lot like this.

A man stepped out from behind the vats wearing a lab coat, a welder's mask, and swim fins. The footwear actually seemed a smart choice on the puddle-covered concrete. He flopped toward them with a curling piece of silicon slung over his arms. "The front page."

Hobart skimmed it, nodded, and passed it to Doreena. The silicon broadsheet was still warm and tacky to the touch. The numerous minute indentations of the embedded quantum dots tingled in her hands. The masthead read *C-Town Traveler*. The headline, Citizens Held Captive: Last Maui Flight Set, ran below followed by: AeroFlux Exports Electric Cars to New West: Still Banned in C-Town.

The scientist lifted his mask. He wasn't a scientist at all. He was a journalist.

The Stew was a traitor. He was running an underground newspaper to compete with *The Mirror*.

"This is why Rock fired you."

"No, Rock doesn't know about this. If he knew he'd shut it down and banish us all." He stepped forward and held out his hand. "I go by Madagascar here."

"C-town's a one paper town," she said.

"Not anymore," Hobart said. "It'll take time. Lots of editions to change this town, but we've started. We're providing an alternate vision."

"That's dangerous," Doreena said.

"It's an adventure," Hobart said.

"That's what you call travel when it gets dangerous," Alonso said.

J-Bay and A-Bay looked at her with mango wedge smiles.

"I think we can help you," Hobart said. "If you can help us."

"Me?" Doreena said. "How?"

Hobart walked over to a stack of folded fresh papers. It was a slim edition with just four pages. One of which was a full-page, full-color ad for The Travel Museum. It was a scaled down version of the HAWAII poster, just like Doreena had envisioned.

"We need more advertisers," Hobart said. "If you know anyone."

Doreena immediately thought of Gavin Traynter and Raja's and began to think of a number of other clients who had turned her down over the years. She wouldn't have thought so before, but she could see now how maybe these businesses didn't like *The Mirror*. Would they be interested in this new vision of C-town?

"I might. I'd have to think about it," Doreena said. If she did, they'd be traitorous thoughts.

She walked back to The Narborough between Hobart and Alonso. The rain had eased, and a layer of fog settled in to the marshy lowlands. The surfers walked in companionable silence, with Doreena awkward among them, but too absorbed in a flurry of thoughts to make conversation herself. The evening hadn't been at all what she expected. The surfers hadn't helped answer any of her questions about the manifestation of the island and they'd raised all kinds of new ones about C-town. Did AeroFlux have a secret importing business that Rock didn't know about? She felt confused and torn between the security and familiarity of *The Mirror* and the strange possibility of joining with the surfers in their underground paper, a possibility that made her feel entirely different inside.

"There's nothing inside them. They're hollow," her grandfather had said about ordinary dolls. He'd wanted her to have anatomy dolls with their insides showing instead. An odd thought, occurred to her, had he'd been afraid that there would be nothing inside her? Maybe she did feel kind of hollow at *The Mirror* office, certainly she had felt still and silent and innocuous inside. Now, she was stirred.

Hobart left them at The Travel Museum and Doreena walked up the stairs to her apartment with Alonso. Everything about his posture said casual complacency. It agitated her. She was fairly seasick from being around him and the surfers. She imagined her insides roiling like hot silicon. She was building up some kind of internal momentum. And where was it taking her?

"Alonso, so, is that some kind of a surf spot too?" she asked.

"No, that's my real name. But I go by lots of things," he said, and gave his easy, liquid shrug. "Right now, my handle is C-town. They say I'm so grounded they gotta call me where I am. My place, my name, is always the one I'm in."

He left her on the stairwell wondering where her place was: with *The Mirror* or the surfers. And that's when the blue haze, like a blur of crowded quantum dots, dropped over her vision again, and sucked her into the island. That wild, nameless place, that she'd managed to forget for just a few hours, overwhelmed her again.

~ 10 ~

BABY SHOWER

Doreena struggled to get her bearings. She'd been flitting in and out of the island frequently and it was becoming harder to keep track of where and when she was. Even when she wasn't on the island, an island-ish feeling lingered so that she did not feel truly present in C-town where no one seemed to notice either her absence or her disorientation. As far as she could tell, the person she was supposed to be in C-town continued to exist and do what people expected. That person, that Doreena, seemed less and less like her actual self, who was really on island time. At the moment, Doreena wasn't sure where she was; everything around her was light-filled and shiny as if she were looking out to sea. Everywhere bright colors dangled like flowering vines, but the overpowering scents weren't of the island. They were forced, stale smelling assaults of musk, rose, and orange instead of drifts of jasmine and lily. Doreena snapped fully into her C-town self when she recognized the reflective glass counters and the hanging displays of necklaces and scarves: Denrigger's Department Store. In her hand, she held the silken straps of a shopping bag. Inside was a puzzling beribboned box gift-wrapped in yellow paper. She could not remember buying anything.

"Have a great time," a voice trilled. Diane was behind the counter rolling a collection of lipsticks under her palm on the glass top. A great time, where? How long had Diane been working at Denrigger's? Doreena searched her face for clues, but it was an illusory sheen of rainbow-colors.

"I'm actually a little sorry I'm going to miss it," Diane said.

"Do you miss *The Mirror*?" Doreena asked.

"I like it here. Rock only gave me a job because he felt sorry for me after the crash," Diane rolled one of the lipsticks at her. "Here, take this, a free sample. The color'll be just right on you."

Doreena dropped the lipstick in her purse. On the street outside the department store, a sliver of sun shone through the clouds. There were quite a few people around, most of them in jeans. It was probably a Saturday afternoon. She pressed her back against the brick wall of the store and waited. Either she'd remember where she was going to go, or the blue haze would pull her away again and it wouldn't matter.

The pull didn't come and the distant winter sun never penetrated her wool coat. Beneath the coat, her legs were bare and her feet chilled in open-toed sandals. The impractical footwear looked like something new she was wearing to please someone else and that reminded her: Marilyn's baby shower. She began to walk the blocks toward Traynter Tower and the loft. She would have taken the bus, but her purse was empty except for the lipstick and a couple of mangoes. Although she walked slowly, she made it to the loft before the island ever came.

It was strange to be going to the loft on a day other than Founder's Day. Even with the sun burrowing its way out of the clouds, there was a cold, gray cast to everything. The street looked dingy. If a parade of C-town's firetrucks, police, and dignitaries were to roll down the street now, it wouldn't fool anyone; there'd be a dearth of civic pride.

In the mirrored elevator on the way up, she applied the lipstick. Marilyn liked her to have color. It was a weird shade called Scarlet Tangier. It made her lips look like wedges of something slightly rotten and emphasized the gray tones of her skin. With all the time she'd been on the island shouldn't she have a little tan? Doreena looked closer. Pulling back the flesh of her cheek below the bandage she was still wearing on her eye in C-town, she examined her winter skin. There was no hint of tan, but there was a strange bluish cast beneath it and a kind of sheen, almost as if one of Diane's metallic makeups had been applied just beneath her skin. When the elevator door opened, Doreena stepped quickly off anxious to escape her reflection.

Her hand poised to knock on the Traynter's door, Doreena worried she'd run into Rock although she didn't think it likely he'd be at the baby shower. If she did see him, for once she'd be glad of his glasses. She wouldn't be able to look him in the eye. He might see treachery. She'd sold ads in the *C-town Traveler* to both Gavin Traynter's Tiki-Tiki lounge and Raja's. Traitor that she was, it seemed wrong to show up at Rock's home, but Marilyn, whose mood of late had been sprightly, had invited her to the shower and she couldn't imagine turning Marilyn down for anything. Marilyn greeted Doreena at the door patting her shoulders in lieu of a hug across her broad belly.

"You made it after all. I was beginning to wonder," she said.

The color of the day was spring yellow. She wore a billowing yellow crepe blouse, there was a glow of yellow across her cheeks, eyes, and lips and a sunny tint to her nails. A blonde woman beside Marilyn offered to take Doreena's present and coat. Doreena was surprised when she removed the coat to find herself in a pastel floral-patterned dress she didn't remember owning in a light, clingy fabric she couldn't imagine selecting.

Marilyn introduced her to a circle of women already gathered on the crème couch. "These are my friends from the club. And this is Dori, she works for us at *The Mirror*." Marilyn rattled off their names: Victoria Fort, Bea Mitchell, Alexis Sand, and Deidre Denrigger. Unlike when she'd been introduced to the surfers, Doreena knew she'd have no trouble remembering names, even if the women were similarly attired in spring dresses. They were iconic: Fort Family Auto, Mitchell's Medical Supplies, Sand Valley Farms and Denrigger's Outfitters and Accessories. These were *The Mirror's* premium customers, the full-page full-color regulars and the businesses that kept C-town operating independently. Fort Family Auto repaired and resold C-town's vehicles. Ed Mitchell was CEO of C-town General Hospital as well as its medical supplier. Sand Valley Farms provided most of the city's food and the Sands were rumored to own the one overlooked illegal import as well, Silver Lake Winery. Denrigger's manufactured clothing and cosmetics and, of course, ran the department store. These were the wives of the C-town City Fathers.

It was strange company for Doreena and discomfiting to be around this new softer version of Marilyn, her professional veneer cracked by the swelling baby. The women settled in on the couch to watch Marilyn open her gifts. Doreena stared out the window to Traynter Tower and wished the island would come soon. Marilyn bent over her belly and picked up a gift from the pile at her feet. She unwrapped a blue button up sleeper and held it up.

For a moment, a familiar, critically appraising look crossed Marilyn's face the one she directed at ad placements and sales figures and Doreena herself. Then she returned to her complacent abeyance and gave a lenient maternal smile. On cue, the women cooed in unison and then one by one as they passed the sleeper around. The blonde woman, Deidre Denrigger, nudged Doreena and thrust the sleeper into her hands. It was impossibly soft like the island sand, or hibiscus petals, or clouds. She smiled in imitation of the other women, but she could feel how it didn't reach her eyes and hoped Marilyn wasn't looking. Her smile caught in the dry cracks around her mouth. Her skin felt dry as sand.

She wanted the island. She ached for it. Worse still was knowing she didn't have to do this. If she went to the island, the women wouldn't even notice. If anything, she'd do this better once she left here and focused on the island. The shell she left behind would do what they wanted and expected and be perfectly behaved. She'd lost all interest in living this C-town life. She didn't care if she controlled the C-town Doreena, if she could remember where she'd been or what she bought, but she desperately wanted to control the island. She wanted to go there now. The worst part about being in C-town was not knowing how long she'd have to endure it. She would have cried, but the terrible dryness made it impossible. She balled her hands into the sleeper, her nails clacking on the teeny-tiny buttons, and noticed Deidre staring. She patted the garment smooth and passed it on.

"I know that look," Deidre said.

"I'm sorry. Just a hard day, " Doreena said. "I'll be OK."

"Honey, it just gets worse. How old are you?"

"35."

She nodded. "Yep, that's about the time it really hits. You start feeling there isn't any time. Well, if you have trouble, Marilyn knows a great fertility doctor. How long have you been trying?"

Doreena understood the woman had mistaken her longing for the island for a ticking clock, longing for a child. Doreena could see the similarity, but if only it were that easy. It seemed easier to get pregnant and have a child than to control her mysterious island. Still, it was nice to have someone to talk to about the horrible feeling. And Deidre's wide expression, her broad face, her leaning forward posture made her easy to talk to. Doreena looked at Marilyn's swollen belly.

"Six months," she said, for that was how long her grandfather had been absent and the island had been growing in her life.

"That's not long sweetie," Deirdre smiled. "Keep trying. Does your husband want children too?"

Doreena frowned. Husband? She hadn't even been on a date. Before the island, her life had been all about *The Mirror*. It struck her now what a strange abbreviated life she'd been living. She'd never even thought about having a family of her own or children. Deidre had turned away sensing she'd asked a sensitive question and returned her attention to Marilyn. Marilyn held Doreena's gift. Doreena wondered what was inside. She worried for a moment that she'd done something odd and wrapped up a mango or a seashell. But her gift turned out to be a plush, yellow, pink, and blue patchwork bag covered with pouches and pockets.

"This is perfect," Marilyn pronounced, swinging the bag over her shoulder. "For all his things."

The women cooed agreement.

There were too many gifts. They paused for refreshments. Doreena clutched her little paper plate with its slice of yellow cake. She'd been eating only island food, fruit and coconut water. She hadn't been hungry for anything else. Still, her new dress was snug across her belly, hips, and thighs. She didn't appear to have lost weight. Out of politeness, she dipped the tines of her fork into the frosting and tasted it. It was lemony in a bottled-up way, like sweetened detergent.

She turned to a shaken Marilyn who was gripping her shoulder for support and tottering. "Excuse me. Just a big kick. Do you want to feel?"

Doreena didn't. There had always been a professional barrier between herself and her boss, and she didn't like the familiar way this new Marilyn kept breaching it. Touching her distended belly seemed disconcertingly intimate, but Marilyn pressed her hand to it anyway. She could feel everything through the thin blouse, the warm swell, the flesh stretched taut over the cushion of water and the undulating life within. The blue haze dropped over her vision, the yellow blouse turning a pale green. The suction surrounded Doreena, but it stretched by extension around Marilyn. She pulled harder to get away, but Marilyn held fast.

"No, it's my place. You'll spoil it," Doreena said, but there was no doubt that the island was embracing Marilyn, too.

As they left, Doreena could see her transparent shell still standing cake in hand, but there's was nothing left of Marilyn in C-town. Her billowing yellow blouse, skirt and matching undergarments dropped to the floor. She simply vanished.

They arrived on the beach together. The colors of the day were peach, dusk rose, and tawny brown. Marilyn was naked except for the double strand of pearls around her neck and the baby bag still slung over her shoulder. Her hair was loose. Whatever clasp had secured it at her neck had been left behind with her clothing. Her belly marbled with blue veins and stretch marks soared out in front of her.

Doreena expected Marilyn to be hysterical and order her about in a panic as she often did at *The Mirror*. But Marilyn did not look in the least alarmed. Her face went through a series of expressions Doreena thought were probably quite similar to her own her first time on the island. Marilyn looked delighted holding her arms wide and her palms up to the island sun. A bit of wonderment touched her smile as she gazed at the tranquil sea. Her fingertips curled as though she wanted to grab the edges of the scenery and pull it around her like a blanket. Then a wary expression crossed her face. Doreena looked to the jungle. She listened for the chilling voice, but there was only the sound of waves. She noticed Marilyn's hands on her belly and saw she'd misread the source of her concern.

"No, there's the kick. He's all right. It hasn't hurt him in the slightest," Marilyn said.

She turned to Doreena and stared into her eyes, but it didn't bother Doreena. Her hands hung comfortably at her sides. She didn't worry about how to hold them. Their nudity didn't bother her either. The island had removed the walls between them, and she was at ease with their intimacy.

"It's some kind of fairy tale place, like my grandmother used to read to me. I should be afraid, but I'm not," Marilyn said. "What is this? You've been here before, haven't you?"

"It's the island."

Marilyn looked up and down the bay and then nodded as if this were explanation enough. "What's back there? Through the leaves?"

"There's fruit, really delicious." She took Marilyn's hand in hers, which felt like the most natural thing in the world to do as if they were childhood friends, as if they were children, and led her up the sand to the grove of fruit. As they entered the grove, Doreena spotted a cluster of five-petaled crème-colored flowers among dark green leaves she didn't recognize, but Marilyn did.

"Frangipani," she said. "Like my grandmother used to grow."

The grove was larger now and there were large-leafed banana trees among the pineapples, coconuts, and mangoes. They gorged on fruit and their chins were dripping with juice when the concerned look crossed Marilyn's face again and her hands returned to her belly. "Is this food safe for the baby?"

"I've been eating a lot of it," Doreena said, but it occurred to her as she did it that the fruit could be responsible for her queasiness.

But Marilyn's concern quickly faded. "I can't imagine anything here would hurt him."

She began gathering the fruit and filling the pockets of her baby's tote bag. "In case we need it for the trip out," she said, looking up the red jungle trail. "Is that how we get back?"

Doreena shuddered. "No, we don't go there. I just go. Just like we came."

"You just go. When?"

"There's a little warning. Things get fuzzy."

"Mmm," Marilyn said. "Well, stay close."

"Come on, let's go back to the beach."

They sat hand in hand staring at the waves.

"I still feel like I should be afraid, but I can't be. I'd be perfectly content to sit here forever. There's *waiwai* here. That's Hawaiian for prosperity. *Wai* alone means water. *Waiwai* prosperity. It's the feeling you get from waves, the sound of abundance." Marilyn mopped her brow. "Mmm. I'm getting really hot. How long will we be here? I just start to wonder."

"I can't say. This is longest I've ever stayed. It's usually just quick trips, flashes really. Why don't we go into the water?"

"Is it safe? There aren't sharks or anything?"

"I never thought so. I've just seen little yellow fishes."

They waded in up to their waists. The water magnified Marilyn's pregnancy, the bottom of it billowed out like a pale pink fish, while the top of it broke through the water sitting on the surface a little island of its own.

"I'm still wearing my pearls," Marilyn said, fingering the strand around her neck. "I guess I really never go anywhere without them. What's your necklace?"

Doreena touched the vial between her breasts. "My grandfather."

"Gave it to you?"

"Yes, but it also is him. His ashes." Keeping secrets seemed pointless now.

Marilyn wasn't disturbed. She laughed. "Was he a pixie? Human remains aren't sparkly blue."

"Blue?" Doreena held the vial around her neck up to the sky. It was the same brilliant tourmaline. "It used to be pinker. More like the sand."

Marilyn examined Doreena's necklace. "Ashes are a chalky beige. I have my grandmothers, in an urn. I looked inside once just to see." As she held it, the blue began to bubble. It twisted in the light changing color: blue to green to yellow and silver. The chain slipped into Marilyn's hand, fell through her fingers, and slid through the waves.

Doreena was quickly after it. She dove under the water but lost track of it in her own turbulence. She waited for the water to settle and then swam down scanning the ocean floor. She finally spotted the necklace pressed into the side of a piece of coral and half covered with sand. Only the blue tint on the whiter sand gave it away. It looked so fluid and translucent at first, she thought the glass had broken and grandfather had floated into the sea.

When she surfaced, Marilyn looked afraid. Again, Doreena looked toward the jungle. It was the only part of the island she feared, but the green wall was still and silent.

"Is the baby, OK?" she asked.

"You were gone so long. You didn't come up for air. I thought you'd drowned. I wanted to come after you, but couldn't," she said, putting her hand to her belly.

Doreena inhaled slowly. She put her hand to her chest. She hadn't felt out of breath.

"I found it," she said. "The last link is missing, and the chain's all tangled."

"You can reconnect it to the next one."

They left the water and sat back down on the beach. Doreena held the chain in the air and tried to untangle the tiny knots. She was no longer at ease with Marilyn beside her and couldn't enjoy either the heat or the color. She could feel the other woman waiting like sitting beside someone at a bus stop.

"I guess this is what it must have been like for Rock when we went to Maui. Now that I'm thinking about getting back. I can't enjoy it. He never really liked Maui though. It's no loss for him to cancel the AeroFlux flights."

"I guess the scenery loses a lot in grayscale," Doreena said.

"I imagine. If something happened to you, could I get back? Would I go by myself?"

"I don't know," Doreena said, still struggling with the necklace. She wasn't even sure what would happen now. She thought she should touch Marilyn when she felt the pull back, but the return trip was faster. It offered less warning, and she wasn't sure how it would work with the two of them.

"Give it here," Marilyn said, holding out her hand. "There's a trick to it."

Doreena handed the knotted tangle of silver necklace over; she'd been making it worse. Marilyn put the necklace down on the sand and slid her finger back and forth over the chain several times. Space slowly opened up between the knots. "It wants to untangle, but you have to remove the resistance. It's gravity that keeps the knots bound. When you put it down, they loosen easily."

When the chain was one loose circle again she picked it up and refastened it around Doreena's neck.

As she did so, the blue haze dropped. Doreena touched Marilyn's arm. "It's happening."

Marilyn hugged her, anxious to get back.

Doreena saw her C-town shell in front of her standing in front of an open door with Deidre and the other women. Deidre was shouting and her words began to register between each crash of the waves, "Where...she...don't...disappeared!" With each word the points of her hair fell back and forth sweeping the line of her jaw like a razor. As Doreena clicked into place. The woman's lemony breath hit her face, "Where's Marilyn?"

Doreena realized with embarrassment that they were standing in Marilyn and Rock's bedroom.

Marilyn was nowhere in sight. Had she left Marilyn behind? Could she go back and get her?

Then a woman screamed. "Call an ambulance!"

The women dashed as one to the living room. Doreena behind them. Marilyn stood there completely naked beside the cake table, exactly on top of her discarded clothes. There was a pleasant look of surprise on her face, but the woman behind her; it was Bea Mitchell whose husband, Ed, directed the hospital, looked terrified. "Call an ambulance," she repeated.

"I'm fine. I'm fine," Marilyn said. "I went to lie down for a spell. You know how tiring it gets."

"I saw you disappear," Bea said.

"And your clothes!" Deirde exclaimed.

Marilyn looked down pointedly stepping off her pile of clothes. Doreena scooped them up for her. The indignant women, who knew when they were being lied to, were blocking the hallway to the bedroom so Marilyn slipped into the bath. Her nakedness did seem unnerving to Doreena now, so she waited outside listening to the women whispering. She clutched her necklace afraid it might have slipped off again in the transition. Her queasiness was at a pitch. Her body felt slack on the outside and watery within. She lurched toward the door and pounded on it. Marilyn opened the door as Doreena's mouth began to fill with water. She staggered forward sloshing. She dropped to her knees in front of the toilet and for the first time in her life vomited. Clear fluid streamed into the toilet and left an iridescent sheen on the surface of the water. Doreena's necklace hung over the toilet and inside it was turquoise so bright, even she could not imagine the ashes bore any resemblance to human remains. Behind her Marilyn, clothed again in billowing yellow, was holding back her hair. Her hands were cold on the back of her neck. Doreena felt better now and pushed to her feet. They stared down into the bowl and looked the sparkling, blue fluid. Marilyn tapped the metal lever and the blue swirled away. Watching it go, Doreena felt the loss of it and almost wished she could drink it up again.

"I want to go home," she said, meaning the island.

"Yes, you'd better. You look strange. I'll call a cab," Marilyn said.

"Marilyn," a woman called. "Are you sick? Is the baby, OK?"

In the entryway, the women were standing looking curiously past Marilyn now at Doreena.

"Good news, actually. She's got morning sickness," Marilyn said.

The women looked skeptical, but then another called, "Marilyn, what's this?"

Alexis Sand of Sand Valley Farms had found the baby tote bag filled with illicit island fruit. She had mangoes, guavas, and passion fruit in a ring around her and was holding up a pineapple. "Where'd this come from?"

"I'll explain," Marilyn said.

"Damn right you will," Bea said.

Behind her Deirde was holding a paring knife, there was an orange opening exposed in the mango she was holding and a small smile crossed her face. She began to cut off slices for the other women.

Doreena made for the door, but before she left Marilyn grabbed her arm. Her voice dropped to a whisper. "Come get me. Next time. I want to go again."

In the mirrored elevator on the way down, Doreena peered at her skin again. The bluish tint was even more pronounced. Her dark eye sparkled, a midnight blue. Doreena looked beneath her bandage. Her eye was healed if there had ever really been anything wrong with it. Grandfather had been right hospitals, were just places people saw sickness. She'd stay away from C-town General. She doubted they had a cure for her. Her body was filled with glittering fluid and the inside of her mouth tasted of saltwater taffy.

~ 11 ~

TIKI-TIKI

C-town gets island-ized

When Doreena concentrated on her work at *The Mirror*, the strange island-ish feeling inside her, the blue, slish-slosh receded until she felt, for the most part, as solid as she'd ever been. Every time she returned from the island, it got harder to orient herself to C-town or feel as if what happened to her here mattered, so she'd been making an extra effort. Doreena spent more hours at work, even while she was betraying the enterprise secretly selling ads to the underground paper.

Doreena wondered about her grandfather's ashes and began to reconsider all his admonitions and the strange way she'd been raised. Her exposure to other people had been monitored. They'd lived in controlled isolation. C-town had been perfect for them. But why? What had he known? Grandfather had told her not to date, but in his absence, she was finally testing boundaries. They were hers now.

She'd invited that tweedy man from AeroFlux out to lunch, ostensibly to sell an ad. Whether a legitimate one to *The Mirror* or a covert ad to the *C-town Traveler* she hadn't decided yet. Then he'd suggested dinner instead and now she was spending more time than unusual in front of the bathroom mirror styling her hair with a new product from Denrigger's.

An open canister labeled Moonbeam Waves balanced on the edge of her bathroom sink. She left two finger-dip impressions in its glistening surface and smoothed her hair with the gel. A collection of new make-ups gave her features shiny angles. She didn't remember buying these cosmetics or these clothes: a blouse with fluttering silk sleeves and a pleated skirt that flapped at her thighs. She imagined Marilyn's critique, "Women of a certain age weren't meant to wear short skirts." At any rate, the fabrics were too light for the weather. Feeling foolish, she was searching in the closet for a sweater when the knock came.

Earnest stood on the threshold holding a cluster of white carnations pinked by the light filtering into the hall. "For you," he said handing her the flowers.

She had no vases.

"Are you still up for this?" He looked at her uncertainly and she stiffened in an off-kilter, disjointed way that increased her awkwardness. There were expectations here, but she didn't know the dating requirements.

This was why she didn't date: the lack of direction. It wasn't just that her grandfather forbade it. "You don't want to be alone with a young man," he'd said. "They get all kinds of odd ideas about women at this age. Be an independent young person." She'd taken that advice to extremes. Her island trips happened so independently; she couldn't depend upon them herself. Besides, Earnest wasn't exactly a young man. He wouldn't have odd ideas about women. Doreena slipped the carnations into the sink and then stepped into the hall closing the door behind her. She was always doing that kind of thing, she realized, sneaking to avoid attention, the way her grandfather had taught her, instead of just admitting she didn't have a vase.

As they left the building, it was silent: no marimbas. On the street, the sunset dimmed to a clear blue twilight. Earnest held the car door open for her. Inside, it was immaculate and pine scented. When he started the engine, a solemn voice intoned, "Photons are packets of energy. The building blocks of light."

Earnest switched the player off. "Let's try and do this without physics."

"I listen to a lot of audio books, too," Doreena said. "Mostly sales stuff for work. The one I'm listening to now is all about how you have to plan to succeed." It put her at ease to talk about work. She was beginning to identify the stiffness it created inside her, but at least it was familiar. "No, the book says it's not enough to just try. You have to do. You have to execute your strategy for success."

"Execute. Which book is that?"

"It's called Motivational Toolkit."

Earnest laughed. "Doesn't sound very motivating."

"But it is," she said.

"You know, you could be listening to the wrong books. Personally, I say why not plan for failure? You learn more from failure. Besides, then you can be audacious. When we take on something big sometimes all we can do is try. If you aren't willing to fail, you'll never push your boundaries."

Doreena thought of the surfers with their little underground press and a couple of ads trying to influence Rock Traynter's C-town or of herself trying to get to the island. She tried now thinking of the blue haze, willing the island to appear. Nothing came.

"Trying doesn't get you anywhere. It's not enough," she said.

As they crossed the overpass, Doreena shielded her eyes. Downtown glowed. The car passed into a blue haze that reminded her of being pulled to her island, but this haziness persisted. All the light here came from the bottom up, radiating just to the tops of the buildings and leaving the night sky shrouded. On the island, the sun-struck colors were crisp and bright. Here, the buildings were just visible through the aura of phosphors. The city looked coated in a numinous gel giving it a sleek wavy look, like her hair. It bore no relation to the smog-stained despair of buildings she passed through every day on her bus ride home. They passed beneath Traynter Tower in the city center. A deep purple veiled its windowed face. Its black light cast a halo of glowing white storefronts around it.

"It's a one newspaper town. I like working at *The Mirror*. C-town is the only place in the United Government that has any stability. I think we'd be crazy to give that up," Doreena said, continuing the argument she'd been having with herself while Earnest parked.

"Look, on the left," Earnest said. "Are you sure you want to go to The Watertown?"

The Tiki-Tiki Room was the brightest spot on Beaumont Avenue. The war for C-town's ideology was being fought in phosphorescence and this was the front of Gavin Traynter and the surfers' resistance. The Tiki-Tiki tangle of phosphors hid any businesses beside it and outshone even Bette's Boutique, Night and Day Chocolate and Coffee, and Sand's Corner Drugstore. Jungle vines glowed around the golden luau font letters: Tiki-Tiki. White flowers spun along the sides. A red and blue flashing parrot pointed at the entrance with its beak. Cars lined Beaumont. Earnest circled and found a free parking space down an alley a few blocks away. The butcher paper cover over the front window was gone and the name was lettered across the glass in slim luau font. Diners milled beyond Tiki-Tiki.

"I can't go in there," Doreena said.

"How can you not?" Earnest said. "Look at them."

The place was packed with people wearing palm frond and flower blossom patterned shirts and shifts. Many cradled fishbowls and sucked red, white, or blue beverages out of them through wide straws. All were laughing.

"I could seriously lose my job just for stepping inside," Doreena said.

"Ridiculous," Earnest said, and held the door open for her. "You can't be fired for eating out."

As she stepped inside, Petey, the animatronic parrot, squawked and trained his cold eye on her. A muggy heat embraced them with layered scents of baked salt and floral spice. A greeter in a plastic grass skirt placed plastic leis over their heads and led them to a table by the window. She handed them menus shaped like tiki idols. The wicker chairs crackled as they sat.

Earnest removed his tweed jacket. Underneath, he wore a short-sleeved work shirt. "Are you going to be too warm?"

Doreena's silk sleeves fluttered below the heater. She was comfortably dressed as if she planned to come here. "Just right, actually."

The place seemed to be trying hard to engage C-town's dormant senses. Gavin Traynter had taken her advice and acquired a lot of relics from The Travel Museum to add to his décor. But for all its brightness, the place was a pale imitation of her island.

"This place reminds me of Imagination Land," Earnest said. "The treehouse with all the singing birds? Come on, I'm not that much older than you. Before the border closed, your parents never took you down the 'Way?"

"My grandfather raised me," she said releasing a sugary scent as she poked at the wax candle adorning their table.

"Well, he took you then. No? Never?"

"We were pretty serious people." She looked up at the painted ceramic birds dangling over each table. "One person's paradise is another's nightmare, he always said."

The menu was boring. It was the same fancied up fish and chips fare that was served at The Watertown. But Gavin, a bartender by trade, had tried to make up for it with the drink menu renaming old standards to fit the Tiki-tiki theme. There was a long list of specialty drinks from Kill the Pig to Voodoo Cannibal.

The waiter interrupted. "Start with drinks?"

Earnest looked at her expectantly. Her grandfather had forbidden drinking too. "Lowers the inhibitions. Makes people do stupid things," he'd said. But it seemed to be something adults did on dates. She was keeping the waiter waiting. When she finally looked up, it took her a few seconds to recognize Alonso in a shirt patterned with orange surfboards hanging down over black slacks. She was used to his wetsuit.

He winked at her. "Hey, lookin' especially *wahine*."

"You too," she said. "You look good in clothes."

Earnest coughed. "Maybe a bottle of wine?"

"Nah, not here," Alonso said. "You want The Great White." He pointed mid-menu and winked again.

"OK, two Great Whites," Earnest said.

"No, one," Alonso said, making a note of it. "Share. You need more, we'll move you up to The Flaming Great White." He winked again. "Don't worry, you can handle one great white. Tiger sharks are the real killers."

When he left them, Ernest bent low over the table. "I meant to tell you; you do look beautiful tonight. I mean, especially."

"It's not me, really," Doreena said.

Alonso returned and placed a huge fishbowl between them. A toy surfer floated on its frothy blue surface.

"Is this what we ordered?" Earnest asked. "The great white? It's blue."

"Yeh, Curaçao," Alonso said. "Now, look in there, and give me a moment."

They bumped heads over the bowl as they lifted up out of their chairs to look in. The tiny surfer even had hibiscus patterned board shorts.

"Sharks. In the ice cubes," Doreena said.

"Make room," Alonso said. He poured shots into the drink from on high, brandished two thick straws and stirred. The shark-shaped ice clinked as the white syrup swirled through the blue. The little surfer boy rocked.

"Hang ten, lil' dude." Alonso said and left them.

Doreena grabbed her straw and sucked. "Coconut liqueur."

"Strong," Earnest said.

They ordered the codfish special, and the food arrived on large blue plates in bamboo holders. It was covered in a chunky red and orange sauce with a golden sheen to it.

"So, your grandfather raised you?"

Doreena clutched her necklace and sipped on the drink. Earnest moved bits of fish from one side of his plate to the other. "I work at AeroFlux. I'm an engineer. It's an interesting place." He paused.

When she didn't respond, he said. "So, I know you're in sales and not much else."

"Well, there's not much else."

"No?"

"No," she said.

He would have made a terrible salesman. His body language was exactly opposite of the confident sales posture Marilyn had taught her. His shoulders were slumped, his eyes were downcast, and his hands were hidden under the table fumbling, she imag-ined, with his palm frond patterned napkin. He was persistent though; give him that.

"So, speaking of hopes and dreams...what are your passions, uh, um, do you have any hobbies? I mean what do you like to do?"

Doreena sucked down the last of the Great White. The surfer boy tipped against the side. "Pretty much this."

She wondered what kind of conversation they would have been having if she were on the island. What kinds of things would she have said? This would be so much easier if she weren't here. Earnest stopped trying to get her to talk instead launching into a long explanation of physics. The drink had been good. She wanted another. She could feel herself growing warmer from the inside out.

"So, it looks like we're ready to move up to The Flaming Great White?" Alonso said the next time he checked on them.

It turned out to be an event drink. Alonso pulled them over to the bar counter. The buoyant accordions ceased, replaced by ominously slinking cellos.

"We didn't want to make a fuss," Earnest protested.

"Too late," Alonso said.

Gavin Traynter came out of the kitchen in his orange and red smeared apron. "Ah, my favorite saleswoman," he said. "I forgive you your employer." He tossed a towel embossed with a parrot over his shoulder. "Everyone gather round," he bellowed.

All around, diners abandoned their plates and circled the bar. Gavin lined up shots in layered colors like a sunrise in front of Doreena. "Suck them down as fast as possible before I light the last one," he instructed waving a tiki-torch shaped lighter down the row of shots. Her eyes followed the flame. The crowd chanted, "Shark, shark." Earnest gripped her elbow. She sucked and swallowed in a boozy rush and then Gavin lit the final float of cherry brandy on top. It flared up and out and then he dropped another little surfer boy on top of it, into the drink. He landed on the turbulent froth of baked waves, ice cube sharks clinking beneath him.

Doreena rocked. The people around her grew hazy. Her skin felt sucked loose like the approach of the island. She already felt warm and far away. She looked for the oncoming waves but saw only the reflection of the bottles and the glasses hanging against the mirrored bar. The bar-goers began to sing. The waves of the song rushed over her. She swayed. They swayed. A swish of grass skirts. Feathers floated down from the ceiling. The parrots, macaws, and mourning doves on their perches over the diners cawed and cooed. This was the best she'd ever felt off island. It was as if she had brought it here with her.

Petey squawked. The swaying stopped. Silence. Space opened up around her, except for Earnest at her back. She carried the song on out into the void, "Your own special hopes, your own special dreams, loom on the hillside, and shine near the streams."

Rock Traynter, the silencing force, the crowd scatterer, looked down on her. He removed one pair of sunglasses. Underneath he wore another, and another, and another and another, as if he had no eyes.

"That's my boss," she said to Earnest. She stared up at the now silent ceramic birds. He'd chased the island away.

"Hey, my brother finally comes to check it out," Gavin said. "A drink, man? No? How about dessert?"

Rock turned from her. Just above his collar, the hair on the back of his neck was trimmed in a neat dark line. "I'm not here to stuff my face."

"Well, it's a restaurant, Rock. That's my business: feed the people. So, how's about it, everyone? In honor of this visit from C-town's illustrious publisher, the one and only, oh, well, not the only game in town anymore. Dessert on the house. Alonso, bring out my new cake. There's plenty to share. How's life in a two-paper town?"

There was a tremulous flapping of nervous applause. Rock stared down the last of the diners until it stopped.

Doreena plucked the surfer boy from the bottom of the glass and licked the last of the burned boozy foam off of his surfboard.

"Do they make these in *wahines*?" she said leaning into Earnest.

Rock barreled toward her. In a black suit, he looked tall as Traynter Tower. He walked past rocking her into Earnest. "Marilyn!"

The crowd parted and towards the back by the kitchen Doreena saw Marilyn in a flaming red dress. A man helped her up from her chair. The dress' plunging neckline drew attention from her distended belly.

"That's my other boss and that's..." Doreena recognized the AeroFlux executive. "That's yours." She said to Earnest. Then she giggled. "Hey, it's like a double date at work."

"Shhh," Earnest said.

Alonso passed out small plates. Slices of her island's contraband mango were splayed over creamy cheesecake tops.

Rock steered Marilyn by. His hand just under the cap of her sleeve made a red band where he gripped her. He pulled her to the bar. "Nice place, Gav. Mom and Dad would be proud. No wait. They wouldn't. And here's our number one salesman."

"She's here on her own time, Rock." Marilyn said.

"Own time? The job's 24-7, keeping this place together," He raised his voice. "Maybe you don't get it. Maybe you're a little too content if you want to risk it all to play at exotics. When's the last time you were out on the 'Way? If C-town isn't good enough, maybe you've forgotten. None of us have our own time or it all unravels."

Rock's face was red around his shades. Doreena peered up at him. What color were his eyes? Steel gray? She touched the lei around her neck and felt the skin soft petals of frangipani. The five petals opened toward her like a hand. She removed it and held it up to Rock on tiptoes. "Any night, any day. In your heart you will hear it. Come away. Come away. Here am I your own special island come to me. Come to me."

"You're drunk," he said shrugging the lei off his shoulder, so the flowers slipped to the floor.

"I want to see your eyes," she said. "Are they purple? Green? I'm so sorry, you can't see all the beautiful colors. You're colorblind."

"And you're worthless. Don't come in Monday. You're fired," Rock said. He stomped on the flowers as he pulled Marilyn to the door. An island perfume rose. Rock yelled at Marilyn on the street in front of his pea green car.

"I finally get it," Doreena said. "C-town's like an island."

"Let's go," Earnest said.

Doreena reached into her purse as Earnest pulled her to the door. She held up the last mango. "Who wants mango cheese-cake?"

She lobbed the forbidden fruit toward the bar. Gavin caught it in one hand.

Earnest supported her on the way to the car. By the time they reached it, she was feeling cold and steady inside again. The drink and the island feeling were fading.

"Do we have to go? I want to go back." The tear she wiped from the end of her nose sparkled. They pulled up in front of the Nar-borough. "No. I don't want be alone. Take me to your place."

"I'm sorry," Earnest said. He walked her to her door.

"Come in," she begged.

"No," he said. "That wouldn't be gentlemanly. Here. Alonso said you should have this."

He handed her a birdcage covered in a buttoned up Hawaiian shirt patterned with orange boards. When Earnest left she peered underneath. Inside, the parrot slept. Petey's feathers were sleek, shiny, and very real.

~ 12 ~

SURFING

Wallowing in the island and taking a lover

On the first day of unemployment, Doreena got up and dressed as usual. She craved *The Mirror* and her routine. Nothing could be more frightening than spending day after day aimlessly in C-town without her position or people: Rock, Marilyn, Tom, the Force. It sickened her to think of it, but there was no sparkling blue fluidity to her illness now. Her mouth was dry. Her stomach tight. It was as if there were sand caught in her chest and throat. She felt strange inside, shifting, as though she could crumble from the inside out.

Meanwhile, Petey preened. The stiff robotic thing had been transformed. Instead of carrying her away last night, a bit of the island had crept over and remade Petey as people imagined him to be — alive. His orange beak clacked against the bars of his cage as he bit at it. She pushed a few slices of mango into his cage remembering how last night the Tiki-Tiki lounge had changed. At first, she'd just felt woozy with the effects of the monster drink. Fishbowls! Only Gavin Traynter would serve alcohol in fishbowls. Then it had felt like the island was approaching, but instead of pulling her away the suction had settled over everything around her. Momentarily, there had been real flowers and birds and probably a

136

grove of fruit back behind the kitchen doors and even the air quality had changed from a stale heat to a fresh circulating warmth.

Rock's entry had swept the island out, but Petey was proof that it was more than a mirage or a hallucination or a drunken moment. And if the parrot was real, then that sloshing feeling inside herself might be, too. Whatever it was, it wasn't comfortable. There was something ominous hidden inside her that she didn't want to explore too deeply, like whatever was behind the wall of jungle green on the island.

"Leave C-town alone, Petey," she said to the bird. "I want to go away, not bring my island here."

She went downstairs and waited for the bus. The uniformity of the street made it easy to pretend it was just another day, until Alonso arrived and stood beside her in his wetsuit. It was always jolting seeing him there dressed like that. When the bus lurched forward, she surfaced, startled, from her thoughts.

"I broke *The Mirror.* I'm broke."

"Don't talk like a regular," Alonso said.

"Where am I going?"

"Surfing, I figure. You brought your board." He swung a dingy yellow board out from behind his blue one and leaned it against her. "My old one."

She leaned her head against it. The peeling corners of the Sex Wax sticker tickled her cheek. The bus was lit by florescent blue overhead. The marshlands outside the windows were dark. The surface of the muck-covered lake, she imagined, was just starting to gleam like a greasy curry as the sun rose. "Surfing, you figure?"

"What else."

"I'll freeze."

He dropped a suit across her lap. She recoiled from its flailing neoprene appendages.

"No, you'll just look like an elephant. What? All baggy-skinned. What? It'll be too long for you."

At the park, Doreena stripped off her wool work clothes and pulled on the clinging wetsuit. Its faded rippled skin stretched over her own. It hugged her, holding her upright. She felt straighter, although it sagged a bit about her waist and neck. With effort, straining against thick, sticky material, she pushed up the sleeves and cuffed the legs. Her feet were bare on the pebbled beach as she waded into the sinking sludge at the shore.

"It's cold. It's gross."

"No, it's a kind of beautiful. Like you in that suit."

"Thanks, I feel like a toad."

It was odd the way, as she entered the lake, the wetsuit kept the water away from her skin, but she could still feel the waves moving around her. She was there, but not there, in, but not submerged, cool, but not cold, insulated from everything. It hid her porous skin. Only her feet and her hands treaded through the chemical-laced lake. She learned to keep her mouth closed so the putrefied algae never touched her tongue. It tasted digested like it smelled.

She never managed to stand up on the board. Alonso didn't give her much in the way of instruction. He was into his own thing, after his own stoke. She could barely see the dull ripples that kept him spired above his board. Left alone Doreena lay on her belly, and, with nothing better to do and no distraction, could not help but contemplate her insides. She began thinking about her grandfather and her parents, whomever they might be, and then about The Force and work, her surrogate family. Who would she be without *The Mirror*? Yet, her thoughts cycled round and round to her own belly distended beneath her and what was inside it: the thing that sometimes felt hard like a stone, grainy as sand or fluid like ocean. Only the thin board lay between her and the gray water. Feeling heavy now, she imagined sinking down into it, the board, and then, the lake.

Alonso came back to her, buoyant with stoke, whatever that was. To him, it was nothing that she'd lost that job, a bad piece of work anyway. So, for a while with him she was untroubled because that's what he saw and expected. Although what she noticed about being with him now was that for the most part, he didn't think about her at all very much or have really any expectations. This left her free to drift — or it left her adrift. She was musing on whether this was good or not. She was used to her grandfather and *The Mirror*. She was used to being held in place.

When she returned to her apartment that afternoon, her clothes were piled in the hallway outside along with her box of photographs and the caged parrot. A red post-it stuck to the door of C-4 said, "Eviction notice." This was Rock's revenge. She'd always known he had that power to take away her livelihood and her home. Alone, with her head in a fog after grandfather's death, it had taken forever to move all the boxes. Her stuff didn't look like much now: wool suits and sweaters, tattered photos under broken glass and the addition of the mangy parrot. He looked like he was in rapid decline for lack of some tropical nutrient. His feathers were faded and loose around his eyes, so his dimpled skin showed as he blinked at her. She picked up the photos and the cage and went downstairs.

Alonso opened his door in a swirl of blue sandalwood smoke. She'd caught him in his black pants and Tiki-Tiki shirt on his way to work.

"I saw all your stuff," he said and waved her in. "No problem. I have plenty of room so long as I make rent."

Actually, his apartment was smaller: a studio with one large window facing the promise of C-town sun. It was cluttered with jade, soapstone, and wood figurines, leering painted masks and fibrous painted mats on the floor and walls. It looked a lot like The Travel Museum, un-C-town, off continent, and vaguely illegal. The mattress rested on the floor covered by yellow and brown batik. Doreena sat and examined the split ends of her curls.

"I can't keep it together."

"The bird can stay, but the cage has to go," he said.

She heard the latch spring and flapping. A couple of red feathers floated in front of her. Petey'd shit all over, but, whatever, it wasn't her place.

"And I don't care."

"I hear that," Alonso said. "Tiki-Tiki is booming. Happy customers. You need something to get by, I can ask Gavin for you."

"About a job?"

"Yeah, work. I don't recommend it. You can totally squat here, but I'm not staying. I'm on the last flight out."

"Maui," she scoffed. "It doesn't matter. All I want is the island. It's all I think about. Never mind."

"Tell," he said. "I like islands."

"It's out of control, really short trips, like dreams, but full-color, full-feeling, texture, breezes." She stopped.

"Maui?"

She shook her head. "Somewhere else, and I bring things back with me: sand, fruit, flowers."

"Mangoes?"

"Yes, the mangoes."

"Good surf?"

"Blue. Waves taller than Lake Traynter."

"Sold. Let's go." He grabbed the two boards, blue and yellow, leaning against the wall.

"You don't get it. I can't control it. I just go."

"Take me." He dropped the board on the bed and sat behind her with his legs around her. "Try now."

"You aren't going to work?"

"I've time."

"You believe me?"

"'Course, there's the mangoes, this parrot, and you. You seem like you've got some secret. Besides, this is just the kind of thing I believe. I've got to. You say you're going to whisk me away to par-adise, I say, yeah."

Alonso breathed on her neck, and it made her skin hum. If she stayed here, it would be on the batik in his bed. It didn't matter whether he liked her, especially. He'd take whatever wave came in to ride and here she was, the next set. It was like he'd made his life easier by deciding in advance: Be with willing people, believe good things.

In a weird way, this reminded her a lot of how her grandfather lived. He'd made a lot of their decisions, a lot of *her* decisions, ahead of time so that there was no need to evaluate anything on a case-by-case basis. Grandfather's rules were just different: Avoid everyone. Don't believe anything. One of his rules had been to avoid situations like these. He'd been frank about sex, curt and clear. He'd described the physiology of the act in all its anatomi-cal correctness. "But that's not the part that concerns me, the nor-mal, healthy human body functioning of a young woman. That's fine. The part that concerns me is what no one ever mentions. It's the part that happens to your brain, the neurochemical reaction. Sex changes your chemistry. It changes you inside. It bonds you to another person. In a way you may not, you won't, be able to control and that will happen no matter who it is, no matter how wrong for you. No one will tell you that it changes you forever. It changes people's chemistry. It bonds you to people before you have a chance to make up your mind about them. You can't be yourself and have sex, before you know it you'll be someone else."

Grandfather's intensity on this point had frightened her, as had her schooling with its graphic and intentionally scary depic-tions of birth, so that she'd never even been in a situation like she was now. Alonso had his hand on her neck, but it felt like he was stroking her inside, reaching into her as though she were a pup-pet, making her insides buzz and hum. The incense smoke in the apartment grew opaque and shiny. The blue haze settled in and the suction throbbed. Alonso's arms tightened around her even before she said, "Hold on. We're going."

The sun touched her face and shoulders in warm welcome. The ocean cast its breath across the shore. The waves sucked in and sighed through the sand. Alonso's chest rose and fell against her back. Her eyes squeezed tight; orange glowed through her lids. Would he still be there when she opened her eyes? He was. His eyes, blue-green with golden flecks, watched the sea. The boards were behind him. They'd arrived. She'd never seen his face so smooth with all the creases filled in. In C-town his skin had a gray cast to it like everyone's. Here, he looked golden. Watching him was even better than staring at the surf or sun. He reflected joy. The breeze flowed through every golden strand of hair on his arms, chest, and thighs. She'd brought him bare-skinned.

She quivered inside warm, ripe, and juicy as island fruit. She wanted him to want her as much as he wanted those waves. She stretched her arms out to him and put her hands on his thighs. "Change me inside," she said.

He didn't even look to wonder at that. He was even more over-come by the island than Marilyn had been on her first time. He was too enchanted by the island to be afraid or question anything. This worked to Doreena's advantage, since she'd decided to have him. Her insides were messed up anyway. Sex with Alonso could only make them better. She wanted what he had: that easy hap-piness and some sense of internal peace. If nothing else, it'd be a chemistry experiment. He held her shoulders for balance. He stroked her sides and his hands, like hibiscus blossoms, covered her breasts. Then he pushed her down onto the sand soft as fine sugar and pink. He moved her up and down against it. She felt like she was being polished like the stones on the ocean floor. When he came, trembling, staring at the waves, she rolled over and sat astride him. Then she watched the waves and rocked them both until their smooth backs and thighs blushed with sand and the raw skin underneath clung to it like a new covering. Now Doreena felt she would stay on the island forever.

"If we brought the boards, couldn't we have brought clothes?" she asked.

"Didn't think of it," he said. "I'm not too attached to mine."

The waves were cresting higher. Alonso reached for his boards. "I've got to get out there."

He handed one to her, but she was in no hurry. He waded into the water. She watched him stroke out to sea and catch some waves, riding high. She sat and the sun, always high in the sky when she arrived, now moved through the sky. When Alonso returned to land, it was late afternoon. He stretched his lean torso. She took his hand and led him back to the jungle trail and showed him the grove of fruit. The voice was silent. They ate banana and pineapple.

"We're still here," she said.

"So where? An island?"

"I've never been further from the beach than this."

He held up a mango, a different kind than she'd seen before, a lighter color. "This is a Bombay. You can only get these on Jamaica, which this isn't. This is some magic place."

"It's not real?"

He shrugged. "Real as paradise. Real enough for me and plenty to eat. Come on. It's time for your lesson. You've never actually caught waves. There wasn't much stoke to be had on the lake. Not really."

"You went there every day."

"I've traveled the world looking for the best waves. I didn't stop in C-town because I found them, I just got caught. Stuck. But stoke is stoke. You do what you have to do to be good wherever you are. Don't be miserable, that's the plan."

Carrying both surfboards, he led her into the water. "Lay on your stomach. Imagine you are moving buckets through the water with your hands."

Doreena paddled mid-inlet on her board and then lay with her cheek on it, feet dangling in the water, rocking on the waves the sun stroking her back. She peered through her fingers, squinting past the sun at Alonso bobbing beside her. He sat up, the board between his legs, looking out to sea and the setting sun. If she saw the island at night, Doreena was sure she'd stay forever. The sun struck only the far side of each two-tone wave. One side captured the shimmering light. The other looked dark and elusive with unknown depths.

"Could there be sharks?" she asked.

Alonso shrugged. "Well, it's the kind of water they like. Warm. Could be anything in a place like this. I think this place is a tulpa. Something I learned about in the Himalayas, in the mountains, BC, before C-town."

"I can't see you in the mountains," she said.

"I didn't like it much. It was cold, heavy. It didn't matter how many layers of gear you had on. The place had a cold heart, no escaping it. I stank too. That was the worst," he said. "Out here, the sun bakes you clean and the sea salt is pure. There, man, I was trapped in a bulky coat with my own bacteria. I could smell them eating off me, getting nice and full."

"Why go?"

"A pilgrimage. My friend said the mountains would be like waves, but taller. The lack of oxygen would be like being underwater but face up. They say there's kind of a euphoria that comes with drowning. It's all about the stoke."

"I don't get that. I don't even know what you mean."

"Sure, you do," he said, still looking at the sea. "What's to get? It's when you are in exactly the right place and time. That's all."

"The Himalayas don't sound right."

"This one night made it. We reached camp on a plateau. We pitched our tent and lit a fire in this charred rock ring. It was a place on the locals' route. We made this tea the locals had given us and spiked it with grog, a local brew, the kind that tastes toxic at first, but then you keep on and there's nothing better. That's what I miss, tasting places: curried pineapple in South Africa, Blue Mountain coffee in Jamaica, mochi in Kyushu. Every shore has its flavor. You can't import it. That was it. That night, just sitting around that campfire. Jeanne called it our trip to Shangri-La. Man, she was a cool girl."

"A girlfriend?" Doreena said. The jealous edge to her voice was unmistakable. So, the sex had done something different to her, just like grandfather had warned. But Alonso didn't seem to notice. He was lost in the Himalayas.

"Yeah. I was the one who'd always said, 'Don't mistake a woman for the stoke. She can be in it, but she never is it.' Then I followed Jeanne into the hills. I lost all cred with my mates, but she was a mad wave rider. All the surfer girls are wild, but she was fearless and then she'd crash down afterwards on the sand, like a sea cat, wouldn't move for anything. Whatever she was doing, she was all in."

"What happened?" Doreena asked.

"We were sitting by the fire. The moon rose with a blue aura around it and these sherpa stepped out of the fog. They were little men, but in these huge yak hides. They joined us by the fire. We shared grog. They were probably our age, but they looked older, wiser with weathered skin, you know. One of the guys had a gap in the front row of his teeth, like he'd lost one to a yak hoof or something. They started telling stories, in English. They must have been guides. They sounded all prophetic the way people do when they choose their words carefully. So, Gap Man says, 'You heard of the village, Vitskaya. They make thought monsters there, like yetis.

They are always thinking there, to keep warm. The tulpas like fog to hide in.' It was so weird. I remember it, exactly."

"I mean, what happened with Jeanne."

Alonso shrugged. "We split at the village. She wanted to stay. I went back to Thailand. My wave bros were merciless, said I'd missed some of the best Thai sets they'd ever seen. So. But my point is, this place feels like a tulpa. Maybe the surfers made it, you know, drummed it into being. We've all been dreaming of a place like this."

Even Doreena noticed the approaching swell, the one that made him swing to his belly on the board. He pivoted and she was looking at the soles of his feet. The wrinkled arcs would fit perfectly in the palms of her hands. She paddled after him pressing buckets through the water and making progress.

"The surfers," Doreena scoffed. She didn't like what he'd said about her island being a manifestation of the surfers' dreams. With Marilyn and Alonso's visits, there were fruits and flowers on the island she had never seen before and it looked much less like her few memories of Maui than it had, but it was still her island.

"Maybe your girlfriend was the tulpa."

She rose as he did when the wave was nearly on them. She clutched the sides of the board lifting up with the wave and then standing. It rose faster and higher with her on top. Up over the sea, her steady haunches held her in place while her torso soared. A sound like a gull's cry escaped her. She sped behind the waves' white emissaries over the rippling expanse of blue gliding toward her island and its pink sand shore. She looked down, in love with the sea that carried her forward, and wobbled. The board dropped away in a moment. She smacked the water. Her neck bent. The emissaries beat her down. Her shoulders scraped hard. Her cheeks bulged with sea. She thrashed and opened her eyes spinning in the wave, twisting toward the light. Pain braced her right arm when she reached for it. She struck out with her left through dark bubbles, then light-filled ones, until she breached, spat seawater and sucked air. Her back stung. The island had turned on her.

Opaque water flowed around her. The horizon held remnants of sun. This was the darkest the island had ever been. A few escaping rays touched the tops of the palms in the distance. Around her the sea lay like black glass, as though she were swimming in the mirrored reflection of the boardroom table in The Meat Locker or in the glass surface of Traynter Tower. She went cold inside. Where it didn't burn, her skin cooled beneath the water. Her face radiated heat. She draped her arm over the surfboard floating by, then jerked back. Not her board. Sharp leather hide sliced her forearm. Purple clouds billowed in the water around her. A torpedo-shape sped toward her and the pointed snout of a shark slid by. Its body followed — a bolt of lavender with black racing stripes. The creature's dot of an eye passed over her as it swayed. Doreena blew out all her breath and sank. The shark snapped around. Then she was clamped onto her and dragged her through the sea. She struck its nose. It released her and she surfaced. The breeze flowed over her cheeks. It clenched her waist and pushed her thigh. He pushed. She looked into Alonso's eyes. They'd turned an anxious green.

"Get up on the board," he said.

They were still in the water with the shark.

"Get up on it. We'll ride out."

She slunk onto the board. He crawled on behind her, half on top of her, his heaving breaths pressing her back. He swam, his limbs in the sea with the swaying shark. The lighter moving patches of water with hidden teeth flowed around them. Doreena clung to the board and willed the shore closer. The blue haze buzzed. "It's ok. It's happening. We're going back."

She reached back for Alonso's hand, but he twisted out of her grip. He slipped off the board, shooting her forward. "Nah, I'll take my chances. Been waiting for this a long time."

The waves behind her were black-tipped fins. Ahead of her were peaks of brown and yellow batik. Then, she was alone on the bed. At some point, she'd have to look and see how much of her was missing. She tried to steady herself to see tangles of torn flesh. She'd heard the warning once: "Shock can kill you."

When she looked, there were just the usual rolls of pale stomach and sprawled legs, intact. Her right arm, more or less the correct shape, was swollen into a disproportionate lump of fierce reds and blues. It would have looked natural on the ocean floor with urchins. But she was not broken or mauled. She was naked, soaking wet with her lips still salty. It had been that close. The cuts on her back where the coral had scraped it raw bled onto the batik.

She stayed in bed all day, and the next, waiting for the island return and thinking about Alonso. The light cycled through shades of lavender: lavender-twilight, lavender-yellow, lavender-orange, lavender-dusk to black orchid night slowly, frequently she was sure, but the blue haze, the fuzzy sheen, it never came. She lay limply, neither hungry nor tired, breathing shallow breaths. She thought of the rolls of her stomach fleshy from sales calls and office sitting. It had been weeks since she'd eaten much and days now since she'd eaten anything, but her body stayed the same. It didn't change.

She lay and waited for the island to return. The waiting hurt. She couldn't make the island come. She couldn't get back to Alonso. She couldn't control it. At one point she heard shuffling at the door and against it. Then she heard voices outside, Alonso's surfer friends. She didn't get up to open the door. She just sprawled. Maybe the sex had changed her inside and she'd never see the island again. Maybe he'd stolen it from her, and she'd lost her grandfather, *The Mirror,* and the island.

Later, a steady pounding awoke her from a nightmare of being shaken in the shark's maw. It wrangled her out of her prone position. She wrapped the bloodstained batik around her. When she got up to answer the door, her legs and arms were stiff as planks.

Hobart stood at the door; her hand red from knocking. "We haven't seen you in a while. I didn't know you were here. C-town in there?"

"Alonso's gone." Doreena said. "He's not coming back."

"He wouldn't head down the 'Way by himself. Oh, had enough cash for that last flight to Maui, did he?"

Doreena shrugged.

"That woman's been looking for you." Hobart pointed at a red notice stuck to the door. "You see this? You know you can't stay here."

Doreena bent her head in her hands. Her curls felt stiff too. "I'm not leaving." The island would have to come and get her.

"The wrecking ball comes through that window Monday morning either way," Hobart said, pushing the door in."

''Gads, vile smell. What's that?"

Doreena turned toward the stench of decay behind her. Petey lay on the floor, one sunken eye looking up at her from his featherless head. She had neglected to feed him.

"Grab your wetsuit," Hobart said. "I'm getting you out of here."

~ 13 ~

DROWNING

Finding a way to control the island and populating it with men

With Hobart's solid influence, Doreena at last left Alonso's apartment. She met the surfers on the shores of Lake Traynter. Their company gave her a fluid feeling. They greeted her casually, and then paid little mind to her. The surfers stayed together, but each occupied his own space and was there for his own reasons. They were all doing the same thing but had arrived at the decision to do so independently. She hadn't thought she would ever miss Marilyn's scrutiny and firm direction, but she did. Mostly, she missed the structure and discipline of *The Mirror*, the way the work gave her a purpose and held her in place. The surfers had no expectations of her. They were companionable, but distant. They didn't mind that she was there and wouldn't notice if she left, but at least coming to the lake with them gave her a place to be and something to do.

"We're here every morning," Hobart said. "A lot of us hold odd jobs or own our own businesses, but we make them work around this. This is where we have to be and then the rest of the day goes fine."

"How about the *Traveler*?" Doreena said.

"It's not making much of an impact. C-town seems the same as it ever was. But we have to make the effort. They've got to keep drumming. It's part of us living our lives the best we can while we're stuck here."

Doreena didn't want to go into the water. The lake never looked appealing, and she was still afraid of sharks. There couldn't be any in that cold, gray water, but it was so dark below the surface that she wouldn't be sure what lay beneath. She wanted her clear island ocean. This dingy, rancid water did not compare. Why should she enter this when the island might come at any moment? It was still fresh in her mind and her longing for it occupied her thoughts. There had to be a way, something she could do to make it come, to get back there.

She sat on the bench beside the lake and watched the surfers, encased in black, solemnly laying their boards across the best waves C-town had to offer. The outfits looked ridiculously alien on the streets of C-town or on the bus, but they had a regal quality like a kind of armor here. She had been sitting here watching them in the mornings for a few days when J-Bay, one of the youngest surfers, came out of the water and sat beside her. He looked like a younger more compact version of Alonso. He had the same dingy blond hair and lithe build, but a shorter torso. His face was smooth and lacked the creases Alonso had at the corners of his eyes. It made J-Bay hard to read.

All the surfers were difficult that way. They had languid hands. They didn't gesture with them when they talked. Their hands rested on their kneecaps or hung by their sides unless they were surfing or drumming. J-Bay's hands were on his knees now. There was a coat of bronze hair across the backs except where the scar cut across his right hand. He leaned on the bench, and it held him propped with his legs stretched out across the sparse grass.

"I don't blame C-town for leaving," J-Bay said.

It took Doreena a moment to remember that he meant Alonso. Alonso's name was wherever he was. She wondered what it would be on her island.

"He's not C-town anymore," she said.

"I thought we were all going to go together. I mean, it happens all the time. Somebody just gets it in their head and goes to whatever surf spot they've heard of and they might tell someone or just go because they get called to a break. It was like that for me once at the cape. I just left and went to Durban. I didn't even tell A-Bay and he's my twin. It was like I had to. A-Bay got choked on that, but he caught me up later and he understood. It happens. But this here, has been different. We've all been stuck since Westport and that bad luck. I thought all for one, one for all, you know. For now, while we're all here, surfing this trash lake. That's what the underground was for, making cash for the Maui flight, for all of us. Then, Rock goes and cancels that way out, too. So, I guess we've all lost, except Alonso."

J-Bay's hands were as loose as ever over his knees, but his voice betrayed tension. Doreena felt a pull across her chest and recognized it as a strain from her new connection with Alonso. She'd been jealous of Alonso's old girlfriend and now she wanted to protect Alonso from J-Bay's bitterness.

"It's not his fault. He didn't go to Maui."

"No? Well, where is he?"

Doreena shrugged and now she heard her own bitterness. She wondered if Alonso, on his end, had spared a thought for her at all. "I don't know the name of the place. My grandfather never took me out of C-town."

"Sorry for you. Sometimes, I hate this place."

He said it with passion, but Doreena marveled at how still his body remained. His hands had moved from the meditative posture over his knees to the bench beside him, but there was no tension in them. They lay like the rest of his body. How did the surfers do it? Doreena was sure she never looked that relaxed except maybe on the island. When she imagined herself, she was always standing at attention beside Marilyn's desk with her hands clenched behind her back to keep them from aimless fluttering. She wasn't laid back like the surfers, except when she'd been with Alonso. Doreena put her hand on top of J-Bay's. It was different than touching Alonso, but similar. Her body eased as her focus moved to the place where their hands touched. Alonso had wanted to see the island. He'd touched her and they'd gone. Could she make it happen again with J-Bay?

"You really want to get out of here, don't you?" she asked.

She leaned into him and pressed against him wetsuit to wetsuit feeling the give of their neoprene skins. She touched her lips to his. They were thinner and cooler than Alonso's. He pulled back and looked around. She wasn't sure how he'd react to her advance and there weren't any clues in his face, or hands or eyes but there wasn't any doubt about the changes in her own body. The neoprene stretched to accommodate the sudden swelling of her hips and breasts.

"Come on," J-Bay said. He led her to a sheltered part of the shore beside the cattails. Their sex there was gritty, uncomfortable, and awkward amid peeling neoprene and sour lake smells. But J-Bay's touch reassured her. The places where they met skin to skin quickly heated up and created the islandish sensations. Doreena thought it was working and they'd make the island come. It took ages, but finally she forgot about the grit beneath her and dissolved in J-Bay's embrace. When the blue haze came, she sighed with relief and pleasure. "My island."

It came with a waft of cool salt and floral scented air.

"What? Are we tripping?" J-Bay said.

He was lying on top of her with his wetsuit peeled down to his knees looking up towards the jungle. He stank a little of lake, but she was naked and her skin felt fresh. She stretched her arms over her head and wiggled her toes in the sand. J-Bay rolled off her, spun around and staggered toward the sea. The surface held only white capped waves and a glaze of sun.

"That's where I left Alonso alone with the shark," she said. She'd been so concerned with getting back to the island; it was the first time she'd thought about whether Alonso might be hurt. "I don't know if he made it."

"Where are we?" J-Bay said.

"On my island." An emptiness gnawed at her, a resurgent hunger and thirst. "Come on, I need to eat."

The broad leaves brushed her body as she led J-Bay into the jungle to the grove. In the clearing, Alonso sat in the middle of a pile of fruit his teeth close to the green skin of a guava. His long body was unblemished. He sucked in breath when he saw her, and Doreena felt his eyes on her. She knew he noticed her body was different now. Although she hadn't been eating, it was plumper. Her hips and breasts felt stretched and viscous. It pulled. It was J-Bay. He was noticing her now and her body was ripening with his attention.

"J-Bay." Alonso said and nodded.

"You made it," she said. "The shark."

"Tiger shark. The board took the damage," he gestured behind him. Her board was missing a hunk in the middle. "A couple of bites and he pretty much lost interest."

"When it came for me, I froze," Doreena said. "But it was like it could sense me."

"They can. In seawater we all produce electric fields and that's how sharks find us. They have these organs, electro receptors, ampullae of Lorenzini, that sense movement in the water. Fascinating creatures."

"Scary. I don't know how it got there." She looked around at the rinds of fruit. There were a few tiny green flies hovering over the rinds. She brushed them away from her face. "Has it been long?"

He shrugged. "Days? It's hard to keep track of time. Listen, you looked great. Just before, I mean, when you were surfing. You have good instincts. When you were up there, it was like your life."

"I did for a minute, didn't I?" She stretched her arms out. "I was flying, riding above everything."

"That's it," Alonso said.

"Yeah, I get it. Then wham!" She clapped her hands. "Fish food!"

She tumbled forward and knelt beside him, a mango between her knees. She reached for him. "Forget about the sharks. I missed you. Hold me."

He touched a curl beside her face and then pulled back. "I can't risk it. It's too good here."

"Hey," J-Bay said. "Man, where are we?"

"When you get out to the waves, you won't care," Alonso lobbed a mango at J-Bay who caught it with an easy stretch of his hand. "Paradise. Bali Hai. Wherever."

He stood and grabbed his board. "Let's go."

"What about sharks?" Doreena said.

He shrugged. "I'll risk it. It's worth it."

He'd risk sharks, but not touching her. As they were walking down the beach the suction came at Doreena pulling her back. She stumbled forward in the sand and reached for Alonso. He pulled away from her and caught J-Bay's arm. "If you want to stay here, you can't touch her. Don't make the same mistake I did, no woman before the stoke. You can't have both."

She returned to the lake alone. Alonso stayed in paradise. When the surfers asked where J-Bay was, she told them about the island.

"I don't know how it started, but I go to an island. There's a perfect beach and waves and all the fruit you can eat: mangoes, coconut and pineapple. I couldn't control it before, when I went by myself, it just happened. I got into an accident the first time because I was driving and then it came, but now I know how to get there on purpose. I can take people with me. I've done it a few times."

"Alonso and J-Bay," one of the surfers said.

"Yeah, that's where they are."

"Where is where they are?" a surfer asked.

She shrugged. It was an easy gesture that she had stolen from Alonso. Now that she was doing it, seeing it from the inside, she could feel what it really meant, not so much, 'I don't know.' as, 'It doesn't matter'. "Alonso called it paradise."

"Kiss you and go to paradise," a surfer said. "Now that's an offer."

"I've heard that one before," said another.

"Hey, it works sometimes, bro."

"I'll show you," Doreena said.

She reached for A-Bay, J-Bay's twin, because he seemed familiar, but he pulled away from her. "Nah, someone else. I don't like to do it...my brother and I don't share girls. It's caused us trouble in the past."

"The Cape Town girl," one of the surfers said. "Legendary."

"Hey, I believe you," another said, the seal-faced surfer. She didn't know him, but she knew his gestures. His hands were limp at his sides and his shoulders low fixed in a permanent shrug. She went to him, put her arms around his neoprene torso and lifted her lips to his. She kissed him with all the surfers watching. She thought of her island and her mouth felt warm and pliable as though she tasted the sun-ripened fruits. A thrill went through her when the suction pulled, the surfer's arms tightened around her. The haze dropped and she brought him over. He was dazzled and unafraid as Alonso and J-Bay had both been. The new surfer went by Barritz. She stayed for a while with the three of them this time surfing and lying on the sand and eating fruit before she came back to the C-town lakeshore where the rest of the surfers were still waiting.

"Where'd he go?" they asked.

"The island. I told you I took him," she said. "What did you see?"

"He disappeared. He vanished."

"And me?" she asked.

"You were still there."

"I saw her for a moment kissing air."

"No, she was just standing."

"She didn't do anything."

"What's the trick?"

"There's no trick," she said. "We just get together and the island comes for us. If there's something really important to you, like your surfboard, you can bring it with you if you're touching it."

They were skeptical, but they kissed her. She took them on top of the gritty sand until it became island soft beneath them. It was different every time. Sometimes the island would come instantly, other times it took a while touching and kissing and making love on top of the surfer's board until the island flowed around them and pulled them into its embrace. Each surfer was the same. He reacted with delight and once there, he refused to touch her. No one would risk it. No one wanted to leave. Doreena wanted Alonso to be jealous that she was making love to all his mates, but he only looked happy to see his surf bros.

"It's fine for you," she said. "But I'm the one who keeps going back."

For a while, so long as there were surfers, she could go to the island whenever she liked, taking the next one in her arms, but the more she populated the island with her men, the more she wanted to remain there to watch them skimming the waves.

When the suction came, she ran at them, she held her hands out to them, pleading with them to try and hold on to her or to take hold and come back with her.

"Come back with me. I'll bring you back," she said. But none of them would come near her outstretched hands and as they saw her desperation grow, they began to keep their distance.

Then only A-Bay was left in C-town as sure transport to her island. He was the youngest of the surfers, by two hours after his twin. She wanted to take him, but she resisted the impulse to do so right away because he was the last. Then she'd be left waiting alone. He didn't have any reservations now. He begged her. "Please. It's my turn. I want to see that my brother's OK."

"He's fine," she said. "Once you get there, you won't touch me either."

"I will. I promise."

"No. You won't. You'll want to stay like all the others, and you won't take the chance. Alonso'd take Tiger sharks over me. Nobody wants to come back here. Nobody wants to get stranded on the wrong side."

It was hard not to touch him when she wanted to and wanted the island. She was in the habit of touching easily now whomever she wanted, and it was hard to resist reaching for him. He had moved into Alonso's apartment with her, and she'd give in soon. Then all the surfers would be on the island, and she'd be in C-town with nothing to do and no sure way to get out. She'd put A-Bay off as long as she could.

"Leave me alone," she said. "Or I won't take you, ever." He knew by now though how desperate she was for the island and how much she needed him to get there.

"I'll wait here," he said.

She went to the lake and found the one surfer she'd forgotten, Hobart. The older woman had kept her distance since Doreena began talking about the island. She'd never trusted Doreena, *The Mirror* salesman.

Now the woman waved her over. "Come on, you're always here, but you're never out here," Hobart pointed to the middle of the lake. "Let me show you how to get a rise out of this."

The surfing lesson was cold and useless. They went close to the enormous, coiled aluminum tubes that spilled ripples of gray-green water. Doreena could not stand up on her board in the little drifts and it stank of amalgamated fish, algae, and chemicals that each, alone, might have been bearable. Hobart tired of her sullen student and left Doreena clinging to her board. Moments later, Doreena looked up and the surfer giantess bore down on her, a dark spire against the light gray sky, looking as if she were pulling the skim of the lake behind her. She crouched in one swift movement and stopped in front of Doreena slipping off the board into the water. A gleam shone in her eye, a touch of enchantment, as though she'd glimpsed the island in the distance as she stood over the lake. That look made Doreena want to climb up the trellis of skin in the corner of Hobart's eye and sit inside that shiny mote of bliss. She didn't understand what it was about this experience on the cold, dank, lake that the surfers loved. But she saw the effects with certainty in Hobart. She wanted to see Hobart on her island, what she would look like gliding on the waves in that idyllic place. She leaned toward her.

"Let me show you the island."

"Don't get ideas," Hobart said.

"But they've all gone. You have to believe me. Don't you want to see it?"

"What, you want to kiss me? You want to make love to an old woman, after all those surfer boys? No, listen, it's not that I'd find it so terrible. Don't look so hurt. It's just that I've been around a while. I like to think I've learned a little. These aren't little pleasures to go into lightly. When you make connections with people, you get tied up in all their shit. That's something to think about. It seems to me like you've got some pretty serious shit to wrangle.

I don't know I want to take all that on. Just touch you. But there isn't any just. Not that I've ever seen. It's never just anything."

"You will, though. You'll just go to a beautiful place and then you won't have to even pay attention to me anymore," Doreena protested.

"Oh, I doubt that. Before this stop in C-town, I traveled the world and it seems to be a rule that once you've been somewhere your odds of going back skyrocket and once you've made a connection with someone, even fleeting, chances are you'll see them again. You can hide for a while. Staying in a small town and keeping to a routine creates a kind of buffer, but eventually, when you move on, it'll open the floodgates and suddenly all those people and places you thought you left behind start pouring out. No, I don't want to get whisked away no matter how pretty. I've seen paradises before. Been to lots of pretty places, and I always wanted to move on after a while no matter how beautiful. I've been running away from my shit all my life. Now, I've started something here in this town and I want to finish it. I started that Travel Museum and I'm attached to it. I like being a business owner. Who woulda' thought."

In the back of Doreena's mind, she recognized Hobart's tone, it was the riff she'd heard from Gavin Traynter, Mr. Elitamby, and even Rock and Marilyn. Entrepreneurs got passionate about their businesses as if they were life-changing experiences. She knew that, but as Hobart talked all she could really think about deep down inside herself was the rejection. It hurt. Hobart didn't even want to try to go to the island with her. It bothered her that she couldn't see Hobart's hands, they were hidden under the lake and under the board. The creases in the corners of the Hobart's eyes looked prominently like laughter.

"You don't want to touch me either," Doreena said.

"What, are you mad about it?" Hobart said. "Seriously?"

Abject, Doreena swam for the center of the lake. She lurched stiffly through the cold water. She felt desperate, awkward, and ridiculous because of it, but that didn't make the pain of feeling out of place, out of time, and out of control any less overwhelming. Something was happening inside herself. She was on the verge of some discovery and she didn't think she could handle it alone in C-town. She stopped when she reached the lake's center and stilled the paddling movements that were keeping her afloat. Her body sank a little into the gray water. She paddled again, softly, and bobbed to the surface. Then she stilled, sank, and went under water. It covered her face and then the top of her head. She hid beneath the water and opened her mouth to let the air escape. The bubbles wobbled out. She sank further into the gray-green darkness until her toes touched the silt. This was exactly what she'd done when the shark had come for her: frozen and sank. She wasn't trying to drown, only submerge her growing panic. She wished there were sharks here now. It would be better if there were a real threat from the outside, better than this hidden, gnawing attack from the inside.

Underwater her mind drifted to a calm, cold place. Maybe the blue haze would appear on the other side, or maybe she'd find a way to stop wanting it. Her arms floated up over head as if detached. She opened her mouth again and the wastewater flowed in. There was nothing she could do to escape. She'd held the trap inside herself all along and now it sprung. She sank into the murky water gaining weight on her way down, daring the haze to rescue her, but the island had abandoned her leaving her marooned on the wrong side of her life. Her toes stirred up a cloud of dark particles when they touched the lakebed. In time, her body leaned over sinking at an angle to lay among the debris. She'd drown or the island would save her, either way, if Alonso was right, there'd be euphoria.

Then her arm was yanked into a vertical position again, her body followed. A hand grabbed hers and pulled. Doreena struggled to stay down, but her kicking lifted her up instead. Her suddenly buoyant body rode up through the water and surfaced. A neoprene arm circled her waist. Doreena gasped for air and stared into Hobart's blue eyes.

"What are you doing, girl?" Hobart said.

As Doreena shook her head, the blue haze dropped. Hobart's eyes became vivid blue and the blue in the world, in the peripheries, around them deepened so that even the gray slick of the lake shone with a cyan coating. The suction wrapped around them and in moments Doreena lay on the beach gasping in the warm sun with Hobart beside her. Hobart's big hands adorned with rings were visible now beside her on the sand. The seal-like wrinkles in her older skin seemed to soften in the island sun.

"So, you brought me anyway," Hobart said. "You gave me no choice. Now our lives are entwined."

Doreena stumbled to the waves and rinsed her mouth of the lake water with its chemical residue. She spat seawater and it left a sweet aftertaste. Doreena looked across the sea. The waves were small and the surface empty.

"Come on, I know where they are," she said. "I'll take you to the surfers."

She led Hobart toward the jungle. As they walked up the beach she noticed how, on the island, Hobart's strange gait finally looked right. It was a spread-legged straddle that kept the thighs apart and came naturally in the heat.

As they approached the trail, Doreena noticed that the beach ahead looked different. It had been bare sand laced with purple flowering pohuehue. Now there were low growing shrubs with fleshy yellow-green leaves bearing white five-lobed flowers among the vines. She knelt to examine it as they passed by.

"Sea lettuce," Hobart said.

Doreena lifted her head and turned back toward the jungle. A heady mix of spice, jasmine and frangipani streamed out of it. The island air had always exuded a light floral scent, but it was perfumed now like the inside of Denriggers. Doreena stepped on the red trail cutting into the jungle. The island continued to evolve. Foliage proliferated. Multi-colored green striations ran vertically from the blue sky to the red trail showing numerous variations on a jungle theme like Pantone swatches. There were plants and flowers she'd never seen before, and the jungle was alive. Restless cawing, clicking, buzzing, and rustling betrayed the creatures hiding in its green depths. Hobart stopped in the middle of the jungle.

"It doesn't make sense," she said, looking around. "Frangipani from Central America, South African protea, Hawaiian hibiscus and this," she pulled a branch with green way leaves and white blossoms toward her and put her face into it. "This is gardenia from Tahiti, Tiare. All these scents are mingling now, but if you could smell this one on its own you wouldn't forget it. The Tahitians' got an international patent on the scent."

She looked up at the trees. "That's traveler's palm from Madagascar. There's a double coconut you only find on the Seychelles, and South American jacaranda. These shouldn't all be growing together. They all require different soils and temperatures and rainfall. This is either a fey place or there's an incredible cultivator somewhere." She pointed up the trail. "Up there?"

This idea bewildered Doreena the way it had when Marilyn had asked about sharks in the ocean. She'd never considered what might be in the depths of the jungle or further up the red trail. She'd heard the voice calling down but had assumed it did not belong to a person.

"I've never been much further than the beach, just a little way in for fruit."

Hobart grabbed Doreena's arm, "I said I didn't want to come, but this island. You're right. This is something different."

The surfers lounged in the grove feasting on fruit. Before it had been a simple stand of coconuts, with a cluster of pineapples growing at the base of the trees and a surround of glossy dense mango shrubs with pink unfolding leaves and flowers. Now trees, shrubs, and clusters of dark green shiny leaves at all heights in the size of fingertips, palms, or entire arms pressed around the clearing. Ovoid green, yellow and gold fruits dangled into the space and lay scattered across the fibrous floor. A cry of "Hobart!" went round, then the surfers returned to languid eating and napping. Hobart handled the fruits and named them. Some she picked up from the jungle floor and tossed in the air, reassured by the weight of them as she caught them in her hands.

"Lime, papaya, papaw, guava, rambutan, durian, passionfruit, jackfruit, breadfruit, Tahitian lime," she said.

"I think it's got everything from anywhere we've ever been," Alonso said. He'd risen from where he'd lain beside a tree gnawing coconut and stood beside them. He stood on the far side of Doreena with Hobart between them. The surfers were wary of Doreena now, her unpredictable leave-taking, and kept her at a distance. In frustration, she'd lunged at a couple of them once or twice when she felt she was about to go. Alonso stepped back from her now. He wasn't even near her and still backed away. He'd felt it before she had. The suction began and stiffened her body.

She reached for Hobart, "Don't leave me."

But Hobart had followed Alonso out of arm's reach.

"I mean to go back. But not just yet. They need me. You need to bury those," Hobart said, turning to Alonso and pointing to a pile of decaying rinds and peels.

Doreena's last glimpse of the island was a haze of brown buzzing flies and then she was in Alonso's apartment at the Narborough. Her hands were a flurry of motion in front of her. She held a suit jacket folded in half over a suitcase. A-Bay sat on the edge of the stripped bed. The bloodstained batik lay crumpled on the floor with a pile of clothing. There was a roar behind her, a thud that made the room vibrate and then the shatter of breaking glass.

"What's that?" she said.

"They're tearing the building down," A-Bay said.

"Why aren't we at the lake?"

"It's closed to the public. They've started construction on Rock Traynter's new resort."

"What am I doing?"

"Packing," he said. "They want us out of here yesterday." He pulled his shirt off, threw it on top of the laundry and grabbed her arm. "Doreena. Please. Just get us out of here."

Doreena shoved the suitcase off the bed and pulled him on top of her. They writhed together on the bed to the roar and crash of the wrecking crew until the haze dropped and the sound became the roar and crash of island waves. Doreena looked at A-Bay his skin gone island gold and his curls backlit by the brightest blue. His face lit up with delight and triumph and tears formed in her eyes. She'd done it, brought the last of them. But before her tear had time to fall, the suction pulled her back. It was her shortest island visit yet and then; she was back on the bed in the Narborough alone. A thud landed against the wall nearby and then a shower of glass crossed the room. Doreena only had time to grab Alonso's tip jar. She left everything she owned and rushed down the dust-choked stairway out onto the street.

Doreena pulled her wetsuit up and zipped it staring as the Narborough fell. Its ordered bricks lay in jumbled piles at the bottom of chalky clouds of dust. She looked through the empty windows of The Travel Museum beside it until the construction workers chased her off the site. Where had all the things gone? She watched them destroy the building from across the street until it began to get dark. Then she rode the bus downtown clutching the tip jar between her neoprene-covered thighs. The bus was filled with islandless strangers who avoided her gaze. There was only one person left in C-town who had shared the island, only one person who gone with her and come back. She went to the Traynter's loft.

"Why are they always tearing down my places?" she said when Marilyn answered the door.

The color of the day was black. Marilyn held her black and white patterned scarf across her nose and mouth. Doreena touched her curls. They were sticky and stiff, matted with blood, salt, and her scalp's own accumulating oils. She was unwashed and layered with scents of stale sex and lake water. She must look frightful and smell worse. But it would vanish once she reached the island; her skin would be clean and pure.

"It's about time. Where have you been?" Marilyn asked.

"Busy."

"You can't stay here. You're lucky Rock's out."

"I won't," Doreena said. She reached for Marilyn's belly. She did not know for certain what it was about these other people that brought the island, but she thought it was something like the pulse of life. The life inside Marilyn, sex with the stoked surfers, and Hobart saving her life. It was that emotion Tom and Marilyn and her grandfather had been hinting that she'd been lacking — passion. She devoted her life to *The Mirror*, all her energy and effort, but some spark within her had held back. She hadn't even noticed its absence, but it had been obvious to others.

"Wait." Marilyn said. "I've been thinking a lot about this."

Doreena sunk into the crème-colored couch. Her wetsuit was stretched and torn in places. She plucked at it while she waited and listened to Marilyn talk on the phone in the other room. After a while, they went down to the street where a silver AeroFlux truck was parked. Marilyn lifted the back of it, inside were crates stamped with maroon wings. She hoisted herself up into it and Doreena followed.

"Most of them are empty," Marilyn said. "Now we're ready to go to the island. Here's what we're going to do.

She grabbed Doreena's hand and placed it on her belly. She put her other hand on the crate. The baby flipped. The blue haze dropped. The suction pulled them onto the island. She landed beside Marilyn and a pile of crates. She was salt washed clean again and floral scented. Her mind, dull and stiff on the streets of C-town, felt lively again.

"What's all this for?" Doreena said, staring at the crates. Around the jumbled stack of gray squares, the island scenery appeared too bright, and it vibrated slowly around the edges of the stack. For the first time, the island itself, the whole scene, looked not quite real, not quite solid.

Marilyn was about to answer when the surfers began to come in from the ocean to see the latest arrival, the unlikely looking stack of crates on the sand.

Marilyn turned to Doreena. "You've been busy."

"What's all this?" Hobart said when a circle of surfers had gathered around.

"Well, good this might help," Marilyn said. "I think it's time we began a major exporting business. I want to start bringing this place back to C-town. The fruit definitely, maybe even the sand."

A murmur went round the surfers as they began to protest, but Hobart stilled them holding up one big hand. Her polished stone rings shone in the island sun. "Wait, this could be what we've been looking for. The next iteration of *The C-town Traveler*. Think about it. This would really change things. This could be a way to open up C-town."

While they talked, Doreena looked for Alonso. He was the last to leave the sea, but eventually he began to stroll toward them. He was one of the few of them that had come to the island unclothed. Most of the surfers had transported their wetsuits with them. Still wet, Alonso's body glistened. She wanted to touch him while he was still cool from the sea.

"Hey bros," he said as he passed them, and kept walking toward the grove.

"I've got a proposal," Marilyn said. With the surfers gathered around her, it looked like a sales meeting on the sand.

Doreena left Marilyn with her new force scheming about an export business with AeroFlux and the surfer's help. She didn't care. She followed Alonso into the jungle to eat fruit. She slipped mango between her lips and let it slide around in her mouth to savor the juice. Alonso gnawed on a pineapple core. He held his muscular torso in his hands with pale pink fingernails. "I eat all the time, but I swear I can feel my ribs."

She heard voices up the trail in the jungle, Marilyn directing the surfers. The palms rustled as they passed.

"What are they up to?" Alonso asked.

"I think they're starting up a business. Try the coconut," Doreena held a chunk out to Alonso. "I never eat, but I'm fat as ever." she patted her hips and swiveled them in front of him. "Feel."

"Is that what's with all the crates?"

"I guess, they're going to bring the island back to C-town bit by bit. I don't care. I don't want to go back there. I don't work for her anymore."

"You sure about that? I mean, you will go back, right?"

"I can't stop it," she said.

"You and C-town are still tangled up."

She reached for his hand, then sighed when he pulled away. "Fine. I'll see what's up." Doreena followed a line of broken leaves, exposed stalks, and bent stems up the narrow red trail through the jungle. She listened for the voice but heard only doves cooing in the trees. A red macaw, like Petey, arched in the sky its wingspan stretching across the path as she reached a clearing where a waterfall fell into a pool beside a yawning cave. It was the farthest she'd ever been up the trail, into the jungle, and off the beach. A line of crates stretched out of the entrance. Inside, Marilyn and the surfers stood around them.

Doreena crept forward and lifted the cover of the nearest one. It was filled to the top with green-skinned mangoes. She thought she heard the voice beckoning within the rush of the waterfall, spun around and froze. Someone grabbed her from behind. She elbowed back punching into hardness before she knew what she was fighting and then going limp when she spied Marilyn's pregnant belly. She didn't want to hurt the baby. Marilyn wrapped an arm tightly around her and pulled her back towards the crates.

Doreena cried out when she saw Alonso coming down the trail. The waterfall muted her, but he turned towards the cave and stepped into the clearing. She reached for him, but he held back watching at a distance. He couldn't help. He still wouldn't touch her.

"What's this?" Alonso asked the surfers. "What do you think you're doing?"

"Saving C-town," Hobart said, barely audible in the roar of the waterfall — no — it was the engine of the truck.

Doreena struggled as the suction surrounded her wicking the moist air from her skin. She forgot about Marilyn and the baby and pulled hard against the suction digging her heels in. She was lurching toward the beach. It had been just feet away. If wasn't fair that she hadn't had any time there. One minute she was struggling in Marilyn's arms and the suction, and the next she was free. She stepped back and her heel scraped a crate and then slid down a metal ramp. She lost her footing and her legs shot out from under her. She tumbled down the ramp and her tailbone struck pavement. Pelting cold rain replaced the mist of the waterfall. She was in C-town again sitting on Beaumont Street staring up the extended ramp leading into the AeroFlux truck.

She looked for Marilyn where she had last been standing inside the truck. But it was empty. She looked back at the stack of crates behind her. The driver in his coveralls appeared looking down at her and over at the crates. He was standing in front of a loading zone sign and Doreena realized what had happened. He had pulled the truck forward, just a few feet, but Marilyn would have reappeared exactly where she'd left C-town for the island. Since the truck wasn't there anymore, that meant in the air over the street.

"Idiot, you moved it," Doreena said.

"What, you wanted to pay for the ticket? Parking ordinances are strict downtown."

Doreena ran around the crates afraid of what she'd find. A cluster of people had gathered and in the distance sirens wailed. The fall would only have been from a few feet up, but even a drop from that height, that and Doreena's fighting, could have hurt the baby. Marilyn sat beside the crates. Strangers held her hands.

"Don't worry the ambulance is on its way," a man said.

The street was wet and dark. Doreena couldn't tell if the spreading sheen over the gravel was a rising coat of oil or slowly pooling blood. Marilyn's face, peering out of her dark overcoat, looked small and pale. The color of the day was black and white.

When the EMT's arrived, Doreena got pushed aside, but before they left one of them yelled at her to ride along. "She could use a friend."

"I'm not," Doreena said, but stopped short. She wasn't sure it was true anymore that Marilyn was just her boss. They had waded into the ocean together perfectly at ease. Maybe they were friends now, on the island anyway. Even so she had to refuse, she would not go to the hospital again. Her eye had finally healed, and she didn't want anyone to see anything else was wrong with her. They could make her sick or worse, somehow cure her of the island. Besides, if Marilyn lost the baby what could Doreena possibly do to comfort her. Marilyn might even be angry. She might blame

Doreena or the island for putting the child at risk. As the ambulance sped down Beaumont, she watched the driver load the crates of stolen fruit into the truck. It wasn't long before her thoughts returned to the island. All she wanted was it, again, soon.

~ 14 ~

INSIDE AEROFLUX

Mirror Island evolves and enslaves Doreena

The next time Doreena returned to the island, it enchanted her again and displaced her fear. Her shoulder blades slunk down her back. Sweat trickled between her thighs and she stepped her legs wide so air would flow between them. Her heels were heavy in the sand and her arms rested at her sides. With her eyes closed, the saline breeze seemed blossom filled. Layers of floral sweetness crested and fell around her. The Hawaiian hibiscus and pikake scent that reminded her of grandfather and home floated somewhere within the flowing breeze, no longer distinct, but still there under the layers of scent.

The inlet around her beach was filled with surfers. They gathered like dark spears and charged toward her to the shore as if they'd scented her arrival. They could hardly have seen her in the glare of the sun appearing on the shore, as she imagined, a blush of honeyed brown blooming on the pink sand.

Doreena turned toward the jungle noticing again its new density and diversity. There were stairways of palms with fringed leaves stretching in the blue sky, crossing over each other and fingering each other's trunks. The vegetation was a Pantone booklet of blue-green, red-green, and yellow-green leaves filled in with purple to black patches of shade. Some leaves were variegated with exposed bright red and white veins. Their shapes were spatulate, pointed, or oblong and they folded, curved and unfurled over each other. Vines crawled everywhere, twining and wrapping around rough trunks. Red and white flowers shone like headlights and brake lights blooming through the jungle traffic. The iron red trail leading up into the jungle seemed wider. It cut a path into the foliage like a leering tongue. The jungle looked impassible anywhere else.

The surfers were behind her now, a half-circle of men baked in neoprene and salt. They, and their stifling scent, were too close to her, as if they were all seated behind her on the C-town bus.

"Where's Traynter?" they asked.

For a moment, she thought they meant Rock and froze trying to remember if she'd brought him and afraid of what changes he would bring to this shifting place. But it seemed impossible for Rock to come here. She would never get close to him and there was nothing island-like about him. Of course, they meant Marilyn.

"In the hospital," Doreena said. "She's on bed rest to save the baby. She nearly lost it."

She shaded her eyes and tried to see beyond them to the empty beach, but they stood shoulder to shoulder in front of her. Stripes of pink sand showed between their wetsuit clad hips and legs but there was no room for her to pass through. The men stood in a quiet arc between her and her beach.

"She'd want us to continue," Hobart said, stepping forward. Her cap of hair shone silver above them. Most of the men's wetsuits adhered to their plank-like torsos, but Hobart, lean as she was, had a small round of belly. Her wetsuit pressed out in just one place like a trapped roll of a wave. Doreena wanted to get away from the woman, but she didn't want to get any closer to the jungle. Instead, she dug her toes into the sand.

"Come see what we've been working on." Hobart said. "It's just up the trail."

"Alonso?" Doreena asked.

"He's exploring," a surfer said. It was seal-faced Barritz, the first one she'd brought over. He nodded toward the jungle. "Come on. Don't you want to take a look?"

"I want to stay on the beach," Doreena said. She'd dug her feet into the sand so it covered them. She wiggled them now and the sand cracked. They were all close around her. The only open space was behind. The tongue of the red trail licked her back. "I'm not here all the time like you."

J-Bay pushed her first.

"There's no time. She could go soon. When she brought my brother, she was only here for a few seconds. We don't know when she'll return so we have to move. We can't be shy about it."

Doreena stumbled back and Hobart walked toward her. The surfers jabbed at her until she stumbled off the last patch of pink. Her feet slid into the warm mud of the trail. It oozed red between her toes. The next shove sent her sprawling forward toward a plant with one enormous blossom mounted at its center. She reached for it to catch her fall, but the tender stem pulled free and she fell with the blossom cradled in her arms. It was the size of a baby's head with feathery fringes instead of petals up its sides. It was one of the foreign plants from far out of C-town Hobart had pointed out when she arrived. She remembered the name, protea. Doreena crashed onto the mud trail and put the sticky protea blossom head aside. She pressed her hands into the mud to raise herself up. It coated her palms and spread up onto the backs of her hands. She shook it off and red flecks landed on the leaves. She wiped the excess on her thighs. It had an eggy mineral smell and, when she touched her tongue to a fleck of it on her lips, a burnt caramel taste.

She walked steadily up the trail with the surfers packed behind her, but the menstrual scent of spoiling fruit made her stop at the entrance to the grove. To one side a swath of melon rinds, lime peels, rambutan husks and coconut shells, stretched beneath of a flurry of tiny brown flies. They moved like Brownian motion.

"Brownian?" she said aloud. "What's that?"

They shoved Doreena on toward the cave. Along the outside of the pool, water lilies stretched over a jade green slurry, but back by the cave a waterfall churned the center of it into peaks of green and white. A stack of crates blocked the entrance to the cave, with the maroon-winged logo plastered up the sides. Beside the crates was cargo: loaves of breadfruit, stacks of strawberry guavas and pyramids of passion fruit and papaya. A-Bay pointed.

"Just touch the crates," he shouted, and she didn't know if he was as angry as he sounded or just trying to be heard over the waterfall.

"I don't want to," she yelled back.

It would have been easy for any of them to grab her and lift her to the crates. But none of them wanted to touch her for long, so they pushed her one-by-one, making her stumble toward the crates. When she was up against them, the surfers stopped. They continued shouting.

"Now what?" J-Bay said. "Are we going to stand here? I saw some great sets on the way."

"Find some way to restrain her," Hobart said.

They bound her wrists and ankles with vines and creepers and tied her to the crates.

"We have to do this. He's got everyone trapped in C-town. This is our chance," Hobart said.

"But you're here," Doreena said. "I brought you. We can enjoy it."

"It's not for us," Hobart said. "There are surfers everywhere."

They left her with her breasts, belly, and thighs pressed up against the rough splintery wood. The waterfall splatter occasionally struck her exposed back. Insects with long legs and translucent glittery wings walked over and pressed proboscis to her skin mistaking her for the open blossoms of the nymphae lilies that they loved. Drops splashed in her mouth and eyes where it fell from the crooks of the jade green rocks perpetually enlivened by the cascade of water pouring down. White veins glistened through wet stones, while the dry cliff beside it stood stolidly matte gray with tufts of course moss growing in its cracks.

When she could no longer hear the surfers, Doreena squirmed against the vines. Immediately, some of them loosened. She was sure she could get free, in time. Maybe she could find another beach, some sheltered cove on the island, the others didn't know about. She would crawl through the jungle and find it. Maybe Alonso would be there. Some of the vines crushed as she struggled. The sinewy strands opened, and their juice slid over her skin. The woodier creepers scratched. The sinewy cords stretched and snapped. Dangling cords swung around her body as she struggled.

"Come see me," the voice called from trail.

She freed her arms and began to tear the vines apart with her hands. All she wanted was to get away from the crates and the voice and be back on the beach. She was almost free when the suction pulled. The vines crawling across her skin began to hiss. She flailed wildly against a blur of green and then gray as she landed writhing on a C-town street. A truck braked beside the stack of crates and released a hissing exhalation.

After that, Doreena spent all her time on the island strapped to the crates. The surfers pushed her into the jungle as soon as she arrived. Her back and arms were covered with rounds of fingerprint-shaped bruises like the spots of some exotic animal. She fought back, but the harder she struggled the harder the surfers pushed and the tighter they pulled when they bound her to the crates. They had ropes now. Her C-town-self had betrayed her, and she had brought them.

At the mouth of the cave, Doreena shivered. Each time became colder and drier: her rough tongue swelled in her mouth. The skin of her hands cracked. Her skin looked pale, shot through with pronounced aquamarine veins. It had been a long time since she'd had any island fruit, but instead of the lightness of hunger, her body felt heavy like freight. Her time in C-town consisted of hazy, half-remembered events. She thought she was coming to the island more often. She couldn't remember what she'd been doing in C-town anymore. The island was all she thought of. She stood with her cheek pressed to the crates and her eyes closed to the drops of water. When she smelled the green nectar of her favorite fruit, her body surged like liquid. Her breasts and hips swelled, and she knew the youngest surfers were behind her.

"Look what we brought," J-Bay said.

He held a mango up and tore through the green skin with his teeth revealing the wet orange flesh. She salivated at the ripeness of it. The rope burned her twisting wrists.

"Let me go," she said.

"I'll feed you," J-Bay said. He slipped a wedge between her lips. The juice slid down her throat. "We need some things from C-town. Bring us women we can touch."

"And beer," A-Bay added from somewhere behind her.

J-Bay moved closer. His arm brushed her breast on its way to her lips with another mango sliver. She stretched her neck up for it, snapped and caught the tip of his finger in her teeth. There was a surge of salty liquid when she clamped down. The suction began. When J-Bay pulled away his flesh ripped between her teeth. Then, he was gone.

Words came into focus in front of her: Quantum. Hawking. Brownian. She was staring at a bookshelf shaking. She spit the fingertip into her palm and closed her fist around it.

"Is that a yes?"

She turned. Earnest knelt on the floor behind her. She recognized him, but not this white-walled place that smelled of orange cleanser.

"I meant to wait until we got to the restaurant." He reached into his pocket and held up a ring.

Where was she? Had it been so long since she'd been lucid in C-town? She tried to bring herself into the moment, but she could still feel the roughness of the crates at her back, the splinters in her thighs, the ropes tight around her midsection and the cold spray of the waterfall across her back. Her chest tightened with longing for the lull of the warm, pink beach and she wished she could take just one deep breath without thinking about it. The pupil-sized round stone on the ring in front of her held a flare of yellow like captured sunshine. The sun: she missed the sun and her grandfather even more. It seemed wrong to love a single person more than the sun, which everyone depended on, but she did. She'd give up the sun to see him.

"Oh damn," Earnest said. "You don't like the ring."

"Earnest." The sound was difficult. Her tongue was dry and light and curled like peeling bark. That was his name, wasn't it? "It's beautiful."

His narrow shoulders in a thin white office shirt shrugged. "Ah, good. There's that. Diane helped me pick it out. She said she was sure you would like it. I should have waited to ask you though. Let's go," he said picking up his tweed jacket and heading for the door. "Forget this. I'll do it properly in the restaurant."

She followed him out and threw J-Bay's fingertip into a juniper outside when he wasn't looking. Earnest held the door to his car open for her. She remembered seeing it sitting on the side of the road beside the landmark sign where she'd crashed the first time she'd gone to her island mid-day. The car was bare inside with the same industrial orange smell. Inside, she ran her pink fingertips over the matching silk of her dress. The wet streets shone with reflected moonlight. The phosphors on Beaumont cut into the dark casting a pale pink skyward over the city.

They parked across from the Tiki-Tiki Lounge, and Earnest held open the door for her again. The silk dress swung round her hips, and she teetered forward on strappy gold sandals. Earnest held up an arm to help steady her. She shivered on the street but in the restaurant the warmth floated quickly up under her dress. The place was packed with people dressed in similar outfits of raw silk and linen in light yellow, pink, or blue. They wore leis of fresh frangipani and jasmine. Live birds, Petey's cousins, perched beside each table preening. White feathers floated down to settle on the bamboo floor. A live band played by the bar. The place had been completely islandized.

"The Steelheads," she said.

The waiter sat them by the window and handed them menus of woven grass. A peach slip of paper clipped to the front advertised the prix fixe menu.

Coconut Satay braised coconut chunks with a side of Tahitian lime sauce.

Savory Tropical Truffle Pie seared plantains and chunks of taro root mixed with shredded coconut covered in a light puff pastry. Comes with a side of braised breadfruit served with mango chutney.

Guava Duff a light fluffy cake stuffed with hot guava compote and served with custard and topped with fresh slices of strawberry guava.

All around them diners were eating and drinking pieces of her island: cooked, braised, sautéed, and pureed. This was where all the goods from the crates were going — or at least many of them. They lifted it to their lips on forks and spoons and devoured it.

"You've barely touched your drink," Earnest said.

There was an orange drink in front of her in a tall flute glass. She took a sip. It was mango and anise and coolly sweet. When she put the glass down, Earnest reached for her hands across the table. She pulled away. His chin dropped with rejection and his shoulders caved.

"I'm sorry," she said and placed her hands in his. It was the least she could do. She wasn't mean like the surfers to deny him a comforting touch.

"I thought about having them make the Great White for us like we had our first time here together. I was going to have them put the ring around one of those little surfers. Listen, I didn't mean to rush the proposal. You know, we've just been so happy these past months. I'm just excited for us to make it official. Especially now."

Months? Had he said months?

"Are you OK? Are you feeling all right?"

"No. I don't know how to explain. If I say it's not you, nothing to do with you, you won't believe me."

The waiter set an enormous golden puff pie between them. It smelled like the end of an island day with the baked scent of taro, plantain, and coconut rising off the sand. She poked through the top of the crust with her fork and it came to her. She knew how to explain what was happening to her to Earnest. She saw the word emblazoned red across the golden puff crust just as it was on the yellow jacket of one of the books on Earnest's shelf.

"At least, wear the ring while you think about it," he said. He leaned in and stroked her ring finger.

The blue haze dropped. She yanked her hand from his.

"Teleport," she said. "I teleport. And you're not going with me."

She left him staring through the rising steam of the pie with a wounded expression. The surfers tied her to the crates again and abandoned her. The dank ropes clung to her skin. A black mold grew on them and the rotten scent attracted iridescent-backed beetles. Her beautiful beach was only 200 feet or so away. Why couldn't she teleport to it from here? The voice called louder from up the trail. It had begun to ask for her by name. On the beach, it only whispered. She drooped against the ropes and closed her eyes. She kept them squeezed shut even when the sound of shifting leaves signaled someone's approach. The ropes slipped off her chest.

"Doreena, it's me," Alonso said. "What are you doing here?"

She shrugged and coils of rope dropped to the wet green stones at her feet covered by a skiff of coarse brown sand by the crates. Instead of the ocean, she saw Alonso.

"Where have you been?"

"Around. This really is an island."

"Is there another beach? A hidden one?"

He shook his head. "Not really. Not that we can get to. It's at the bottom of a cliff. No way down."

He finished untying her and she reached for him, but he still refused to touch her.

"Even now?" she said. "Come with me. I'll bring us back to that beach you saw."

"You can't control it."

"I'll try. Don't you trust me?"

"I trust you. But my time here, it's too precious."

The surfers came quickly. They must have been just below in the grove eating fruit. J-Bay, the first up the trail, called back, "It's Alonso."

"What've you been doing?" Alonso asked.

"Saving C-town," J-Bay said.

Alonso pointed at the crates. "Like this?"

"We've got a little export business going."

Hobart arrived leading the rest of the surfers. "It's not just us. Other people are stuck."

"Yeah, and what if we want to go back? What if we get bored?" J-Bay said.

Doreena looked for a way to get past them to the beach, but the only clear way was up the path where the voice called. Maybe though, if they were distracted by Alonso, she could duck into the jungle a little and get past them. It wasn't very far to the beach. She just wanted to feel the pink sand under her feet and get a little warm before she left. She had decided to try it when her skin tingled and the suction began. She sighed.

"Get her to the crates," J-Bay said. "She's got that look."

The surfers turned to her. J-Bay pushed her but as he did she grabbed his wrist and climbed this arm. She threw herself onto him, wrapping her arms and legs around him and digging her nails into his shoulder blades. J-Bay rocked off balance and stumbled toward the pool. The surfers crouched around shouting but no one, not even Alonso, made a move to help either of them. As the suction gripped them, A-Bay finally lunged and grabbed his brother's shoulders, but he slipped on the rocks and tipped the three of them into the pool. J-Bay pushed away from her chest and neck, pressing against her throat and submerging her even before the cold water rose over them. The chain of her necklace became an icy collar. It loosened and slid down her neck. She forgot the twins and grabbed for it, clutching at her watery collarbone, ribs and hips, but it sank toward the dark rock bottom of the pool.

She was sucked away from it, sinking toward a sheet of white. When the suction released her, she smacked up against ceramic tile. It chilled her cheek as she lay on it with the pink silk of her dress slid up around her hips. She was in the bathroom of the Tiki-Tiki lounge, but, for a moment, with The Steelheads pulsing through the floor, it felt as if she were back in her apartment at the Narborough. Doreena got up and stumbled to the sinks. She squeezed coconut lotion onto her hands and wrung them together while she got her bearings. In the mirror, she stared first at her bare neckline, then at the emptiness of the bathroom behind her. The Narborough, that's where A-Bay would be. She'd taken J-Bay to the island from the shore of Lake Traynter, but she'd been in the Narborough with A-Bay. But where was her necklace?

Two women entered the bathroom one in silver sandals and the other in bejeweled thongs. "Did you lose something?" they asked.

"My necklace," Doreena said. She scanned the shiny white floor expecting the necklace to emerge from a reflection or in the lines of grout.

The sandals and thongs walked back and forth across the floor with her for a while.

"I don't think it's here. Sorry," sandals said.

Thongs stood beside a small grate in the floor. "It could have slipped down there."

"No," Doreena said. "It was too big."

Sandals pivoted toward the door. "Then it's definitely not any-where in here."

Doreena followed the women out past the band and the bar and the bamboo partitions. Earnest sat at a table by the window. Across from him was a half-eaten slice of pink cake and an empty chair. She sank into it, but her chest, bare without the necklace, felt as if it were floating.

"You were saying an island? Which one?" Earnest asked. "Where?"

Doreena looked around trying to recall where they were in this conversation.

"I never understood where all this could come from," Earnest said. "In the old days, there would have been someone asking questions, but now all we've got is *The Mirror* and no one's doing any investigative reporting. But this can't all come from the same place."

"It does," she said.

"When does this happen?"

"It just did," she said.

"You were here eating cake," Earnest said.

"I leave some part of myself behind. Like a shell. It does things while I'm gone."

"Like eat cake?" Earnest said.

Doreena touched her hand to her chest. "I've lost my necklace."

Earnest looked at her then ducked his head under the table. When he popped back up, he raised an eyebrow, at her and said, "I remember it. You always wear that one. It's very unusual. Can you show me where you went?"

"No." she said avoiding his eyes and watching the band instead. The Steelheads' lilting rhythm rose above the metal drums. It seemed disconnected from the objects, emanating directly from the players' fluttering fingertips. "You wouldn't want to come back. And I always do. I always come back. I know you can't believe this."

Earnest tapped his fingers on the table. "Well, in theory, it's plausible if not probable. What you're saying reminds me of quantum entanglement. You and this other place could be connected like entangled particles. Einstein called it 'spooky action at a distance'. But when did you first teleport?"

"After my grandfather died. After I moved into the Narborough," she said. "I think that was the first time. No, I am sure it was."

"The Narborough across from AeroFlux," he said. Then his voice dropped, and he muttered. "There could be side effects."

"What?"

"Let's get out of here. Stay with me," he said. "I want to show you something."

Earnest drove them to the industrial part of town. Across from AeroFlux a gap rose in the night sky where the Narborough had been. She looked at the patch of sky that had been Alonso's third floor apartment. There was rubble below. Would A-Bay have appeared there in the sky? Would he have fallen? Couldn't the island have placed him somewhere safely on earth? It had dropped Marilyn, but only a few feet. Chain link circled a collection of cranes and bulldozers. She could imagine A-Bay sprawled with his limbs twisted over the crushed rocks, but she didn't tell Earnest to stop as they passed the site. She couldn't believe the island would do that to him and what was she supposed to do, explain to Earnest how she'd had teleportation sex with all the surfers?

Miles passed. They entered the forest at the edge of town and the pavement ended. They turned onto a dirt road. The forest was even darker than the city without phosphors. She could barely see the road behind them.

"Where are we going?"

"We're almost there."

They parked in a clearing. The moon shone just over the tops of the evergreens, casting a silvery light on the long grasses so it looked as if they were flowing over the small hill. Earnest leaned out the car door. He stuck his hand into the hillside and she caught a gleam of electronics. The hillside began to hum and the side of it opened. A road dipped into it. Inside, it opened like an airplane hangar. Its sides were lined with cars.

"We're in AeroFlux," Earnest said. "Those are the electric cars they've been selling to New West and the UG."

"Cars? AeroFlux? The future of flight is cars?"

"With all the flights grounded, what were they supposed to do? But yes, one of the possible futures anyway."

They drove past miles of the small, green cars packed alongside the tunnel like jungle leaves. After a while their rounded hulls, grew slimmer and pointed. They looked like nothing she had seen before, a completely new design.

"The latest models," Earnest said. "The flying cars. But this isn't what I want to show you."

They parked beside concrete steps where the road ended. Earnest led her up them and down a dark hall. He grabbed her hand, and it reminded her of trailing her grandfather at his job.

He'd worked as the night janitor at her school and the halls had had this same chemical smell. Earnest unlocked a door that opened into darkness. The air moved freely over Doreena's head and opened up far out front of her where distant surfaces glimmered. The room vibrated.

"We're in one of the sub-level mechanic bays," Earnest said. "Let's wait for our eyes to adjust."

As her eyes began to distinguish color in the darkness, Earnest strode toward an enormous teal tube. It looked like one of her old sleeping pills, giant-sized, and ringed with metal clasps. She hadn't bothered to try to force herself to sleep in some time. Earnest tapped the tube with his fingers and she half-expected it to chime. Instead, there has only a dull thud against the thick metal.

"This is it," he said. "We used the inside of an autoclave— an enormous heater used to bake composite materials, the heat changes the chemical structure so that they become an entirely new material stronger or lighter."

He hovered over a screen filled with spinning numbers. "AeroFlux is visionary. That's the secret to its longevity. That's why it's been around so long. The concept from the beginning was flight, not just hunks of flying metal. Not airplanes, not jets, but flight. This is where all the experimental projects are done. Not just flying cars, but ways to fly. This is one of them. In a way, teleportation is flight, the most efficient form. This could be the source of your island right here. They've been testing it a lot. There could have been unforeseen side effects."

The teal capsule thrummed as Earnest waved his hands about explaining.

"I think I meant to marry you," Doreena said.

He stopped; his hands drifting to the side.

"I got all dressed up," she said. "But I can't. Whatever this machine has to do with it, I think, I'm definitely that, what you said earlier, that tangled up effect."

"You really don't remember us, do you?" Earnest said.

"I've been gone. On the island. And I haven't told you the really spooky part. I haven't told anyone. It's calling me from the top of the island louder and louder and I don't know how much longer I can ignore it. I'm afraid. I hear a voice."

"Shhh. Me too." Earnest grabbed her hand and pulled her into the tube. They huddled at the back of it and heard the door open.

"We're moving," she whispered.

"It's vibration, like super-sized Brownian motion," Earnest pulled her close and took her hands in his.

He whispered. "Doreena, we have to get married. You wanted to." He squeezed her hands so tight her fingers ached. It was like shaking hands with Rock Traynter. "Maybe you don't remember us, but you have to remember the baby."

Earnest pressed his hand to her belly, and she felt it suction up to his touch.

She stared down at the little swell. "Baby?"

Then footsteps echoed through the chamber and the opening to the capsule clanged. Large eyes peered down the tube into the darkness at them.

"Thanks kids, I never would have found this without you," The Stew said.

~ 15 ~

AEROFLUX PRESSER

The demonstration of teleportation fails, Doreena loses the island

The next day, The Stew's handy work was all over the front page of *The Mirror*, "AeroFlux in export scam, City Fathers to meet." AeroFlux executive Dalton Rees called Doreena at Earnest's apartment.

"It's pushing our timeline, but we have to show them teleportation. They need to see that the opening of C-town's borders is inevitable. I'm calling a press conference. We'll give a demonstration of the new technology," Rees said.

"What does this have to do with me?" Doreena asked.

"I want you to tell them about the island."

"You know about it?"

"Earnest and Marilyn told me everything. Listen Doreena, you work for AeroFlux now."

Everything was happening so fast. Doreena couldn't keep track of it. All her life, C-town had been one stable, steady place. It was devoted to recreating and preserving the comforts of the past. The City Fathers discouraged innovation as part of the city's Growth Management Act.

"That's a losing strategy," Earnest explained. "You can't defy entropy. It's impossible to stay in stasis. If you're not moving forward, you're falling apart. You always have to be looking ahead."

"That's just a Western way of thinking," Doreena said. It was something her grandfather had often said as he read the C-town CounterPoints, the space where Rock aired dissenting voices on the editorial page of *The Mirror*, so that he could rebut them. Doreena didn't know what her grandfather meant by that, except that he wanted things to stay the same. But where was Eastern? On the other coast of the UG? Somewhere off-continent? And if grandfather liked this different way of thinking, why hadn't her shared it with her?

Now AeroFlux was breaking ranks, creating new flying cars and exporting them and researching other modes of transportation such as teleportation. Somehow, she'd gotten herself tangled up in that too; AeroFlux wanted to annex her island as though it were just another business line. Doreena couldn't believe she'd gotten involved with AeroFlux, until she checked her bank account. It was loaded. She no longer had to worry about buying lunch or paying rent. But she had found herself worrying less and less about these things anyway, since the island made it unnecessary.

In the same way, these new events, this heightening tension between *The Mirror* and AeroFlux troubled her little, even though she seemed to be right in the middle of the two companies and the two executives. These were the troubles one read about on the front page of the paper, not the ones that normally impacted her life, and she thought the island would absolve her of any complicity in the mens' schemes. It would come for her in time. She depended on it.

Earnest dropped her at Denrigger's on his way to work. Doreena met Diane. "Look at my bank statement. Can this be right?"

"Only if you're involved in something illegal," Diane said.

"Exactly." Doreena said. "I need to do some shopping. I have to look like the kind of person who belongs on an island."

"Follow me," Diane said. "Island clothing coming up. We need the fourth floor, and you can afford it."

They switchbacked up the escalators. The goods displayed on each floor grew brighter as they rose. Wealthy people weren't afraid to attract attention. On the fourth floor, they'd left behind any traces of basic black, beige, or brown shoes, handbags, or undergarments. A flurry of silk in macaw-like colors draped the racks. Doreena looked through the glass sides of the escalator to the last of the business suits below. Eggshell, lavender, and sea-green were in for spring. The blue, black and gray suits were on sale. Diane fluttered ahead of her through the designer dresses. "I know just the thing. I've been eyeing this all month."

"The thing" was a mannequin wrapped in yellow. Doreena couldn't look away from the pheasant feathers curled over the top of the mannequin's head.

"We have a saying here at Denrigger's, Diane *non est disputandem*," Diane said. "It means: Diane is always right about clothes."

The dress cost more than a month of sales at *The Mirror* even before the accessories Diane threw in: the matching boots and cape-like shoulder wrap. But if there was one thing Marilyn and *Stellar Sales* had taught Doreena, it was the importance of looking the part. Since her island experiences had begun, Doreena had noticed how other people's thoughts had a physical effect on her whether she felt stiff or fluid. She could feel what they thought and feel herself becoming what they expected. Now she wanted them to see her as someone who belonged on an island.

The Denrigger's clerk emptied her bank account and handed her a striped crème bag. It swung at her side, feather-light, holding her return in trade for all the time she'd spent tied to those crates. There are royalties to come, Dalton had assured her, "What they wouldn't do for a little tropical fruit." The surfers had been delivering the island fruits to C-town, but AeroFlux had plans to export her island goods to the rest of the UG.

"I'm wearing it," Doreena said. She put the dress on in the fourth-floor lounge, adjusting the swath of fabric across her hips until it clung to her frame, folding into the places she put it. Outside, she paused beside the mannequin. The dress hung loose on its stiff figure.

"It's good," Diane insisted. "You look like I've always imagined you. From the first time I saw you, I think I saw something islandish inside you."

"Really?" Doreena said. It was strange the way people saw things sometimes, and strange to think they noticed her at all. She was always busy watching others, she never thought of herself as the kind of person who was seen. "I'm surprised you thought of me at all. And how could you know about the island?"

"Well, maybe not the island, but you were kind of far away and thoughtful and you seem exotic," she said. "Didn't you think about me?"

"We thought you wore too much eyeshadow and weren't very good at sales," Doreena said.

"Both true."

"And you seem very birdlike, exotic, too."

On the way in to AeroFlux, Doreena stopped by the black and white photo and picked her grandfather's face out from the team of astronauts standing among the proud crew of mechanics that had worked on the AF-897 spaceship. They wore flight suits with the old AeroFlux logo; the same wings but in a cubic style with blunt, shorn-looking feathers. The modern logo was streamlined, its wingtips like blades.

She'd researched the flight since she'd first seen the photo and knew how heroic the men had been. The astronauts were going to stabilize the world's economy; they were seeking a new energy source on a distant planet. It had worked for a while too, until the mining operation had caused the new planet to implode. How had grandfather survived and come to raise her? He must have been so much older than he looked. She clutched at her necklace, but her hands cupped air. She thought of how she would look to him. Exotic, Diane had said. Ridiculous, her grandfather would think.

Grandfather would not have liked it, her being here in this get up or being here at all about to get up on stage in front of everyone and take a stand against the status quo in C-town. She was going to attract attention, exactly what he'd always wanted her to avoid. Ever since grandfather had died, it seemed, she'd been defying him, breaking rules she hadn't questioned before. It was no way to honor his memory. But he'd left her with so few memories, she thought angrily. Maybe if he'd told her about her mother...Then, what? Would she have lived a different life? She was no longer sure what she wanted. She realized she had never known. She'd had no deep desires until she'd ridden the island wave. Now it was crashing over her.

The belly of AeroFlux was already full when she arrived. Suited people sat in row after row of metal folding chairs. Workers in red AeroFlux coveralls flanked them on one side of the room and the union workers in their green shirts stood behind them on the other.

"You're here." A young woman guided Doreena up a metal platform. An AeroFlux banner swathed the teal tube behind the stage and gave wings to its jet-sized bulk. Vases of red anthurium lilies flanked the stage. AeroFlux flouted its island contraband. The City Fathers sat sternly in the front row with Rock at their center. The Stew scribbled in his notebook beside them.

"They want to shut AeroFlux down," Doreena said.

Dalton Rees looked fresh and confident in a linen suit. "Not after this they won't. The island changes everything."

The chairs buckled and squelched against the concrete floor as the crowd shifted, waiting for them to begin.

"After you," Dalton said. The top of Doreena's boots flexed around her thigh as she ascended the platform. She could feel Rock glaring at her through his double-glasses. She'd still never seen his eyes. Were they gray like the concrete floor, or teal like the teleportation tube? She had not expected to make it this far without feeling the pull of the blue haze. She had not thought that the island would abandon her to this. She adjusted the useless yellow capelet around her shoulders. It was still cold.

Dalton commandeered the microphone. "Welcome to AeroFlux," he began. "The inner bowels so to speak. This is where the real work of our company gets done. As you know, AeroFlux has always been about flight: from the days when our jets sailed the open skies of the United Government, until our fleet shrank to flights out of C-town airport, until a few years ago when all flights out were cancelled except those regular trips to Hawaii and then last week when our very last flight to Maui left and the City Fathers eliminated the rest. Today, C-town is an island, isolated, no longer a peninsula even with a single line of contact to the outside world. We've all been grounded. AeroFlux has been criticized for defying that destiny. Yes, we've been selling cars to our neighbors to the south, New West. But while I am grateful to the City Fathers for what they have done to protect the way of life in C-town, and I appreciate the insulation they created from the chaotic world out there, I don't apologize for fighting their isolationism or for trying to keep your jobs open. As you know, AeroFlux is not about jets or airplanes. We've never been about mere machinery; we're propelled by an idea: flight."

Dalton paused and looked from one side of the room to the other across the sea of red and green. The standing workers were leaning forward now, swaying on their feet. Like a conductor, Dalton pointed from one side of the room to the other. The floor rumbled as the AeroFlux employees began to stamp. "The future is flight," he said. The workers cheered. "That's right. And we'll do whatever it takes. Whether it's jets or flying cars, we *will* fly into the future. Today, we are here to demonstrate a new technology which will change the direction of C-town and the UG for all of us."

Dalton turned to Doreena, "They're ready."

She swayed uncertainly in her boots. She couldn't believe she was still here. She'd stayed through the speech. The City Fathers and Rock glared up at her, their hands stiff in their laps. There was not the slightest tinge of blue in the yellow-gray, fluorescent light of the room. The cool, dry air flowed around her. Where was the haze and the suction? When would the island rescue her?

"Let's skip my part," she whispered. "Go to the demonstration."

But Dalton stepped away and gestured to the microphone, "They're ready for you."

Doreena's breath reverberated through the hangar in time with the whir undulating from the jet-shaped machine behind the platform. Earnest, among the red coveralls, caught her eye. He nodded. For once she heard the words repeating inside her head in her own low voice, not Marilyn's or Stellar Sales', "Believe in your product. Be persistent. Speak as if to one person you care about." When had she become her own employer?

"I." The microphone squawked as she began to speak. "I want to live on an island. We all do. But not the kind the C-town fathers have created," she looked down at Rock in the front row, "the bleak fantasy of a colorblind man." He stared up at her from behind his two pairs of glasses and even though she could see no trace of his eyes or feeling she didn't like to look at him. All he'd ever done was give her a job and ask her to work hard for *The Mirror*. The trade had never seemed anything but acceptable, and now here she was cutting down his dream. The security and longevity of C-town that Rock had sustained would evaporate. "I've been to a place with sun and light and tropical breezes. I've been to this place. I've teleported. The future of flight is teleportation."

That said, she was a traitor, just like The Stew.

Rock sat unmoving with his fists clenched on his knees.

"Yes, I think, a demonstration," Dalton said.

The workers behind them shuffled. The machine thrummed. While it came to life, Earnest took the microphone and explained the science. Doreena recalled some of what he was saying from their conversation over dinner, "light waves travel 300,000 kilometers per second...oxygen molecules travel 480 meters per second...there are 26 trillion particles for every 70 kilos of body mass."

Doreena raised her arms, reaching for the island sun, eager to shed her awkward shell. The machine popped. The sky flashed blue; an effect which Earnest had explained was caused by the charged Fermi sea of electrons and polarized photons. There was a chemical smell of lithium niobate crystals used to steer the photons down the optical fibers hooked around the room. Doreena looked for the waves but saw only an ocean of black suits shifting on their metal chairs.

A worker joined Dalton on the stage. They turned toward the teal tube, their backs to the crowd. Doreena looked at Rock as he sat leaning back on the metal, his hands steepled in confidence. The doors at the back of the room swung open and the surfers, in wetsuits, cut a black swath through the divide of AeroFlux red, and union green, workers. Doreena looked up at them in wonder. How had her surfers, her islanders, as she now thought of them, returned without her? All those times they'd let her go, never knowing when she'd return. She'd left them stranded on the island, but they'd never minded. They'd never been afraid. They looked afraid now, and angry, the island had released them when they wanted to be contained.

"She's there," J-Bay shouted as the surfers ran down the aisle of chairs in their squeaking neoprene shoes. AeroFlux security blocked them at the stage. There was a grayish cast to all their faces and their wrinkled wetsuits hung. They were all back, every one of them, and they looked like starved seals. It was clear that the island fruits had not been truly feeding their bodies. And yet, all she had been eating was island fruit, too, and she was as fat as ever. Her body was sleek and swollen from it, while their bodies had wasted away. Only A-Bay was missing.

"I didn't have anything to do with it," Doreena said, before Dalton took the microphone from her. "It's this machine."

"Obviously, we had to rush this demonstration in light of today's headlines. Apparently, we don't have the power to move this much mass. But, if we can isolate it within the tube, we can continue the demonstration with a few volunteers," Dalton said. "Go. Let's keep it moving."

They descended the stage, and he pushed her toward the machine. The Stew hustled forward with his notebook and security waved him inside while holding back the reaching and shouting surfers, "We'll go. Doreena!"

"I'm sorry. There isn't room for everyone, perhaps one of the City Fathers?" Dalton asked.

Rock stepped up. "I'll stand in your machine."

Doreena wanted to back away from his gray bulk, rather than crowd with him into the tiny tube, afraid that any contact with him would be razor sharp. She also feared his effect on the island.

"Perfect," Dalton said. "Maybe one more. Doreena?"

Doreena turned from the desperate faces of the surfers. She could see how they blamed her for their reappearance in C-town. But what had she ever done? She'd delivered them to paradise and borne back the fruits of their labors. She pointed to Earnest. He'd wanted to marry her. He'd given her a ring. And he was the one who'd explained how all this technology worked. She felt guilty to betray her own tribe, but Earnest quickly stepped inside, and the decision was made.

"I'll come back for you," Doreena said to Alonso and Hobart and the rest of the islanders as she stood in the dark, pressed closed against Earnest and The Stew and the two executives. The tube reeked with the competing scents of their colognes: chemical earth versus chemical sky.

The arrival of these men on the island would be a kind of pollution, she thought, now that they were close around her and preparing to embark. First, Marilyn and then the surfers had come to the island, and they'd changed it. Marilyn's fears were responsible for the sharks. The surfers had made the island bigger and diversified the variety of plants and animals. These powerful men would shape it too. She could have tried to stop the demonstration, but Doreena desperately wanted it to work.

It had been too long since she'd seen the island. She felt brittle and afraid. She put her own desire ahead of the island's preservation. What good was it, if she wasn't there? She was already planning to escape to the far side of it, to find a way to another beach either the inaccessible one Alonso had seen or one he had missed. She would even climb up into the jungle if that were the only way. The workers closed the metal lid with a clanging staccato and sealed them inside.

"Now, we teleport," Dalton said.

The machine thrummed. Earnest took hold of her hand. The blue current flowed around them. Shapes circled in the dark around the scratching of The Stew's stylus. There were many sensations similar to the onset of her island. There was the hazy blue light of the Fermi sea. The claustrophobic press of bodies in the dark suctioned around her.

Earnest had told her a few different theories about how teleportation worked. The most likely, and most demonstrable, being that it was not a transfer of matter or particles at all, but a transfer of the information carried on them. He had described things that were very small, and she found hard to visualize. She did not have a scientific background, but what he said meshed with her own island experience. It was likely that she had not been transported to a new location at all, but simply copied, which explained how she continued to live her life on C-town. The information that made her had been replicated.

Then, Earnest had gone into a long and complicated philosophical discussion about the soul. Scientists, he said, had discovered a lot about matter and mind, but there was a level of understanding, between the microcosm and macrocosm, they could not grasp. Earnest called this, "the mysterious gap". Neuroscientists, in their studies of the brain, didn't know what caused consciousness. Quantum physicists, in their studies of matter, didn't understand the behavior of specks of it at the smallest levels. Earnest made it sound as if these two remaining mysteries were connected and about to be revealed.

In short, he could not say what had happened to her soul. Most likely, it did not replicate. "That's the no cloning theorem," he'd said. "Quantum particles can't be duplicated." But it might remain in two places at once entangled in C-town and on the island. The danger was decoherence, that the connection was fragile and if they tried to pin it down it might disappear altogether, he said.

Earnest explained about entangled particles, how bits could remain together acting in tandem even when separated. He used the term nonlocality; which meant that time and space did not matter. Doreena, who had always been discouraged from thinking about anything mysterious or theoretical, found these musings perplexing; except that it all fit within the realm of her recent experience. But she remained concerned about her soul. She had often felt like her soul had been split between the two places: C-town and the island. Often in C-town, she had felt soulless. A terrible thought occurred to her: What if she and the island had always been entangled, long before she'd ever actually experienced it? What if much of her soul had been living on the island unknown to her? This felt true. The idea resonated. There had been so many times that her grandfather and Tom and Marilyn had accused her of lacking something, some intangible quality, some passion, some happiness without which all her stalwart devotion fell short of some ineffable standard. They'd said the same thing over and over again bewildering and confusing her, now their words carried a clear meaning: they'd been calling her soulless.

In the AeroFlux teleportation tube, after a series of pulses, there was a single bang and then a painful pop passed between her ears. The lid clanged open. Dim light shone through the porthole. Doreena peered around Rock's shoulders wishing she had the strength to shove his bulk aside in her haste for the island, but something was wrong. The island was nowhere in sight or feeling. Cold air flowed in at them off the AeroFlux factory floor. Doreena thought she could collapse from weariness and the weight of her disappointment, but her body was so stiff it upheld her. The surfers, gray-faced, stood shivering. Their hands usually so languid at their sides, twitched with sadness. They looked cold and exposed even in their suits. Even Alonso and Hobart looked drained and fidgety.

The islanders were the flaw in Earnest's theory. While entanglement described her experience perfectly, it did not explain what happened to the islanders or Marilyn. They did not appear to live two lives while on the island. They disappeared from C-town returning to it exactly where they had left. Earnest had had other theories of teleportation. It was possible, for example, that it worked more like reincarnation. In order to teleport, a particle had to be destroyed and rebuilt. Maybe only the soul could teleport. Maybe that's what had happened to hers and where it had been all along. There were other ways it could work, but Earnest's science could not explain why she was different. Doreena thought she knew: It had to do with how she was tangled up in the island. It was her place, and they were only tourists. Their souls could visit, but not inhabit it. The failure of the demonstration proved it. It was her island, and it was gone.

She was the last to leave the tube leaning stiffly into Earnest, letting him help hold her upright. Rock took the stage. He applauded and the City Fathers joined him. "A marvelous demonstration. Truly. It reminds me what's at stake. We're not experimenting. We're preserving our way of life. That's something no outsider can appreciate. Although all you'd have to do to understand is step out onto the chaos of the 'Way, Mr. Rees here makes it seem like C-town is a prison, yet nothing prevents him from leaving. Certainly, we encourage him to go."

"We," he gestured at the silent teal tube, "cannot be affected by this machine. We cannot rely on technological solutions to innovate for us again and again and pull us back from the brink of disaster. That is not the answer. We all remember how that works. It may prevent us from plunging into the abyss, but we remain poised on the brink and eventually, inevitably, we fall. The spaceship, the new power source, the mining of another planet; you remember. All that saved us for a while. But eventually it imploded, and we plunged into economic ruin anyway. Even if this teleporter worked and brought us goods from the outside, it wouldn't do what you wanted it to do for long and it would create further dilemmas. The only thing that can prevent chaos, and make our society safe and sane and whole, is political will and personal responsibility. We draw a line in the sand, and we step back from the edge. We step back from the edge. We don't wait for a crutch, or a savior, or a mechanism to wrench us away. Citizens of C-town, the answers are within our grasp. All we have to do and continue to do is make choices. It is within our power to move: in our minds, our bodies, our hands."

His voice made the microphone redundant in the hollow hangar and as he spread his arms wide his hands, long and spatulate, the ends of them looked as if they could pull the room together. Beside him, Dalton looked reedy; with delicate hands suited to fine-tuning. In a tug-of-war, Rock Traynter would win.

Earnest squeezed Doreena's arm. "I was wrong."

"It was supposed to be possible," she said.

But Earnest's science seemed a flimsy thing now, just as Alonso's tulpa theory had seemed when she'd been in the very real jaws of the shark. Earnest's scientific reality was too fanciful, and Alonso's fancy was too real. Doreena didn't know what the answer was, but she didn't like feeling trapped in C-town when all she wanted was the island. It actually felt worse now that the surfers were with her, the opposite of what she'd been thinking and would have expected. It had been better when she could imagine others enjoying her beautiful place, better than imagining it emptied. The new plants and flowers that the surfer's thoughts had fertilized would be drained of life and left wilting and then rotting in the island sun.

"For the longest time," Rock continued. "We've struggled to keep our standard of living at accustomed levels. We've sacrificed. In a few months, we will be rewarded. Traynter Resort will open — all the luxury of the world in your backyard. The next time we meet, you won't be disappointed. Traynter Construction and Traynter Hospitality Services are hiring now. Turn in your applications today. Thank you very much for joining me here to see this very powerful demonstration. Nothing happens without *The Mirror*. We all see where we are truly going now."

The security guards let the surfers pass into the blue machine. They laid hands on Doreena at once and they kissed her, but nothing happened. Hobart and Alonso bent over the control panel, but the machine stayed silent.

Earnest held her. "So, there's no island."

"There is," Doreena said. "I've been."

"Are you sure?" Earnest said.

"Of course, she's sure," Alonso said. "We were there, too."

"All of you?" Earnest said. "You brought them all? Then how are you here?"

"Last night, we all landed in Traynter Lake not long after J-Bay left."

"You guys come back to where you left from," she said. "But I am always somewhere else."

She was still trying to get her mind around how the island affected her differently, what it could mean, and whether that was the key to getting it back. All she knew for sure was that neither science nor myth would transport her.

She remembered her argument with her grandfather when he'd abruptly left her for Maui. She'd felt betrayed that he planned to go without her. "But you always said, home is where I am." she'd said. "Where will home be when you are gone?" Where was grandfather now? When people died, they disappeared, he said. That was all. It hadn't bothered her at the time. But it did now. She clutched again at the empty space at her breast where her grandfather's ashes should have been. An idea came to her and then went when J-Bay interrupted it.

"Doreena," he said, and it was difficult to look at him because his face was so drawn with famine and the gray of C-town. "Where's my brother?"

"A-Bay and I left from the apartment," she said. "But the apartment isn't there anymore. It's been torn down. The third floor, all of it."

Doreena and the surfers walked across the street. They cupped their hands against the window of The Travel Museum. Everything was gone. The walls were bare brick, stripped of every poster.

"I can't believe I let it happen," Hobart said. "I should have been here. I said I'd come back. What did they do with it all?"

Next door, the construction workers were erecting the Lakeside Hotel, part of Traynter Resort, in the footprint of the Narborough. Doreena pointed to the empty sky where she'd held A-Bay close in the apartment. "There."

They stepped onto the site and wouldn't leave when the construction workers confronted them. "You can't be here without a hard hat. It's not for tourists."

The manager stalked toward them in a bright orange vest. When he looked up from under the shadow of his hard hat, he stared at J-Bay with a haunted look.

"I'm looking for my brother," J-Bay said.

The construction worker was stiff and silent for a long while with his hands hidden behind his back. "Your twin, must be," he finally said. "I'm sorry. We didn't know who to call. We found him this morning." He pointed at rubble beside a pile of steel girders. "We didn't know who he was." His voice dropped and he looked away from J-Bay. "They took the body to the morgue."

She looked at the surfers, cold and haggard and saddened by the loss of one of their own. It wouldn't be long now, she thought, until they would leave her. After, the island they wouldn't be able to make do with the cold waters of the lake. Doreena looked up at the drifting clouds. The island had placed A-Bay, its supplicant, in the empty sky and dropped him. This was what it was capable of: abandoning him and her and all of them, disregarding their safety and their fates. Still, no matter how uncertain she was of the island in principle, she still wanted it.

~ 16 ~

ROCK TRAYNTER'S RESORT

Withdrawal; the island abandons Doreena and her islanders

Doreena and her islanders came together again in the Labor Temple, in its dripping rooms permeated with silicon stench. They waited for the island to return. The drum circle went silent as soon as Earnest entered. The AeroFlux employee didn't belong here.

"It's OK," Alonso said to the islanders, as Doreena rose and followed Earnest into the hall. "She'll be back."

In the pressroom, Doreena leaned against the wall while Earnest talked. The presses were still and silent now. The *C-town Traveler* had been neglected and then abandoned. The islanders had given up.

"Nothing's going to change this place," J-Bay had said and not even Alonso or Hobart argued. But they still loved drumming; it was all they had left now that the lake was off-limits. The plaster shook as they resumed their beats.

"Come back to the apartment with me," Earnest said.

"I told you I'm waiting for the island. You don't believe me."

"I love you," he said. "Let's work this out. You said you were pregnant."

"Then I lied. And if I were, you might not be the father. Those guys in the next room, they've all been to the island all except you. How do you think they got there? We went together kissing and making love, our bodies connected, creating a magical island energy which you've never experienced. You couldn't with your cold steel tubes, your factory, and your machines. You broke it. My connection to the island was fragile you said. Now, it's gone."

"You're, this is, crazy. You're blaming me? I'm sorry, but I can't take this anymore. I've tried to help you for the baby's sake," Earnest said.

"Look at me, what baby?"

"Fine. I'm leaving. I won't ask you again." In the dripping hallway, his retreating figure grew shadowy as he walked upstairs to the street. "You said you heard voices." he called back, casting echoes. "Maybe you should see someone."

Alonso joined her in the hallway and wrapped his arms around her.

"If the island's a delusion, I still want to have it," she said. "I'm sorry I made you miss the last flight to Maui and now you're stuck here with me."

"It was my choice," he said.

The islanders that went out to work reported that C-town looked more C-town than ever. The Tiki-Tiki Lounge closed. They began to talk about leaving.

It was worse here without The Travel Museum and the lake to surf on, and still no sign of the island. "We were going to steal one of those flying cars," J-Bay said. "But they're gone too. The tunnel's empty. Still nothing?"

"Whatever it was, is gone," Hobart said.

"We can't stay here. I think we should take our chances out on the 'Way, just walk 'til we get somewhere. Anywhere's better," J-Bay said.

Hobart nodded. "If I thought I could, I'd go."

They looked to Alonso. He nodded. "We'll go, but let's get some things together first. I want us to have a chance at making it somewhere. Soon."

When Doreena left the Labor Temple, no one tried to stop her. The islanders, or maybe they were just surfers again, weren't like that. They were used to each other coming and going and finding their own way. They let each other make their own mistakes: like when Alonso had left the Thai set to follow the chick Jeanne to Tibet or J-Bay and A-Bay had tried to share the same girl in Cape Town or Lonnie had surfed the Tank Roll on a day when no one else would touch it and he went under forever. Everyone had known those decisions would bring pain, but that was life, and death was life, too. Loners came back to the tribe a little wiser, with scars to heal. Or, as in Lonnie's case, if they did not come back, the surfers all went out to the sea together to sit upright on their boards and link legs and tell the stories of a man's stoke quest through the night until the sun rose.

Doreena walked across town to see the condominium rise where grandfather's house had been. Staring at the crisp, beige squares of building over her childhood home and the absence of hibiscus, she felt empty and faint. She was neither hungry, nor thirsty, nor sleepy. There was nothing to take her mind off this either. She wished she could go to work. There, a feeling like this wouldn't even register. She returned to Traynter Tower. It was overcast and in the reflective surface of *The Mirror* building she stood: a yellow blur like a remote sun in the slick gray surface. She sank to the street, and huddled.

In the morning, the pressmen in their gray coveralls and then the sales force in their suits entered the building. No one looked her way or spoke to her. Rock's pea green car rolled up, its chrome fenders shining through the timid morning light, into its reserved space along the street. At night, a waft of silicon from the presses followed the men out. Doreena stuffed papers into her boots, now a grimy shade of yellow. She tucked her boot legs under her, pulled her capelet around her shoulders and insulated herself with silicon sheets. The headlines read "Traynter Resort: C-town's Paradise in Progress." She stared up into the pink glow of the phosphors and the dark line where the top of Traynter Tower intruded. The long, still night passed. When the sky began to gray, she rubbed her back. The ridges of the brick wall were etched along her spine.

That day, not long after he'd arrived, Rock Traynter left *The Mirror* building. The editor, Vic, followed him out.

"So sorry for your loss," he said.

"My son, my son," Rock said, pushing Vic away. He lurched toward his car; his feet twisted over each other, and his broad shoulders sloped to the street. A noise like a gull's cry rose from his throat as he hung on the open door of his car.

It was hard to see Rock like this, his stalwart form and voice eroding in waves of grief. Doreena watched the editor turn away. She knew at once what had happened, the only thing that could have affected Rock Traynter like this. Marilyn had miscarried. The bed rest had not saved his son.

Rock tore his shades from his eyes, both pairs in one fluid motion, and pressed his hands into them. There was a flash of light color: his eyes mounted in the winter sky. But, which: gray, violet, amber, green?

He sank into the car, head bowed. His black-suited leg stuck out of it trembling. "My son."

Then he looked up. It was as if he held the island in his piercing blue eyes. The color looked powerful enough to transport her and she wanted to go to him and find a way into his eyes, bright with sorrow. But her body was heavy and slack on the street. The car door slammed, and Doreena shrugged off her soggy translucent pink broadsheets. She bent her legs and, like an animal mired in mud, struggled to rise off the street. The muck-colored heels of her boots caught in a crack of the pavement, and she lunged forward. She lurched for the car as it pulled away, "Marilyn." She sat on her heels and brushed a skiff of dust away. It came from her side, moldy brown with a sheen of gold like the bottom of a dry creek bed. She picked at her clothes and a chunk of brown crumbled in her hand. She rose quickly and nearly fell. A ring of mud circled the place up against the building where she'd been sitting. Clouds of black gold dust drifted from her shoulders. It fell around her as she walked across town to C-town General. The doors opened automatically. She stepped into the sick place, crumbling.

"Marilyn Traynter," she said at the front desk, her voice raspy. "Marilyn Traynter's room."

The receptionist didn't acknowledge her but reached back for her sweater. "Hey Joe," she said. A security guard who'd been staring into a fish tank turned around. "You wanna' step out for a smoke?"

With the receptionist gone, Doreena used the computer herself to find Marilyn's room. She left smudges of golden-black glitter across at keyboard.

The room was on the third floor. She made her way up unnoticed. Marilyn sat in bed staring out the window. The color of the day was gone. Everything was white, as if all the color had congealed in Marilyn's black eyes. Even her hair, frizzed up against the pillow, had a dull cast to it. Doreena approached uncertainly, but Marilyn turned and regarded her at once. Doreena instantly felt more solid.

"Why didn't you come sooner?" Marilyn said. "They say that I have had a miscarriage, but they haven't been to the island, and they couldn't possibly know. What's happened to my boy is beyond the reach of medicine."

Doreena stared at the grime-filled lines in her hands and pushed her thumb across the powder. The muscle in her palm arched. The bones splayed across the back of her hand showing through her gray skin. "I'm so sorry. It's my fault."

"He's on the island. I left him there," Marilyn said, she reached her arms out. "Take me to him."

Doreena knew she meant the baby. Marilyn didn't know the island had left them without consolation. They had only each other. In sympathy, she bent close to Marilyn to let her arms enfold her. At first, it seemed Marilyn's arms might pass through her muddy clothes, but they finally caught her around and gripped her waist. But when the hospital room remained, Marilyn released her.

"It's gone," Doreena said. "Whatever it was, AeroFlux's experiments or the islanders' tulpas. We'll have to go on without it. There is no island now."

"No, my son is there," Marilyn said. "He is. Other things people want are there. Things not possible in C-town."

"Yes, but those are only small things: fruit."

"But he is small, so small, and like a kind of fruit."

Doreena was silent. She found herself wondering whether it was possible. There were still so many things about the island she did not know. Maybe they would open up one of the fruits on the island, a durian or a coconut, and find Marilyn's son inside it nestled like a seed. How could she argue with Marilyn? Why say it was impossible?

"I left him. How could I have done that?" Marilyn said, staring into her hands. "It was because I didn't want him trapped here. No one likes a cage. With even a little open door to Maui, we coped. We adapted. People do. But he shut us in completely. Stupid. You have to leave people a way out to make them feel safe and accept their containment. If you trap them, people will start looking for a way out and they'll find one, like rats. Try to close all the gaps and a new one opens. Leave an opening and the majority will stay in, they won't even notice." She looked up and her black eyes darkened. "That was your mistake, Rock. Shutting down those flights to

Maui. Hardly anyone could afford them anyway. You should have left them hope. Then I never would have gone to the island, and my son would still be here in my arms."

Doreena turned and saw the man behind her barricading the doorway. She clutched her hands to her chest. She wished for the ghost-like quality she'd had before, so that he couldn't see her, but her hands were cleaner now, her usual honey-brown tone coated with an ordinary layer of dirt. She was any laid off worker. And even though Rock's eyes were hidden again behind his double-glasses she could feel the vise of his attention. His fists were clenched. "Why are you here? Get out."

"Wait," Marilyn grabbed her wrist. "It's bullshit about AeroFlux and the Islanders. I've been there with you. You can get it back."

She scrutinized Doreena. Her gaze felt like girding. It made Doreena hold the posture of *The Mirror's* top salesman. "Where's that necklace? Your grandfather, you said. Blue. You vomited blue."

Doreena grasped at the air between her breasts again. "It's gone." She balled her hand into a fist. "Oh. Gone."

It had been in one of the twin's hands as they passed into the blue haze. Inside J-Bay's scarred fist. And then, A-Bay and J-Bay had fallen away from her. She'd dropped to the tiles in the Tiki-Tiki Lounge bathroom. A-Bay had fallen through the sky and J-Bay into the lake with all the other islanders after him once she had lost the necklace and their connection to the island.

"That's it," Marilyn said, whispering quickly. "You remember where you saw it last. Listen, my mother told me it's difficult for women to manage other women. We resist each other, the way we resist our mothers; because we see in each other what we dislike in ourselves. You see in me the cold reserve and the need for security that binds you. I see in you someone too adaptable and weak-willed to act independently. But we must accept ourselves now. We have to accept authority, but only so that we can learn to outgrow it. Do so now. It's not our fault we live in C-town and have had to operate within its perimeters. Don't punish the child for it. Go. Get the necklace. Bring back the island to me. My son is there, alone, and too small to forage, too young to eat fruit. Please."

"Get out," Rock said from behind them. He grabbed Doreena's arm and spun her toward the door. He looked startled when he laid hands on her. "I've seen you around. Stay away from *The Mirror* and my wife."

"But Rock, she can get us back to our baby. There's an island and I'm still pregnant there. I know I am. He's there. The doctors said there wasn't anything of him to bury. Nothing came out."

"Stop raving," he said. "You lost the baby, Marilyn. It's gone. It's over."

"No," Marilyn said. "He's there. I'm pregnant still. I am."

"She's more pregnant than you," Rock said.

Marilyn ignored him and pleaded with Doreena. "Promise me, you'll go back. Promise me you'll find him."

Doreena remembered how they had walked on the island beach, not holding hands exactly for it was too hot, but side by side with their fingertips occasionally touching.

"Of course, I will," she said, feeling the burden of the promise in her belly.

With that, Rock turned to her furiously. If Doreena had not seen his naked glistening pain-stricken eyes earlier, she would have thought him monstrous. "Find your own child. Ours is lost. Lost. Leave us."

He pushed her through the door, and she fell to her knees in the hallway. That morning, in her fragile state, such a push and a fall to the floor would have crumbled her, she had been close to becoming another layer of grime on the C-town street. Now she caught herself. The flesh of her hands and knees pressed against the mopped Formica. Talking to Marilyn had restored her solidness, although there would be a black-gold glittery cast to the bruises forming on her knees and a pit weighing in her center as if she had swallowed a stone.

The islanders hadn't left the Labor Temple. They'd stacked their backpacks in a corner of the room. When she told them about the necklace, Alonso and Hobart agreed to help her search the lake before they went. J-Bay threw up his hands. "I'm done."

"One last try," Hobart said. "There's something to it."

At night, they walked the three miles along the road and climbed the chain link fence to get to the shore. The marshes and cattails were gone, replaced by sands that glowed in the moonlight. Alonso massaged a handful of the coarse grains in pale green, pink and yellow. "A synthetic."

They entered the sanitized lake in wetsuits. The cool water held no smell. It thinly splashed her bare hands and face. They strapped lights to their foreheads like pilot fish and swam ahead into the beams. The phosphors in the grains of the synth sand, newly thick and three feet down, glowed as they combed through it.

"It will be further out," Doreena said. They couldn't see anything in the glow anyway.

"We landed far out," Alonso said.

The synth sand covered the bottom of the lake for 20 feet, but the same old muck lay at the lake's center. Its bottom was green-black gunk, a mixture of decomposed fish, algae, and C-town effluent. They dug through it raising particle-clouds into the murky water. The brownish silt looked like a dull version of the slough of her body on the street. They found a bicycle tire, rusty cans, glass bottles, fish bones, and folded remnants of *The Mirror* that swayed like kelp.

"When I get to the bottom, I've got just enough breath left in me to stir up the sediment," Hobart said when she surfaced. "Could be anywhere in there, buried. Or," she looked to shore, "Back there in that fake stuff."

"But we know it's here somewhere," Doreena said, casting an arc of moonlit waves as she turned round. "Somewhere in this circle."

"Unless it slipped through the filters," Hobart said. "The ones they're using to clean this. I'm sorry, but it was small enough. Are you even sure it was J-Bay grabbed it? Could be buried under that new hotel."

"I'm pretty sure I remember seeing the scar on his wrist," she said.

That first night of searching the three of them dove until the first gray tinge of daylight. On subsequent nights, they swam straight to the middle. Hobart tired after ten or so dives and waited for them on the shore. After a week, she stopped going with them.

"I still think it went through the filters," she said. "You're still trying? It's raining tonight. So, you really think it will bring back the island?"

"Either way, it's my grandfather. I should find it." Doreena said. She clutched the hollow of her chest. "I know it's there. I can see it, you know."

Alonso walked with her through the rain. She snagged her wetsuit on the chain link. The surface of the lake rose in onyx peaks but underneath the water her view of the cloudy bottom was no more obscure than usual. It was even a tinge warmer below the lake than above in the pelting rain. But they didn't find it that night. On Friday it was clear and Alonso dove with her again. She surfaced and found him floating on his back staring up. "Just resting. Beautiful moon. You should take a break, too."

"I can't stop looking when I know it's there," she said.

"I think you'll have to. This isn't good for you," he said.

Even without mirrors at the Labor Temple, she knew what he meant. She'd noticed the blue-gray cast to her arms and legs and how the dry cracks in her hands had swollen and filled in with overlapping lines. They hung at her sides like damp gloves. She'd become accustomed to the cold water; she never slept. She barely needed the headlamp anymore. She could see better in the dark and she'd begun, faintly, to glow like synth sand.

At the end of the next week, J-Bay said he was leaving. "Who's coming?"

"Wait," Alonso said. He threw a copy of *The Mirror* down on the floor in front of the islanders' drum circle. "Traynter Resort Opens July 20," the headline proclaimed in the biggest point type since the AeroFlux crash.

"One last try. In daylight." Alonso said.

"Fine. One," J-Bay said.

"That's all we've got. The public can come to the opening, then members only," Alonso said. "They'll keep us out."

On July 20, the islanders wore half-wetsuits leaving their arms and legs bare. They were ready to try the wave machines, only Alonso talked about searching the lake. Crowds covered the beach along the resort even early that morning. The new hotel fronts gleamed beyond. Vendors sold shaved ice, caramel apples, and chilled pears along the walkway. Nearby The Steelheads were setting up their marimbas. Boats zipped across the lake's surface close to the hotel. Parasails with rainbow chutes rose behind them. The place was pleasant, but uninspiring. The islanders ran over the multicolored faux sand with their boards overhead, slipped into the water and headed for the waves. Alonso and Doreena swam past them to the center of the lake. The water had been filtered to a clearish green like colored glass. Sunlight shone through the clouds of stirred silt as they searched. After several dives, they came up empty-handed.

Alonso came up for air and inhaled: a long anxious ah. "I still can't stay down long enough. We may not find it."

Doreena remembered looking for the necklace in the island's ocean when it had slipped through Marilyn's fingers. The water had been clear and lit. She remembered gliding back and forth over the rippled sand. When she'd returned with it, the giddy island flush was gone from Marilyn cheeks.

"You were gone so long," she'd said.

Doreena didn't remember that "ah" of inhalation or being out of breath when she'd come up from the island's ocean.

She dove again, this time without taking the many small breaths to permeate her blood with oxygen as Alonso had taught her. She imagined the fine links of the necklace's silver chain. She combed a large square of the lakebed muck with her fingers. Then, pressure wrenched her chest. She shot up to the surface and sucked air.

Alonso swam to her. "You, OK? I was worried. You were down so long."

"Don't," she said. "Let me look alone."

"What's wrong? Listen, we may have to accept it's just lost."

Doreena held up her hands. The sun shone through the gray, clammy edges of her skin. "Look. I can do this. I need you not to worry. I want to find it. Let me do this."

She went under before he could reply. His legs churned the water above. The pressure circled her chest. She fought to stay down: Just don't think about it. Find the necklace. He wants me to find it. The wetsuit weighed on her. It held her limbs close. She unzipped the suit and peeled it off. The water flowed over her bare skin. The disembodied wetsuit floated above her, its limbs dangling. She opened her mouth. A puff of sparkling blue billowed into the green lake. Yellow fishes appeared in the specks and grew as they swam. Her body, heavy and fluid, began to sink. She followed the fishes down to the murky lakebed.

She reached for the first glint of silver, expecting it to flash away from her hand. It stayed. She tugged at a buried loop and a bright chain uncoiled from the drenched loam. A vial floated on the end of it. She rose with the necklace in hand and broke the surface in silence. Alonso swam to her, and she could not read the expression on his sunlit face. His hands were cool on the back of her neck as he fastened the necklace for her. They swam together past the boats with water-skiers and parasailers toward the celebration on the shore. The islanders glided off the wave machine induced crests to follow them when Alonso beckoned.

On shore, the islanders crowded around her to hide her nudity. Loudspeakers screeched and spread a distortion of voices over the crowd as the ceremony began. There were familiar faces in the throng, members of the salesforce, barely recognizable, out of uniform, in linens and Hawaiian shirts. They raised flutes of sparkling wine. Marilyn stood beside Rock and the City Fathers, in dark suits, and their wives, in floral dresses, on a platform in the center of a swimming pool. The color of the day was gray. A plane flew overhead trailing a Traynter Resort banner and leaving a wake of colored smoke across the cool blue sky.

On the beach, Doreena opened the vial and dumped the contents of the necklace into her hand. The ashes were gray as the lake bottom. She took a pinch between her finger and thumb. She would not risk being parted from her grandfather, or the island, again. Like charcoal, the first pinch caught in her throat. The next was flakier and saline. Pinch by pinch, she ate the ashes. The last few were pink and sweet like saltwater taffy. Finally, she licked the traces of sweet blue that stained her hand. She looked up past the blue tip of her tongue at Earnest.

"I thought I'd find you here. I've missed you," he said.

A faint blue haze ebbed into the edges of her vision.

"It's coming," she said. "The island. Get me to Marilyn. I promised I'd bring her."

Alonso pressed her back, Earnest held onto her arm and the islanders surged forward through the crowd. She could hear Rock ahead of them his voice reverberating through the microphone giving the kind of speech one would expect, filled with the same pride-filled language of Founder's Day, all about C-town: unity and strength, loyalty, and tradition. As they neared the front of the crowd, Doreena could make out Marilyn standing on a stage erected on a platform across a swimming pool. But there was some of kind of commotion ahead of them in addition to the fanfare of the resort's opening day.

Suddenly there was a swath of green around her, as though she had stepped into the jungle and was running through it. A group of people near the front of the crowd had unzipped their coats and shrugged them off to reveal their green union sweatshirts. Their shouts rose over Rock's voice, tinny through the microphone. At first, she thought, they were yelling, "Fight, fight, fight!" and Doreena was afraid that if fists flew, she and the islanders might never make it to Marilyn. But as the voices coalesced. They gained strength and resonance. They were saying, "Flight." Not, "Fight." "Flight, flight, flight, flight," they chanted. "The future is flight!"

They raised white-backed posterboard signs, blocking Doreena's view of the stage. "Marilyn," Doreena shouted and the islanders echoed her. They continued to push her through the waves of bodies with white placard crests. They broke through the crowd and waded into the pool towing her along past people standing in the water, drinks in hand: Dalton Rees, Rock, and the City Fathers. Marilyn reached for her, bending down from the stage. Rock was behind her with his arm around her waist, pulling her back. "Stay back. She's crazy."

Sparkling wine splashed from Marilyn's cup down to Doreena's outstretched hand and bubbled through the raised hairs on her arm. They stretched fingers toward each other. Doreena felt a hand on her thigh, Alonso's, lifting her up and Hobart pushing at her side. With a pang in her abdomen, Doreena stood in the center of the mass of reaching people as the blue haze dropped and the tentacles of the island grabbed hold and yanked.

The suction squeezed her tight. It juiced her making every drop of her island. Through the blue haze she could see the jumble of them; the salesforce, the union protesters, and the islanders; the City Father and their wives; Tom, Diane, and Marilyn; Rock and Dalton; and Earnest and Alonso. She could see the front of the protest signs: "Maui forever!" "Jobs now!" and "The future is flight!" They were all touching someone who was touching her. Those desperate to be caught up in the chaos and those desperate to avoid it all tumbled toward the island. Some of the islanders had grabbed green bottles of sparkling wine as the haze dropped. They lifted them to her, grinning.

$\sim$ 17 $\sim$

THE CAVE

A surrogate mother, Doreena gives birth

They arrived on the beach in the middle of a hurricane. The wind, keening, whipped around Doreena. Her hair flew across her face. She held a handful of it aside and peered out at the crashing waves beyond the gritty, streaks of air. The ocean churned rank with the contents of its upturned depths, seaweed, and decaying fish. Up the beach, palm leaves slashed from the ends of bowed trunks. Sand shot into her eyes. She shoved her fists into them until tears came. A hand grabbed her shoulder.

"Is this it? Your island?" Earnest said.

Her hair whipped forward to curtain their faces. They shouted to hear each other over the pained wail of the wind.

"The others. The others are here," she said.

He pointed up the beach and she began to crawl. Through the pelting rain, a cluster of people huddled in knots across the sand with their heads ducked to protect their faces. Most were naked, their backs gray and the bones of their spines arcing up to meet the whips of sand. Others, an opaque hunch of shoulders, still wore their suits. The City Fathers and Rock began to rise. The sleeves of their suits hung with the weight of the rain. The naked ones lifted pale faces. The Stew unwrapped his body from around a camera. A harsh light swept over them. Doreena shielded her eyes.

Rock squinted. His eyes were naked crystal blue. "What is this?"

"It's not usually like this," Doreena said.

"We need to get out of this storm," Earnest said.

Doreena pointed to where she knew the trail began. A field of slick vegetation thrashed around the opening, hiding it. "Follow me."

Marilyn's shoulder brushed Doreena's. The color of the day was white. One hand fingered her pearls and the other lay across her flat belly marbled with stretch marks from where it had expanded more rapidly than her flesh could follow. Marilyn had hoped to be pregnant again on the island. She was not.

"My son is lost," she said.

"It's my place," Doreena said. "I am the one who is entangled in two worlds at once. I am the only one who can carry it inside of me."

Suddenly, Doreena's belly swelled. It felt like unfurling. Her belly blossomed, then it gained weight. It hung low and stretched until it looked ready to burst. Doreena pressed her hands to it. When she did, she could feel the entire island inside her, but when Marilyn looked at her the island kicked, and she was a surrogate mother about to give birth to Marilyn's child. The first contraction rolled Doreena like a wave. She fell forward, legs splayed in a lurching step. Sparkling fluid gushed between her thighs. It splashed a blue lined pattern across the sand and pooled. Doreena grabbed Marilyn's arm and pulled her to the trail. "Shelter."

She took a last look back at the beach before they ducked under the thrashing branches. By the sea, the surfers, with their black arms raised, were dancing. In the center of them, Alonso leapt. His whoop rose over the wind. His arms and legs scrawled across the sky. The wind caught him, and he hovered before he dropped to earth to leap again.

Up the trail, the lagoon beside the cave bubbled with sand. Eggy steam rose off its surface and the keening wind gained words, "Come see me. Come see me." Doreena pulled Marilyn into the cave. The warmth of it stifled like *The Mirror* office. With each step, the ceiling of the cave lowered, and the heat and sulfur grew. They went deep into its low angle where a black, damp moss coated the stone walls. Doreena sank to the cave floor with her back against stone so hot it burned when she shifted. She could barely see her arms and legs in the darkness, only the rise of her belly and its pale glow.

Rock had followed Marilyn up the trail, with the City Fathers huddling after him, too frightened to be left alone on the beach and depending on Rock, as always, to lead them to safety and shelter. But the men stopped when another round of contractions sent Doreena's cries echoing off the cave walls. They stood in the entrance to the cave blocking the light and leaving the women inside to their mysterious business.

Marilyn touched fingertips to Doreena's forehead. "You're going to have my baby. Just breathe."

Doreena clenched her fists. She did not have to breathe, or eat or sleep, but this task required the anatomy she had played with and pretended to have as a child. This was not the time to relinquish that. She puffed; she panted; she tilted her chin to the roof of the cave where the dark fuzz of rock above her shifted. Two glinting ovals appeared, and the rock grew features and became familiar. She knew that face, those three long lines across the forehead and that sun-darkened spot beside the cheekbone where she had liked to kiss and inhale the traces of hibiscus pollen.

Between her legs, Marilyn's fingers brushed her opening. "I see him. That's right. He's coming now. Push."

Grandfather's head and shoulders pushed through the ceiling of the cave. His hands slipped free of the rock and reached for her. His arms were angled and black, then round and blue and finally his familiar shape and flesh color. The rock singed Doreena's back. Her ankles were in a vise. Marilyn screamed and backed into a crook of the cave. Doreena caught grandfather's hands, warm and soft, in hers and pulled herself closer to him again.

"I've missed you. Is this where you've been? I thought you were gone."

"I was supposed to grow old and die," he said. "People do. I tried to follow the rules and managed to make myself age in the normal way. It wasn't hard to be what people expected. When they saw an old man, they didn't pay me much attention. But I didn't know how to make myself die. What we are does not have a lifecycle with such an obvious beginning and end. I didn't want you to have to care for me through some long illness that would have been a lie. I just wanted to disappear so that I wouldn't worry you. But I never have had the strength to let you alone. And I could not completely leave you."

"Tell me who I am," she said.

"We are inorganic helical structures made of plasma with a collective consciousness. We had never experienced an individual identity until Leonid Moriena joined us. He and his family died a long time ago, but his desire to know you was so strong that our empathic systems responded to his pain and preserved his identity. To fulfill his desire, we created the first individual among us: Doreena Flora Moriena. We learned "I". But it felt wrong, to be one person in a unified world. I saw us as a kind of pollution, hardening the place. But I did not want to give you up, so I brought you here to C-town to hold you in place and protect the rest of them. I wanted to keep you, but it was selfish, and I am sorry."

"You could have told me," Doreena said.

"If I had, it would have changed you."

"What about my mother?"

"Don't you see? She doesn't exist."

He pulled his hands from hers and the flesh color pulled away with them. His hands were gray and black underneath a hard sparkling shell beneath a thin flesh tone.

"Wait," she said, and her words held him steady above her. "Stay for the birth of your great grandchild."

"There's no child," he said. "You shouldn't be doing this."

Doreena pointed at Marilyn who, overcoming her fear, had begun to move closer. "But I am."

While they had talked, Hobart had joined them crawling back into the cave beside her. She took Marilyn's place between Doreena's legs. "I've got it. We're in new territory here."

When the baby finally exited her body, it came out in an easy gush, Hobart held it up. There was no umbilical cord. Strands of deep blue crisscrossed its tiny body.

Marilyn grabbed for it. "My boy. My baby boy."

Hobart pushed her aside and laid the baby on Doreena's belly. It huddled there, its skin a translucent pale blue tingling silently.

"Is he OK?" Marilyn asked.

Hobart leaned close to Doreena. "She's not breathing."

"Yes, she is," Doreena touched the child's back and its lungs lifted under her hand. Grandfather's hair had begun to fall. It drifted down in blue sparkles.

"Tell me the truth," she said.

"You don't want to know."

"I do," she said.

"Then I must tell you she was an ugly thing. We became her, but she grew stiff and hard among us, she clung so fiercely to her shape. She wanted everything to be like it had before on her own planet. I smashed your father and then I smashed her too. I destroyed them, but I coveted you. I took you from her arms. I held on to you when I should have let you go returning to the fluid blue, the electrically charged plasma sea. When I took you to C-town and you grew up and began work *at The Mirror* I could see you becoming like your mother. I thought I wanted you to be solid and permanent, but when I saw the dark reflection of your mother in your face, I felt only regret. I wondered what you could have been, if I hadn't been so afraid of losing you."

The keening voice rose commanding Doreena to come deeper into the jungle.

"Isn't that her?" Doreena said.

"No. Now, listen, you've recreated Doreena. What will you do to her this time? Who will she please?"

The wind blew against grandfather. It carried away his flesh-toned surface, revealing t the dull gray, then navy and amethyst, jade, and light blue agate, and finally the palest blue particles swirled away in the wind. Shimmering blue showered her and the baby. Doreena, he'd called the child, too.

"Then who?" Doreena asked. "Who is up there, above us?"

"We must soften. We all go together." His face crumbled down to his lips, the powder of them caked and the words fell with them, "soft, soft."

With grandfather gone, Marilyn grew bold and approached. She lifted the baby off Doreena's chest and powder fell. Doreena unclenched her hands and two handfuls of pink powder dropped with a shifting sigh.

"Put it back." Hobart said. "It needs to nurse."

Marilyn placed the baby at Doreena's breast, leaving her hand on its back. Doreena sat up to see it. It was a boy now: warm, pink, and mewling. He suckled at her breast. He might grow up and ask, "Who is my father?" Would she tell him Alonso, Earnest, one of the surfers, Rock? How would she explain? He would be uncomfortable and awkward in his humanity as she had been. She would evade his question fearing to distort him with the truth. Answers would never give him a solid sense of sureness. Like rain on sugar, information would dissolve him. She understood now why grandfather had never explained her identity. He barely understood it himself. They were alien to each other and, also, made of the same stuff.

A rumbling erupted from deep within the cave. A belch of sulfur filled the air with a scalding steam.

Hobart pulled Doreena to her feet. "Get away from the cave," she yelled to the others.

Outside, the voice said, "Come, come. Don't make me wait any longer. I am his heart."

Doreena wanted to run to this voice. Nothing would stop her from reaching her mother.

~ 18 ~

CLIMBING

Doreena discovers an island of skin

The women were all outside when the shaking earth collapsed the cave. Its wet rock maw crashed closed. The wind whipped by them, and the voice cut through it crying, "Come see me." The lagoon roiled. Marilyn, focused only on the newborn's face, held the child up to Rock. "Our boy. It's him."

"Their skin. I see. All the colors, in there." Rock turned away as if blinded.

The child's skin changed colors as they examined it. The child had yet to make a sound, but the shifting colors wailed at Doreena. When Marilyn spoke, it looked apricot pink. When the City Fathers looked on, it faded to shades of ashen gray. The child had been Marilyn's idea, but now Doreena reached for it.

"Give it to its mother," Hobart said.

"Please," Rock said. "You can see that is not our child."

Marilyn's features stiffened into her sales manager mask. Her lips all but disappeared as she handed the baby to Hobart, who passed it to Doreena. "You have to nurse him," Marilyn commanded, but she looked lost with her arms still outstretched. "He's cold without a blanket."

Doreena remembered all the blankets Marilyn had unwrapped and held up at her baby shower in light yellows, pinks, and blues. There were none here. There had been no preparation for this birth. As she brought the baby to her breast, Earnest peeled off his jacket exposing his thin shoulders to the wind. It pressed into his white shirt and the whorls of his chest hair showed through the thin cotton. He swaddled the baby in the suit jacket. It still held oil and cleanser smells as it had when he'd pressed it around her after her car accident outside AeroFlux. He'd thought she was stuttering from shock, and it had felt nice to be cared for then. With him standing close, she almost thought she could parent this child that clung to her breast. Then sated, the child released. Her breast dripped a sparkling blue liquid that shared only the density of milk. The child's mouth shone with it. The voice screamed again, and Doreena began walking up the trail. She could not mother this child in ignorance. She had to know her history, how everything fit together. Wet leaves brushed her body as she began to push through them.

A thunderous sound shook the jungle, but the report came from a precise point on the trail behind her instead of filling the sky. Doreena turned back toward it and Alonso and Earnest followed. The color of the day was dusk gray. Marilyn wore an abrasion of stress across her taut face. The revolver waving in Rock's hand shone silver and surprising as the inside of an oyster shell. The things people brought to the island. They clung to the objects that made them feel secure. She'd arrived naked and empty-handed but for grandfather's ashes. Marilyn had brought her pearls, Diane still wore seven-shades of eye shadow, the surfers brought boards and wetsuits, the union workers had their signs and sweatshirts, the City Fathers had their suits and Earnest his tweed jacket. She'd expected Rock to have his glasses, the double-layers protecting his sensitive color-blind eyes from the light, but his eyes were unguarded. Instead, he had this weapon in hand.

"Here?" Doreena asked.

"Some kind of devil," Rock said.

A body lay face down across the trail. A red wound peeked between the plucked pink nubs in its back. Blood trickled from the hole into the rust red of the trail. Hobart turned the wounded man over. Dalton's slack eyes looked up at them. The AeroFlux executive had arrived on the island with vestigial wings.

"Take him down to the beach." Doreena said. The islanders hoisted him. The earth rumbled and Doreena turned back up the trail. She had to get to mother and get answers before the place fell apart.

"Where's she going?" Rock said behind her. "We should all go back to the beach and try to signal a ship."

"There's no ships in a place like this. Surely you can feel that? It's her," The Stew said. "You have to touch her to get back."

Doreena hurried up the trail. Rock was coming now, after her, the revolver in hand. She fell up and then slid down the path, mud coating her legs up past her knees. Alonso caught her arm and pulled her up in one swift motion, she went lightly to her feet momentarily weightless. She stepped into the greenery along the side of the trail and a mash of vegetation and mud formed a crust around her feet until at the top of the trail her feet slapped stone. She climbed a series of ledges until her thighs ached. Drying strands of blue afterbirth clung to them. They looked like external veins on top of her translucent skin.

She was turning into one of her childhood dolls, her seven invisible women. She saw now grandfather's reasoning: he'd wanted her to learn anatomy so that she would grow correctly on the inside. She wasn't sure now if she had. She'd never been sick, and yet, she'd given birth. She cradled the pale blue, shallow-breathed baby inside the suit jacket. Hot as stone, the child radiated heat. Through the jacket, her fingers burned, but she hugged the babe closer. It reminded her of the heater blasting her fingers around the steering wheel. The baby was so hot she could hardly bear it, but if she let go, she was afraid she'd lose direction.

The City Fathers grunted, tearing through the foliage as they came behind her. At the top of the trail, the jungle opened and dark sky showed through the slats in the broad leaves. Alonso reached from behind and parted them. Wind blew in. Diane, Alonso, and Earnest stepped into the clearing after her. They were drenched and smeared with mud. Moss and bark crowned Alonso's matted curls. Doreena brushed fuzzy wisps of tangled green out of her eyes. A clearing of lawn ran right down to a bluff. The manicured swath looked like grandfather's front lawn, but the sea crashed below, and the air smelled singed and salty.

Alonso brushed her shoulder and pointed left at a tower of land inclined into the sky. Clumps of green wound around its base but thinned towards the top to sparse tufts in rock clusters. A plate of stone angled down from the top. A bolt of faint blue struck the pinnacle, illuminating two spires. The voice called down.

"I hear it too," Alonso said. "Up there."

"Mother," Doreena said.

"Get back here. Get us out of here," Rock said. He stood with the City Fathers in the clearing and smeared red across his thighs as he wiped his muddy hands on his slacks. Doreena began to climb the hill stepping on the patches of grass between the stones. She held the baby in one arm and used the other to steady herself as she ducked low to the rocks, so the wind rushed over her back. She would reach her mother.

"Enough," Rock said, turning to The Stew. "Bring her down."

"I don't work for you here," The Stew said.

As Doreena climbed, the incline narrowed and grew rockier. In the dim light, it was difficult to tell which rocks were solid handholds and which stones would crumble when she reached for them. Doreena clung to the tower of land, Alonso beside her. Earnest and Rock followed below.

Where the tower became more sky than stone, Earnest stopped ascending. "I can't," he said.

Rock searched for handholds. "I can't see where to put my hands."

On the lawn, The City Fathers held Marilyn back. She strained between them leaning into the wind.

Doreena climbed dangling the baby. With each hoist, the ground dropped away, and the wind rushed in. Alonso climbed beside her. "We can make it."

A shot fired behind them. This time, Doreena knew the lonely sound came from Rock's revolver. It was there in his hand. He had stopped climbing to fire it. A hole gaped in her thigh and red trickled out like it had from the wound between Dalton's pubescent wings. She moved the leg and pain flared through it. The block of flesh hung. It wouldn't bear weight. She wouldn't be able to go higher. She would never know who she was or where she came from. She would have to go down now, as Rock wanted, to take them all back to C-town where everything would be the same as when they had left it, nothing changed. She would feel the same way as she had before: awkward, trapped and stifled but now she would be aware of it and there would not be even one escape.

"Do you want me to take her?" Alonso said.

Doreena held the baby in one arm swaddled in the suit jacket. "No."

"You have beautiful tears," he said. "You could bottle them."

The tears evaporated as the wind burned across her cheeks. Glittery traces flew through the air in front of her. Doreena bent her head to the baby and whispered. "I won't let it hurt you."

She looked down at her thigh and watched the red deepen to purple. It shimmered out of the wound. There was so much she'd found she hadn't needed: hunger, thirst, sleep, breath. Of all those irrelevancies, pain was the hardest to release. She'd always been uncomfortable encased in her skin, uncertain how to stand or where to put her hands every time she'd been in Marilyn's office. She'd strained to make the movements that seemed so natural to others, to go out to lunch, to talk. This pain seemed an extension of that. Discomfort was the way she moved through the world. It clamped her into place as she walked the streets of C-town. But what scared her most was how much she'd grown to need it, even as she grew numb to it. Without pain, she wouldn't need release and the island wouldn't matter. She wouldn't want it so much anymore.

Still, she let the pain go because she wanted to see what would happen if she allowed herself to be different. It faded. The wound with its deep blue core remained. She reached for a higher rock and pressed her foot into a step above. Her leg renewed, braced her. Alonso stared at her the way he watched an approaching wave, more awed than afraid. It was just the expression she must have had the first time she'd gone to the island and found herself standing on the sudden stretch of sand, wanting to take all the sun inside of her.

She had arrived effortlessly, immediately, and naturally. She had allowed that feeling to wash over her again and again: This is who I've been all along. But it hadn't lasted. The island hadn't been something she could control, and she had never been alone in her desire for it. They were all looking for an untamed place like this: the surfers, the City Fathers, the sales force, the AeroFlux executive, Rock and Marilyn. They were all refugees and they'd stirred the island up.

"I never, ever, ever wanted to leave the beach," she said. "All I wanted was to stay there. I would have stayed and stayed."

"I know," Alonso said. "I get that."

Her legs lifted her up to the top of the island. More gunshots and shouting chased her through the air, but the bullets missed her, and she climbed steadily up. Alonso followed. The wind met them at the top of the plateau with a push. The slab of rock, shining wet with rain, capped the jungle mount. Violet lines ran through the gray stone, the same dark color as the billowing clouds above. Thunder shook the hillside and far off clouds flashed white underbellies. Most of the island, surrounded by dark sea, was visible. Jungle green cut down its side. The cave lay far below under a distant overhang and a deeper emerald patch marked the location of the lagoon. The beach, however, was hidden. She imagined it calm and empty but remembered her islanders had taken Dalton there. His body lay somewhere on it bleeding. Still, the beach was the safest place on the island. Maybe the only safe place anywhere.

The City Fathers huddled at the base of the pillar. Rock, once he had emptied the gun, had climbed back down to them. He stood like a column with his arms crossed over Marilyn. Earnest clung to the stone, white, where she had left him. The plateau she and Alonso stood on stretched wider than the island below, a teetering black plate. An onyx path led to crumbled stone ruins where the two pillars stood. Doreena and Alonso followed the path and stood beneath them. They were two statues, seated on rock thrones, with familiar features etched on their chiseled faces. Doreena knew them from her grandfather's description.

"My parents," she said.

She listened for their voices, but even the wind silenced. Doreena took Alonso's hand, and they walked around the statues. There, a woman, with powder blue skin, sat. A pale blue hibiscus blossom held waves of hair behind her ear.

"Grandmother," Doreena said.

"Come sit, child." Grandmother patted the grass. "Put Doreena down."

Doreena knelt and set the baby down on the lawn. She crawled toward the woman, kittenish.

"Your grandfather brought you to Maui because it was so soft, on island time, with everything in motion. You were thriving but growing more and more autonomous and independent, foreign, and hard for us to understand. You wanted to touch everything, and we were forever pulling you back and reforming your fingers and afraid of losing you. We teach our own to tune — *zza, zza, zza* — to the vibration of togetherness. But for you, he carried a pocketful of stones and shells and when you got too excited sat you down and made you count them to keep you focused on each separate object and make you solid in yourself. But that place was too loose and flowing. Time and space and individuality were subdued. So, he took you away to a place where it would be easier to contain you in rules and schedules and borders. He suffered there; except he loved you. When he was lonely, he'd watch the hazy motion of the hummingbird wings that reminded him of home. And we stayed here on this island of our own and waited."

"What happened to my parents?" Doreena said.

"Your mother's dying thought was water, your father's too. We don't know anything as certain as death only hard and soft the way water can be. They are not those statutes, but the sea that surrounds us. Leonid thought he killed them, but he only destroyed his own idea of them: the part of them that only cared for self-preservation. It grew hard and stiffened everything it touched. Your grandfather wanted to save the softness in us, but he wanted you too. We could feel you starting to solidify in C-town, becoming uncomfortably stiff and slow. We brought you here to help you and now feel."

The woman touched Doreena's chest and she felt the slosh, slosh of waves in her breast. "We missed you. We are always with you. We came to find ourselves again, explorer."

Grandmother looked at Alonso. "Some are soft inside. Some are stiff."

"Like my mother and father?" Doreena said.

"Like fear. Your grandfather was afraid to see you as you could have become on Maui. Like this," Grandmother swept her pale blue hand across the lawn.

A mound of blue powder lay on the grass where the baby had been. Doreena could see the movement in its dust, the constant flow beneath the surface of a calm sea. She reached for the child and black sparks shot across the loose surface.

Grandmother's hands clenched the grass. "Mustn't fear."

Doreena reached for the baby and stroked the soft pile until its back reappeared. Its tiny limbs reformed. Then she picked it up and held it. She thought this baby pink and human again. She held it to her breast. "Is this what happened to me?"

"Yes. Your grandfather held you. He wanted to know you," the grandmother said, weaving vines with trumpet-shaped blossoms through the grass. "But you were never really born, we made you out of us, a kind of cultural misunderstanding. We did not under- stand individuality, really. You were always unhappy alone. We're going home now. Will you come be with us?"

Doreena plucked at the grass: smooth and slick and spiked. Am- ber light outlined the rolling clouds above. Alonso held her hand.

"I'm too stiff now," she said. "Too human."

Grandmother reached for Doreena's right hand. She held it in hers. "Relax." She shook Doreena's hand and stroked her palm. As she did so, Doreena's skin paled and stretched smooth and pools of cobalt blue appeared in the center around a remnant of flesh with the faint trace of her heart line across it. Alonso anchored her left hand. It tingled in his tight grip.

Grandmother dipped her fingertip into the pool in Doreena's palm. Waves flowed in over the island of skin. "We are together. Explore more but stay soft." Grandmother gazed up at the pillars, which flashed gold and then darkened to burnished black. "The stiffness must go."

As Grandmother dissipated in a blue haze, Doreena felt dust falling on her face and hands. The thrones were crumbling, toppling to dust. The sky boomed. Doreena and Alonso began to run down the incline. It slid with them becoming less steep with each step. They rejoined the citizens of C-town who stood now at the edge of the bluff. Behind them oncoming rolling dunes of black gold dust enveloped the mountain, the stones, the trees, and the jungle.

"Get us out of here," Marilyn said. Her voice felt hard like stone.

"Doreena?" Alonso asked, and his voice ran over her like water.

"I'm not going back," Doreena said.

"You have to," Marilyn said, she reached for the baby. "We have to go. We can't stay here."

Doreena looked over the side of the cliff. Far below was another beach, a half circle of white around a bay filled with white water cresting over the pink sand at the bottom of the red and white striated cliff. It was the last calm untouched spot; the place she had wanted to get to when she was bound to the crates freighting cargo from the island to C-town. Now that she could see it, it seemed difficult to get to, though not impossible. Could she fly down to it or sail around to it from the side? There would be flowers below and another grove of fruit and she and Doreena could live there peacefully if no one would ever bother them. But a human child couldn't grow there in such a soft place. That was the reason her grandfather had taken her away from Maui. The baby would dissolve into pink sand and blue water, and she would go with it.

Or she could take this child back to C-town, where it would relive her own life. She could never raise this child to understand itself differently. She saw how it would grow up into the same solid uncertainty as she herself had. She could see the baby standing here at the edge of some other precipice or maybe the exact same precipice and also trying to decide. It was not unique. It was part of herself. She could give it to Marilyn to raise, but she knew in a way she had already done that, given herself over to *The Mirror*. They would mummify the child to hold it in place. She looked around at the islanders, Hobart and Alonso, they could care for her, but they would not know how to raise a child in C-town. This new Doreena would get no further in understanding than she had, if she could not help it begin its life at some further point of discovery.

"We don't need her to get back," Marilyn said to Rock. "Touch the baby."

It was true that they needed a way back and she was the only one who could provide it. Doreena leaned far over cliff, she held up the child, a baby girl again now as when she had been born, parted her arms and let her drop between them. Immediately, Marilyn began to scream. Doreena's mind went with the baby as it fell and she felt herself in two places at once: falling from the cliff and standing upon it. As the baby fell, its shape grew nebulous, and she felt the passing rush of wind and the fearlessness of her fall through the sky towards the sea, which looked both hard and soft from a distance. The red and white striped cliff running down to the sea passed like scenery. After the first few tense, disorienting moments, she began to enjoy the glide.

Then Marilyn leapt off the cliff after it, and Rock teetered on the edge. "Damn it, woman."

He spun and jumped, flailing. Marilyn's fingers stretched toward the child, but midway through the sky the blue blur of it stopped as if it had hit a wall. A swath of blue blanketed the dark sky, calm washed over Doreena, and then it was gone. That part of herself she had cast away, burst into a portal over the sea holding a door open to C-town. Another boom shook the island, but everyone stared at the infant light and the would-be parents falling toward it. Marilyn hovered in the sky above the blue nebula and Rock caught her up and held her. They swung in the sky together around the sparkling sea of air and then slipped through. The portal shuddered and contracted as they entered it. The light flashed out, then reappeared, a blurry teal glow over the sea.

"You have your way back." Doreena said to the others. "Leave me and my island alone."

The mountain behind them thundered and now the air grew thick and hot and sulfurous. Black plumes of smoke rose over the towering cliff. The Stew leapt first, followed by all the suits and the reporters and the union workers, naked and clothed. The sea below looked hard and flat, but they all took leave of her in their way and blinked through the wavering portal. Even the ones who fell short were sucked into its tide. Finally, only the islanders stood beside her on the precipice.

"Time to move on to the next waves," Alonso said.

Hobart led the way. "Come on," she said, and the islanders followed her, diving off the cliff into the portal's center. They left Doreena, Diane, Alonso, and Earnest alone on the cliff.

Earnest took Doreena's hand. He pulled her toward the cliff. "I love you. Come back with me," he said.

Doreena released him as he neared the edge. He tumbled back over it. His limbs flailed as the portal took him in.

"I'll stay with you," Alonso said with an easy shrug. The corners of his eyes and mouth were slightly raised as always. Behind him lay the crumbled ashen remains of her island.

"Let's go back down to the beach, one last time, anyway," she said.

"Is it still there?" Alonso asked.

"I want it to be," she said. "So, yes, I think so."

~ 19 ~

THE ISLAND AT NIGHT

Experiencing Mirror Island at night

With the others gone, and Earnest still plummeting toward C-town, the eruption of the island stilled. Its decay blew out over the cliff on a zephyr. The spot in the sky, the infant pool, blinked out. Translucent darkness replaced the opaque smoke and billowing ash. The rumbling faded. The black-gold dust cleared into a gold-starred sky and the sea-struck air cooled. A current of jasmine cut through the sulfurous fumes. A purple nimbus around the moon glowed over the ocean. The sea lay like black silk with rumpled, pearly waves.

Doreena and Alonso turned from the cliff, hands clasped. Pawing animal noises came from behind the jungle leaves, where insects began to whir and sing. In the dark, Doreena couldn't distinguish between the red of the trail and the green of the leaves. Was this the way the jungle had looked to Rock? With each step down the trail, she stumbled as if on the edge of some dark pit. Curled fronds brushed her bare arms too tender to catch her. She no longer trusted the solidity of the land beneath her feet — the island was a transient, a traveler.

Heading down the jungle path in the dark was more frightening than falling toward the sea. The blackness flowed around her arms and legs, and it looked like the dark beneath her feet could drop away. Each step surprised her, when the island stayed firm with just the give of mud and moss beneath her feet. She and Alonso began to run plunging headlong into the dark. Ferment rose near the opening to the beach. In the fruit grove, huge luminescent eyes watched.

"Those eyes," Doreena said.

"It's a lemur. He looks a little like The Stew."

Near the opening to the beach, they examined a body-shaped indentation of sand, stained and tacky with drying blood.

"Where's Dalton?" Doreena asked.

Alonso shook his head. A stir of air made her look up into the palms with their green fringes visible mostly as fluttering movement in front of the night sky.

"Bats," he said.

"Where did all these creatures come from?"

"They came with the people, I think. People and paradise. You can't keep them separate. They always find the secret spots."

"And ruin it," Doreena said. "We bring turmoil."

Alonso shrugged. "Or calm."

"Calm sea meat. That's what I heard grandmother say at first. She meant, 'Come see me.' but I was afraid, inert. I guess I already knew that a big change was coming. Until I was ready, I wanted to stay on the beach and not do anything."

"Yeah, like that. We're calm sea meat, until we're ready. But we can't be still forever."

"No, but I didn't want someone else to tell me when I was ready for change. It might have been nice if I had listened, easier, but I wanted to feel it for myself. My time to move."

Ocean debris littered the beach. Shells decorated the sand flows. The moon, as if it had dropped down to them, was even larger here than on the cliff side. The beach shone like a strand of pearls circling the inlet of sea. It reminded her of Marilyn and how they'd waded into the water together. Marilyn had been afraid of sharks, but she'd gone in anyway seeking the coolness, naked except for her pearls, the waves magnifying her pregnancy. Marilyn had jumped back to C-town following the infant mirage. What would happen to her in that hard place?

"Do you think there are still sharks?"

"No, those were someone else's idea, your parents were just trying to scare you into action. Now there are only Spinner dolphins," He stroked the back of her hand. "You know, their skins so soft you can't wear rings, or you'll scratch them."

"I don't have any rings," Doreena said. "Earnest wanted to give me one, but I wouldn't let him."

"Just your necklace then," Alonso said, putting his hand over the glass where it lay empty on her chest.

"This is the first time I've seen the island at night. How can it be more beautiful?"

"As beautiful, anyway." He bent and retrieved a bottle from the sand. It was one of the celebratory wines snagged by an island-bound surfer meant for the opening of Traynter Resort. He swung the sparkling wine with the silver label as they approached the sea. The sand shifted and the waves rushed into the stillness. Alonso sat and offered her the open bottle. She waved it away.

"The stiffness, it's a kind of death," she said. "If we go too far from fluid consciousness, we can't get back."

"Not easily," Alonso said, sitting in his loose way. His knees were bent, and his elbows propped on them, the bottle swung between them with his wrists crossed over the opening. She imagined all the islanders sitting in a row with their languid limbs draped across the sand, Alonso the most liquid looking of them all.

"What will you do? You can't get back. To C-town, I mean," she said.

He tipped the bottle to his lips, so they gleamed wet when he answered. "Everything works out. I've never been stuck. Even in

C-town I found a way to surf and found my way to an island. I'm lucky like that."

"Maybe. Marilyn said if you close up entirely, another way opens."

When he offered her the bottle again, she took it. The storm-battered label had begun to peel but the phosphors in the ink still glowed: Silver Lake Sparkling Wine. Silver Lake was a real, natural lake surrounded by vineyards outside of C-town. Marilyn said it looked just like the label. It was another trade route, Doreena realized. There were always openings, always exceptions. There were ways to get to every island if not by ships and planes there were always bridges of land hidden, waiting beneath the sea. She sipped at the wine and let the tart fizz flow over her tongue. She moved between Alonso's legs and, kneeling, placed her hands on his shoulders.

"Grandmother liked you, your gentleness."

"I really like her. I really like this place."

She straddled him letting her thighs rest over his to match his languid posture. She wrapped her arms around his neck and held the bottle against his back. He placed his hands over her breasts. The warmth of them made the rest of her skin feel cool by comparison for a moment until the feeling faded into the muggy night. His hands caressed her and her skin warmed. She tucked him inside of her. They rocked together as they had when they'd first arrived on the island, just the two of them, with Doreena's knees buried deep in the sand. Under the skin of her palms, her grandmother had showed her blue pools. She imagined Alonso, now, deep inside in the waves at her blue core.

They moved together clinging like strands of kelp in the ebb and flow offshore. Strong cycles of tide seemed to pass with the moon filling the sky above them. The island slipped away into the darkness. She was connected only to Alonso until she began to forget him too and resided only in her own body until that fell away also and her mind rose up to join the moon. Then there was only the moon, but its light touched the entire island. The wine bottle dropped from Doreena's hands and the last of the wine seeped into the sand, but she felt drunk with it, her insides filled and sparkling.

"Oh, love," she said at last.

"Those tears." Alonso caught her hands and stroked them with his thumb. The light touch made her feel the flow beneath her skin like the tides within the powder blue baby.

She stared at her hands so full of human gestures. She'd studied these movements so carefully for her job, not knowing why they meant so much to her. She'd listened to the tapes Marilyn had given her again and again with slavish persistence, somehow knowing how much she needed to learn. To fit in, she had become an expert. Foreign beings filled her insides and subconscious, so she made being human a conscious external act.

She freed her hands from Alonso's and repeated the gestures she knew. Palms up, people were open to receive. Palms down, they were ready to pull away. Fastened in a fist, a hand betrayed insecurity or anger. Fingers pointed up meant leadership or hope. Hands touching the face indicated boredom or disinterest. Hands over the mouth betrayed dishonesty or secrets. Hands could serve as clasps to fasten the arms across a body protectively.

She stood and made the movements bigger. Pressing hands to the hips made a person look larger, more threatening or in control. Hands behind the back, portrayed confidence or obedience depending on how the hidden hands were arranged: fastened or folded. Hands could dangle near the thighs or flutter and fidget through the air with nervous energy. They could touch, hold, feel, grasp or clench. They could fend off or embrace. She performed a kata of humanity across the sand and ended in front of Alonso standing with her hands clasped over the place where her heart lay still for just a little while longer.

"To create a feeling of sympathy. Put your hands in the same position as the person across from you. Subconsciously, they will see you as like themselves," she said, repeating a line from Chapter 1 of *Stellar Sales*. "Some neurons react empathetically, 'mirror neurons' they're called, when you imitate others they fire. They create a connection inside of you that extends beyond you to a person outside of you, even to a whole group of people if you are speaking to a crowd. This is possible for anyone. It isn't only me. It's just easier for me, someone of my heritage."

Doreena lifted her hands to the night. The stars shone around her fingers. Her connection to C-town lay in the thin barrier of her skin. She displayed her humanity in 10 digits. Her human experience was etched into her palms, but there were pools and islands inside of them. She stood and raised her arms to the moon stretching her fingertips up into the purplish glow.

Alonso wrapped his arms around her waist. "When did you feel it for yourself? When did you know you were ready to change?"

"When I was falling. I was in two places at once and I didn't want to be."

"Where did you want to be then?"

"Without limits, I think, everywhere. I want to experience all earth's islands."

She looked at her hands, once more, and let them go. They changed color as she released them: pink, lavender and teal. When they reached powder blue, she waved and the blue sparkles shook — *zza, zza, zza* — through the moonlight to the sand. The blunt ends of her wrists jabbed the sky. She began to spin slowly in the circle of Alonso's arms.

Her hair fell first, the curls sparkling down. Her skin swirled like the inside of an oyster shell. It looked as though she'd torn a rent in the sky and the stars were glittering down. The last thing she saw, from beneath her fringe of blue eyelashes, were the crinkles around Alonso's eyes caked with blue sparkles. She'd stuck to his tears. But still he gave her only softness. He let her dissolve without protest. As she released her container, the island, her ancestors, embraced her. They loved her not for the infant they had once coveted, but for the person she had become: *our explorer.* The peace of their mind flowed through her and she understood: They could not be separate. There were no places distant from them.

She lay at last, a blue flow pooling in the prints she and Alonso had made sharing passion in the sand. Alonso pressed his hands into her. She flowed around his fingers. His hands stirred her. There was a sensation of salt, the cut of the tiny crystals, as she mingled through his tears. So, this was what grandfather meant. He'd warned her about men, about sex, and here, at last, were the consequences. She'd been forever changed by the contact. Even now, she would not leave them. She loved the surfers and that called and carried her back to them like an island. Alonso dropped the necklace down into her and she ran over the knotted squares of its chain and into the smooth, glass vial. Then the weight of it within her was lifted. The clasp clicked closed. It fell against Alonso's chest, and she rode there, some of her, so close beside his heartbeat she vibrated. The rest of her filled the empty wine bottle. She spilled from Alonso's cupped hands, down his life and heart lines, into it and shook side to side against the glass.

Alonso sat holding her in the wine bottle while Doreena settled into her new state of being. Her sense organs were gone, but she could still sense everything. Her mind flowed between the fake containers: the glass vial of the necklace with its ornate silver top and the corked wine bottle. Now she was content, perfectly at ease in her containers, but she thought of the islanders and the citizens of C-town who were still trapped. She and Alonso were marooned on the beach through most of the night, but it was still dark when wings beat down and Dalton landed beside them. The island had healed the aerospace executive and given him the wings he had so firmly envisioned. In the necklace and in the bottle, Doreena sensed the wings above her. The billowed tents were AeroFlux red attached to Dalton's lean body. He agreed to fly them off the island and back to C-town if it were possible. In Alonso's embrace, in the necklace and in the bottle, Doreena flew up as a hazy blue powder soaring over the ocean.

And, of course, she also remained on the island.

~ 20 ~

WORLD TRAVELER

Doreena Flora Moriena, world traveler

Exactly as advertised, AeroFlux flew them into the future. Dalton held Alonso's waist as he flew and Doreena, shifting like sand in the necklace on Alonso's chest and in the bottle in his hand, left the island flying over the ocean under Dalton's wings. In moments, La Merde and the other drowning islands in the rising, reddening Rust Sea appeared. Then, they flew over the scalloped coastline of Cascadia and the nearly abandoned coastal town of Westport, whose breaks had lured the Islanders into the area and then left them stranded on their way out in C-town, passed beneath them. Inland over New West, they crossed the smoky Freeway swarmed with refugees, entered the green splay of wilderness, and found the vineyards twining around the shores of Silver Lake. From this height, the scenery, even the dark 'Way, looked placid and pristine. Anything that fell from the sky would sink under the pools of color — blue, gray, or green — and be gone. The land looked as if it would not break a fall.

Then Dalton swooped toward C-town and rock cliffs spiked out of the forest. The fir tops pierced the sky and even the dirt road into town rose threateningly. The neck of Doreena's glass bottle warmed where Alonso squeezed it. They landed on the edge where

246

pavement marked the entrance to C-town and return to solid ground.

"Are you sure this is where you want to be?" Dalton said. "I could take you anywhere."

"I'm sure," Alonso said. "There are people we need to see."

"Well, I can't go in winged. I guess I thought they'd disappear."

"No, you can't," Alonso said. "I meant me and Doreena."

"Maybe I'll fly back East. The trip from the island was easy enough."

But it wasn't any distance, Doreena thought.

"Do me a favor," Alonso said. "Wait for a while at Silver Lake. I want you to take someone with you."

There was no audible reply other than the expansion of wings. The air churned as Dalton struggled to lift from the earth again. A faint sulfur and sea scent departed with him. Doreena imagined him gliding again over the evergreens with the flat map of the world beneath him, blue rings around all the islands, her uncharted island floating not far off in a hazy nimbus. Alonso carried her the rest of the way into town on foot and in her softness, she felt the rhythm of his walk.

They met Hobart inside the reopened Travel Museum along the boardwalk at Traynter Resort. Doreena shifted inside the wine bottle as Alonso explained to Hobart what had happened to her and the plan they had concocted that last night on Mirror Island. Then Hobart showed Alonso the space. New construction smells of paint, plaster and pine floorboards masked the stale traces of mold and incense that rose off the few world-worn curios displayed.

"Doreena saved everything. We found it in one of the AeroFlux trucks. I haven't unpacked it all yet."

Hobart thumped the lids of a couple of the wooden crates. "You really want to reopen this place? I don't know how you'll find room for everything."

"I'll manage," Alonso said.

"What does Doreena think?" Hobart gazed into the bottle.

Doreena swelled and pressed the glass sides, but she stayed soft. Alonso lifted her away and the bottom circle of the bottle came to rest on the top of the crooked wood table. It rocked to the side.

"She doesn't say much these days."

Rubber band glissandos released the museum's cache of scrolled maps and posters, and they unfurled across the new floor.

"These are the places; all the best and softest places," Hobart said. "Do you think you can remember them all?"

"I love the names: Protection Island, Captiva Island, Deception Island," Alonso said. "I might forget the rest."

"Leaves more to be discovered," Hobart said.

A match struck and flame sizzled up against a stick of incense. The oily smoke rose, freeing jasmine as it dripped ash. Hazy blue wisps carried the inaugural scent through the store.

"There's nothing holding us here anymore and we all feel braver," Hobart said. "The City Fathers say they're opening this place up to trade. I think we'll go out now. Tonight, will be the is- landers' last meeting."

At dusk, Alonso took Doreena to the Labor Temple. She shook against the glass up each stone step, entering the familiar drip and clank of the building. The meeting had already begun. Alonso set Doreena down in the circle of drums. Each jolt elevated her up the glass vial in the necklace and up the glass neck of the bottle. She lifted and dropped as the islanders' hands tapped the drumheads. Their voices joined and the names of earth's islands washed over her as they chanted.

Alonso dropped a bundle of maps. The dank air echoed through the paper tubes. "These are all the places we want to know; we want to share."

Each of the islanders picked up a place.

"North Island, New Zealand," J-Bay said.

"I won't make it far. Maybe Protection Island," Hobart said.

"Don't worry, me and my boys have got Kyushu and Sri Lanka. We'll get there somehow." J-Bay said. "For my brother."

"AeroFlux has reopened on the East Coast and I've heard rumors you can catch flights out of some little island up north outside the UG," The Stew said.

Doreena imagined his eyes wide and glowing like the lemur's in the dark.

When they'd all decided where they would go, the islanders gathered around her, kneeling, their knees thumping the cold concrete. Alonso uncapped her bottle. Space opened up above her releasing a breath of sour wine. The islanders' exhalations stirred her, followed by the tap and click of many lifting lids. Alonso tilted her bottle, and she precipitated down into all the differently shaped containers: ovoids, triangles, circles, ellipses, rhomboids and squares. She slid around tin, wood, glass, stone, or shell sides. Fingertips pressed into her tamping her down and she clung to the whorls. In time, she'd know each islander by his fingerprints. She stiffened a little, gaining a chalky weight, as she adjusted to her division and the myriad sensations of her separated selves, but then she stilled and softened again. *This is natural*: she heard her grandmother say.

"You'll make it," Alonso said to the Islanders. "Just remember, you'll affect her."

"Travel soft, or not at all," Hobart said.

"Go soft," the Islanders said.

And they stilled inside, she felt their thoughts soften even though they were all nervous about what awaited them outside C-town. They all made the effort, even The Stew. She shifted side to side with each of the Islanders in the various containers. They tucked her away into pockets, bags, and backpacks. She lay in these dark nests as calm and warm as the island night. This is the allure of islands: places to let go and still be contained, she thought.

She would journey with the islanders, embodying the experiences for her ancestors. When they arrived on the islands, the islanders would pick a place and pour her out onto the sands and she would become part of those places, assisting to preserve their softness forever. She imagined it like sales calls. That was the plan she and Alonso had come up with that night on Mirror Island.

As she traveled, however, she also stayed behind in the slim vial around Alonso's neck that had once held her grandfather. She swung through the air or rested in the thrum of Alonso's particular slow heartbeat. The portion of her in the necklace, she imagined, might have once been her human heart, or the nerve endings clustered between her legs or perhaps the primitive place in her brain, the almond-shaped amygdala that loved instinctually. But she knew there was really no distinction between the part of her here, and the part that traveled. Alonso's hand embraced the vial and she clung to the warming sides of the glass.

"What about you?" J-Bay asked.

"I'm still going by C-town. I'm staying here with the museum," Alonso said. "And they've reopened the lounge. I got back on as a waiter."

"You're kidding. Here? The world awaits and you want to stay C-town?"

Alonso gave his easy shrug. As they were leaving, he pulled Hobart aside. "Head to Silver Lake." He explained to her about Dalton waiting with his maroon wings. "You might get farther than you think."

"Red wings, like a cardinal?"

"Not exactly, more like stretched skin. Bat like," he amended.

"I feel like you just said the devil take me." Hobart said and laughed. "But then I've never heard of an island underworld."

With the islanders, Doreena went out into the world and with Alonso she stayed in C-town shifting — *zza zza zza* — like sand. Her fluid form inside the many traveling vessels felt easy and companionable she wondered how she had ever survived 35 lonely years in one sole, solid body. In the mornings, Alonso poured her out into his palm, and she settled into the hooks and spirals of his fingertips and flowed down the long deep river of his lifeline and crossed the broken arch of his heart. He read aloud the headlines of *The Mirror*: C-town Opens Trade with New West, C-town Allows Refugees to Return, C-town to Begin Negotiations with the UG. Slowly, C-town was letting go, too.

At night, after a long day showing curios to passersby at The Travel Museum and evening waiting on diners at the Tiki Tiki Lounge, Alonso and Doreena surfed. At first, they just went out on the lake, where Doreena glided around Alonso's neck over the mechanized waves. But the island never felt very far away. When the weather turned warm, one Sunday in spring, Alonso walked Doreena to the street where she'd grown up. He bent down among the rounded shrubs planted in front of the condominium, its terracotta-colored siding still newly bright and clean. He scooped out a handful of the thin dry soil, lifted the silver top of Doreena's home and tilted the necklace over the shallow indent. A little of Doreena wafted down onto the soil with its infertile smells of paint and aluminum. The next morning, a hibiscus bloomed before the glass front doors.

Once believed to be extinct, the succulent petals of the white *kokio keokeo* native to Hawaii glistened faintly blue. Most hibiscus have showy, scentless blossoms, but the *kokio keokeo* is one of few with fragrance and this one's sweetness carried to the houses across the street and rose up through all the open windows reaching even as far as the 32nd floor. By the time Mrs. Dammerung, the widow who lived there, had taken the elevator down, a crowd of neighbors, the people usually only seen together at occasions such as chimney fires or ambulance calls, had gathered on the front lawn before the bush. Mrs. Dammerung wished she'd brought a plate of her grandmother's pfeffernusse cookies dusted with powdered sugar. The cookies used to be so popular at office parties and potlucks. She'd given the recipe away a thousand times.

"Have you ever smelled anything so exotic?" someone said.

As the crowd grew quiet remembering, Doreena Flora Moriena — the wanted child, the abandoned adult, the salesman, the surfer, islander and lover, ashes and dust, inorganic consciousness, world traveler and explorer, and now, the hibiscus flower — gathered all the thoughts that plumed from the neighbors enchanted by the fragrance. The globules of exotic thought, yellow tufts like pollen, stuck to her pink knobbed stamen. One day they too would blossom, flowing out into the islands of the universe and becoming so tangled up in everything that it would be impossible to be separate, impossible to stand still.

Shel Graves is a reader, writer, and utopian thinker who lives by the Salish Sea. She is a solarpunk author published in the anthologies *Glass and Gardens: Solarpunk Summers* and *Glass and Gardens: Solarpunk Winters* from World Weaver Press edited by Sarena Ulibarri. Shel earned her MFA at Goddard College, Port Townsend, a utopia which no longer exists. Shel is an ordained animal chaplain with the Compassion Consortium and as Shel Graves Animal Consulting, www.shelgravesanimal.com, aims to create a culture of compassion and pay attention to animals.

May we all be confident, at ease, playful, and safe.